MW00462515

MURDER AT SEA
CAPTAIN'S INN

Melissa Bourbon

MURDER AT SEA CAPTAIN'S INN

A BOOK MAGIC MYSTERY

MELISSA BOURBON

LAKE HOUSE PRESS

Copyright © 2021 by Melissa Bourbon

All rights reserved.

No part of this book may be reproduced in any form or by any electronic or mechanical means, including information storage and retrieval systems, without written permission from the author, except for the use of brief quotations in a book review.

Published by Lake House Press

Art by Dar Albert, Wicked Smart Designs

Print ISBN 978-0-9978661-6-2

NEWSLETTER SIGN UP

Join my newsletter mailing list and receive a free exclusive copy of *The Bookish Kitchen*, a compilation of recipes from my different series.

For Gee Gee Rosell, proprietor of Buxton Village Books on the Outer Banks. You inspire me!

To readers, if you ever make it to the Outer Banks and head toward Cape Hatteras, visit Gee Gee at Buxton Village Books. It is a magical bookshop.

PRAISE FOR THE BOOK MAGIC MYSTERIES

"A combination of magic and mystery, 'Murder In Devil's Cove' by Melissa Bourbon is a deftly crafted and impressively original novel by an author with a genuine flair for originality. While certain to be an unusual, immediate and enduringly popular addition to community library Mystery/Suspense collections, it should be noted for the personal reading lists of anyone who enjoys Women's Friendship Fiction, Cozy Animal Mysteries, or Supernatural Mysteries..."

–*Midwest Book Review*

"The unraveling of the mystery involves Pippin's family history (it goes all the way back to Roman times in Ireland), hidden clues, a long-lost keepsake, and a secret room. For mystery fans who enjoy amateur detectives who rely on mystical insights rather than Holmesian deductions, Murder in Devil's Cove will provide an entertaining read."

–*Seattle Book Review*

"A magical blend of books, mystery, and smart sleuthing. Melissa Bourbon's Murder in Devil's Cove offers mystery readers everything they crave and stands out in the crowded cozy genre. This captivating new series will leave readers spellbound."

~*NYT and USA Today Bestselling Author, Ellery Adams*

"This tightly woven mystery spins a web of intrigue where magic simmers, waiting for the perfect time to surface. I can't wait to read more about Pippin and what awaits her in the next Book Magic adventure."

~*Dru Ann Love, Dru's Book Musings*

Praise for Murder in Devil's Cove

This book had me at 'book magic' and wrapped me up in its unique plot from start to finish! . . . I really enjoyed the set-up, the plot, the characters and the setting; they all added intriguing layers to the story. . .

~*Reading Is My SuperPower*

I thought the author beautifully intertwined magic and mystery...Murder in Devil's Cove is an intriguing tale with forbidden books, a departed dad, family folklore, mysterious magic, renovation revelations, and one bewildered bibliomancer.

~*The Avid Reader*

This book totally sucked me in as the story tells the past as well as the present . . . a truly magical read for fans of cozies with a slight magical flair.

I totally loved it so I give it 5/5 stars.

~*Books a Plenty Book Reviews*

Filled with quirky characters and atmospheric descriptions of the quaint town of Devil's Cove, Bourbon hits all the right notes for a cozy: amateur sleuthing, several possible suspects, bookstores, and a touch of romance.

~*Elena Taylor, Author*

Blending a family curse and a hint of the paranormal with an intriguing mystery MURDER IN DEVIL'S COVE is a fantastic start to a new series.

~*Cozy Up With Kathy*

Praise for The Secret on Rum Runner's Lane

The Secret on Rum Runner's Lane by Melissa Bourbon is a fantastical book that I loved diving into. It was great from the first chapter to the ending.

~*Baroness' Book Trove*

This is the prequel to this new series and it had me hooked on the concept, the setting. and the characters.

~*Storeybook Reviews*

It may be a short story but it gives a thorough introduction of the characters as well as a picturesque view of Devil's Cove. Sure to pique the interest of cozy lovers looking for a mini-mystery to draw them into a new series.

~*Books a Plenty Book Reviews*

. . . this was a quick read about characters that you immediately care about in a picturesque setting (two, actually).

~*I Read What You Write!*

THE SECRET ON RUM RUNNER'S LANE captures the uncertainty and underlying strength of women searching for their place in the world. It allows readers to get a glimpse of the past while seeing the glimmer of what's to come.

~*Cozy Up With Kathy*

The Secret on Rum Runner's Lane is a layered story with a well-developed backstory for a character whose decisions in that time period set the path for generations to come.

~Reading Is My SuperPower

The setting is enchanting with realistic characters you can root for. The mystery is perfectly solvable based on the clues hidden within the text. The paranormal aspect is an original idea.

~Diane Reviews Books

The author brings the story to life with her character development and vivid setting. I could feel Cassie's pain dealing with her family curse. I was totally transported into her world.

~Socrates' Book Reviews...

THE LANE FAMILY TREE

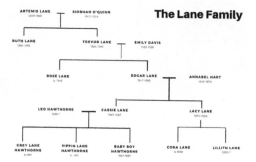

The Lane Family

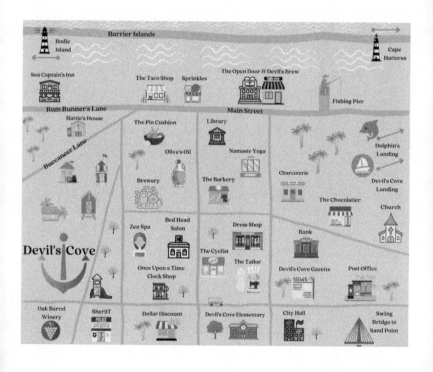

MURDER AT SEA CAPTAIN'S INN

PROLOGUE

"Seanabhean is ea mise anois go bhfuil cos léi insan uaigh is an chos eile ar a bruach." / "I am an old woman now with one foot in the grave and the other on its edge."

~Peig Sayer's opening gambit, 1936

For Pippin Lane Hawthorne, being in her father's secret study was akin to wrapping herself up in a cashmere blanket on a chilly afternoon. It had become her safe place. It was the room in the big, rambling house where she could forget everything and everyone. Where she could focus on the Lane family curse, picking up where her father, Leo, had left off.

She hadn't gotten very far. Jamie McAdams had tapped into his expertise as a scholar of medieval Irish to translate the writing on the scrap of papyrus they'd found hidden behind the mechanism of a clock hanging on one of the study walls. It had been a stunning discovery. "This is an ancient text. An historical document. A primary source," he'd said, tracing it back to the first century.

Knowing that had gotten them nowhere, and now Pippin sat on a pillow in the center of the small room, a collection of items laid out around her, no closer to an answer.

To her left was a hardcover book of poetry by William Butler Yeats that belonged to her father, Leo Hawthorne. Next to that was a goldenrod envelope that held a small plastic sleeve, which in turn held the worn, thick piece of papyrus. On her right side was a miniature carved ship in a bottle cradled in the wood frame where she found her mother's necklace. She touched the cool metal of the medallion hanging from a silver chain around her neck. She had very few of her parents' belongings. The books in this room; her father's notes and maps; and the circular pendant embossed with a Fleur de Lis on one side and two trees and something else indiscernible on the other. The pendant had been terribly tarnished when she first pulled it from its hiding place, but she polished back its shine and hadn't taken it off since.

Next to the maritime art was a transcription she'd done of the family tree her father had created and pinned to a large beige rectangular bulletin board hanging on the back wall of the room. It detailed the Lane family's ancestry with Artemis and Siobhan Lane, Pippin's great-great-grandparents at the top. The rest of the family-members' names cascaded down like an expanding waterfall. Annabel and Edgar Lane. Their children, Lacey and Cassandra. Lacey's children, Cora and Lily, who lived in Oregon. And Cassie's kids—Grey and Pippin.

Artemis and Siobhan were at the top, and above their names was a single word—Ireland.

On the floor directly in front of Pippin was a letter she'd received from her great Aunt Rose. It was written on a pale blue sheet of stationary. Pippin picked it up and reread it for what had to be the hundredth time.

My Dearest Peregrin,

What an odd coincidence that I should receive a letter from you today, after so many years and across so many miles. Just yesterday, I was cleaning out a cupboard and discovered your mother's copy of The Secret Garden. She loved that book so much. I think she must have read it a dozen times or more. Her name, with the curlicue "C," is inscribed on the flyleaf, and I spent moments just tracing it with my finger, remembering your mother's smile. I swear the flowers in the garden used to turn their faces to her, because she was brighter even than the sun.

But then the book fell to the floor, almost as though it were pushed from my hands, and when the pages fluttered still, I saw the words your mother was trying to give to me: "It was in that strange and sudden way that Mary found out that she had neither father nor mother left; that they had died and been carried away in the night."

It sent a chill down my spine, Peregrine. A harbinger of death. But whose? I do not know. I was just overwhelmed by a fear for you and for Grey.

Please be careful, my dear.

In your letter you mentioned that you found a fragment of a document among your mother's things. The letter from Morgan to her soldier, Titus. I wonder if it is related to the parchment that was tucked in your mother's book? It was just a scrap, written in some old language. But the torn fragment was wrapped in a piece of notebook paper, and it looks like someone--perhaps your mother--had made an effort to translate. It's just a handful of words: "Lir," "pact or contract," "descendants," "tribute? offering? sacrifice?"

Life has taught me that there is no such thing as coincidence. Finding your mother's book, finding the fragment of parchment, and then receiving your letter, out of the blue, the very next day? It all means something. The family curse has been quiet for years, since your mother's death, but I feel that the magic is rumbling to life again.

With deepest love,
Your Aunt Rose

PIPPIN DONNED the pair of white cotton gloves that had been in her father's desk before she picked up the goldenrod envelope, undid the clasp, and slid out the plastic sleeve protecting the ancient scroll remnant. She gently removed it from its protective sleeve, holding it for just a moment before replacing it and laying it down in front of her. She wondered if the parchment from her mother's book was the missing half—two parts of a whole, an entire country apart.

She removed her gloves and focused again on all the items laid out before her. There was the common theme of Ireland in all her father's research: Yeats, her family's country of origin on her mother's side, the ancient language on the old papyrus, and the random words written in her father's hand and in Aunt Rose's letter: Lir; Tuatha de Danann; Morgan Dubhshláine. She just had to weave it all together. She started with what Jamie had translated from the fragment they discovered, filling in blanks from the missing half.

Morgan Dubhshláine wrote to her Roman soldier, Titus, telling him she would wait for him.

Pippin recalled what Jamie had told her about the Roman Empire in the first century. They never landed on Hibernia—the Roman name for Ireland, he'd said. The small island country was never conquered.

But—and this was an important caveat—recent archaeological discoveries supported the idea that the Romans actually were there between the first and fifth centuries. "Artifacts have been discovered in Leinstar, close to Dublin, and they have unearthed burials on the island of Lambay," Jamie had said. This meant that what might have been nothing more than a fictional story in her family's history now had a historical basis.

She looked again at the words *Tuatha de Danann*, written in her father's hand inside one of his books. *Tuatha de Danann* were the Gaelic deities in the pre-Christian world of Ireland. Her research had shown her that Lir, mentioned by Aunt Rose, was part of that supernatural race. Part of the Irish mythology.

An idea had started to form in her mind. What if Morgan had made some sort of pact with Lir? She couldn't have known what that promise might really mean. If Pippin believed in magic, which she was beginning to, Morgan may have unwittingly cursed all of her descendants. The Lane women were destined to die during childbirth, and the men would be taken by the sea. It had proved true, generation after generation.

Her father had been trying to break the curse. To save his beloved wife, Cassandra. To save Pippin's mother.

But the curse had won.

Pippin wrapped her hand around the pendant at her

neck again. It had become a touchstone, as much of a comfort to her as being in this room.

Pippin gently touched the book cover of Yeats's poetry. Her bibliomancy, something she was still experimenting with and refining, had led her to a specific poem. The message revealed was titled simply *My Descendants*.

She hadn't understood at the time, but now she was beginning to. Her understanding felt as fragile as gossamer, though, as if the whole thing would tear apart if she pulled too hard.

She held tight to the silky strands of information, trying to weave them together into something more substantial. Morgan Dubhshláine, who Pippin thought must be her oldest known ancestor, had made a deal with the devil—in the form of an Irish sea god. In turn, Lir had cursed Morgan's descendants, taking payment with their lives.

A shiver snaked through Pippin. It was fantastical, yet in the deep crevices of her soul, she knew it was true. And if she didn't finish what her father started...if she didn't end the curse—she and her brother, Grey, were destined to suffer the same fate as their ancestors.

She jumped at a sharp tap on the sole small window in the room. A bird sat on the outside sill. A crow. She held her breath and waited for a feeling of dread to spread through her. The crow. A harbinger of death.

But no darkness came. Only the many strands of her family's story flopped around in her mind, untethered. Salty Gallagher swung wildly among them. What did he know about her father? About the curse? About her mother? She touched her necklace again, letting the weight of the silver ground her. He hadn't succeeded in taking it from her. Despite that, he never fully left her mind. She still needed answers from him, but for now he was rotting away at the

Dare County Detention Center. Just thinking about him ratcheted up her nerves.

Pippin worked to quiet her thrumming heart, turning her thoughts back to the curse. As long as she didn't get pregnant—not even a remote possibility—and as long as Grey stayed away from the sounds surrounding the island of Devil's Cove and from any body of water, because the curse didn't care where in the world you were—they were both safe for the time-being. But she knew fate had a way of catching up to a person. Case in point, their mother, Cassie. She survived childbirth when she and Grey were born, but the curse had taken her at the end of her second pregnancy.

No Lane could ever be safe while the curse lived.

Pippin scanned her father's bookshelves. "Which book, Dad?" she muttered. Which of her father's carefully curated collection held the answers? Her father's own writing had led her to the Yeats book. "Dad, give me another clue," she said softly, half hoping a volume would simply fly off the shelf.

She held her breath waiting. When she looked at the window again, the crow was gone.

Chapter 1

A widow's walk is "derived from the romantic tales of those loyal women who continued to keep watch for a ship that had long gone to the bottom of the coral reef."

~James A. Michener, *Chesapeake*

*O*n a clear day, the widow's walk at Sea Captain's Inn provided a dazzling view east across Roanoke Sound. The Bodie Island Lighthouse sat in the distance, the treacherous waters of the Atlantic beyond. Of course, Bodie Island wasn't *actually* an island. Not anymore. Not for more than one hundred and fifty years. Centuries of storms passing through closed the inlets turned the island into a peninsula that was now known as Hatteras Island.

Cape Hatteras, the majestic 170 foot brick lighthouse, was barely visible from Devil's Cove, and then only if you knew where to look. Pippin Lane Hawthorne stood on the widow's walk staring eastward. Even in the waning evening light, she knew exactly where to find the black-and-white striped structure. It was nothing more than a speck, if even that, but there, nonetheless. She closed her eyes as she breathed in, feeling the summer air expand inside her body, filling every cell.

Devil's Cove.

This house.

This air.

She was home.

"Pippin?"

Ruby's voice floated up to this isolated part of the old house. "Up here," she called. She scooted around the chimney, which took up the center of the widow's walk, and leaned her forearms on the railing, facing west. The sky was a watercolor painting with filmy streaks of color brushed in broad strokes. Across the street, the houses on Rum Runner's Lane were smaller than the one she and Grey had inherited from their parents, but no less charming and colorful. The island had a definite coastal vibe, which attracted tourists all summer long.

"There you are!" Ruby Monroe suddenly appeared at the top of the ladder, popping up like a Jack-in-the-Box.

"You scared me!" Pippin said, hand to her heart. She'd been lost in her thoughts again. The floor below hadn't creaked, and Ruby's sandal-clad feet hadn't made the slightest sound as she'd climbed to the scuttle. But there she stood, her black hair a halo around her head and pulled back with an orange headband. A purple sundress fell like a wave over her slim body, and her smile was as wide as the ocean.

Ruby put one finger to her smiling lips. "Always quiet as a mouse."

That silent presence Ruby possessed meant she could make herself invisible to her customers as they socialized at

Devil's Brew, her coffee shop on Main Street. The bartenders from The Brewery or hairdressers from Bed Head Salon had nothing on Ruby. She could compete with the best gossip on the island.

"What're you doing up here?"

Pippin moved over, making room beside her. "Just watching the sunset."

Ruby draped one arm over Pippin's shoulder. "I feel like I haven't seen you in forever."

It *did* feel like forever. Since the soft opening of the inn, Pippin scarcely had time to breathe. The treat of a leisurely morning and an iced coffee at Devil's Brew sounded heavenly, but opening an inn—even one as small as hers, currently with just four rooms—was a twenty-four-seven job. "I admit, it's been a lot of work. More than I imagined. When my head hits the pillow, I'm *out*."

What she didn't say was that most nights, as she drifted off to sleep, she feared she'd bitten off more than she could chew. She'd been on her own since Grey had decided to start his own custom woodworking business on the north end of the island. It probably wasn't fair to him, but she felt a sense of abandonment. As if, truly for the first time in her life, she was alone, and it terrified her.

There'd been plenty of days when her twin's pep talks over the phone were the only things that kept her going. "You can do it, Peevie," Grey had said more times than she could count. The comfort of him using his childhood nickname for her was always reassuring.

She came right back at him with her own encouragement. "We *both* can, Greevie. Forging our own paths, and all that."

New paths. Wasn't that the truth? If she said it enough times, maybe she would believe it. She and Grey had been raised in Greenville since the age of nine, on the mainland, not far from the island. They returned to the place of their birth after Grandmother Faye died and they discovered that they had inherited their parents' old house. *This* old house.

Forgotten memories had surfaced and neither one of them had wanted to sell the old place. Instead, they decided to renovate it and turn it into an inn. Pippin thought they'd do it together, but Grey needed to go his own way. Follow his own dreams. This wasn't the first time the two had been apart, but this time it felt different, more permanent. While Pippin had wandered for a period after high school, it had been temporary. She'd always known she would come back to her brother, and she had. This time, though, Grey was the one to pull away.

Ruby squeezed her shoulders, bringing Pippin back to the widow's walk. To the house. To now. "Welcome to the joys of running your own business, where there's rarely a day off and everything comes down to you. You're the boss now. You'll have to make a hundred decisions a day. Nobody else can make them for you. And you can't just take a break when you need one because you *are* the business."

Pippin wanted to step back in time and give more thought to her impetuous decision to turn the house into an inn. She knew nothing about running a business. What had she been thinking? "You're kind of scaring me."

Ruby smiled as she shivered. The temperature had dropped enough that a light sweater or jacket was useful.

"Nah. I'm just saying it's a big responsibility, and it never goes away."

Pippin saw goosebumps rise along Ruby's arms. "Take my jacket."

She started to pull off her white windbreaker, but stopped when Ruby said, "Nah, I'm fine."

They stood in silence, staring at the sky. Suddenly Ruby turned to her. "You know that feeling you get, like something's going to happen?"

Pippin nodded. She knew it well. That was the Lane curse. "Hey. Are you okay?"

Ruby shook it off. "Yeah. No." She gave a short laugh. "I don't know. I just need a vacation. Ignore me. Now, what can I do to help out for Saturday?"

At the mention of Saturday, a million little things suddenly raced through Pippin's mind. It was the official grand opening of Sea Captain's Inn. The two-room suite and the two singles were booked and the food and beverages were ordered from local businesses, including the Chocolatier and Oak Barrel Winery, the tasting room on the island. Zoe Ibis—thank God for Zoe, her only employee—was ready to pitch in whatever way Pippin needed. In her mid-twenties, she'd been looking for a job at exactly the right time. Pippin was at her wit's end, trying to get everything ready for the soft opening. Zoe saved the day. Now she was making her way through each room in the house, giving each a deep, methodical cleaning. She'd done the guest rooms first. Once the open house was behind them, she would resume her deep clean, starting with the bunk rooms on the third floor.

Pippin made a quick mental list of her last-minute tasks. Bring in ice. Lots of ice. String a no trespassing rope across the bottom of the stairs. That was critical. Set up the food and drinks. Do a final cleaning. The top floor had the guest rooms and a back staircase leading down to the mudroom, and the third floor had the bunk room and another bathroom, both of which Grey and his team had finished, but she hadn't gotten around to furnishing or decorating. That space wasn't quite ready, but would be soon. There were two storage rooms, a sitting room, window seats in the dormers, and, of course, access to the widow's walk. The second floor and above were off-limits during the party. With Zoe's help, she could manage. "I think I'm good, but thanks."

Ruby squeezed Pippin's hand. "After it's over, you'll settle into a routine."

"I know." Ruby was right. Sea Captain's Inn had only been open for sixty-one days. In some ways, those two months felt like a lifetime. She crammed so much into each and every moment of each and every day. From the time she woke up until she closed her eyes at night, it had absorbed her. What Grandmother Faye had always said was proving to be true. "The devil was in the details."

Pippin had quickly learned that owning an inn was about much more than the blueberry muffins she baked. It was about taking care of the guests, and anticipating their needs.

Still, things really *would* begin to settle down once the official grand opening was over. She hoped.

Chapter 2

"You know, many people believe that we archaeologists are just a collection of old fogies digging around in the ruins after old dried up skulls and bones."

~Griffin Jay

*D*r. Monique Baxter, one of the first guests at Sea Captain's Inn, stood in front of the stand-alone pub height counter Pippin had turned into the guest check-in and concierge area. Dr. Baxter leveled her considerably intense gaze at Pippin after she had her room key in hand. "Am I your guinea pig?"

Pippin looked at her, puzzled. "I'm sorry?"

"You just opened, right? Will you be ironing out your procedures and processes while I'm here?"

The questions might have been lighthearted if they'd been posed by someone else. This woman, however, had the bedside manner of a porcupine and the harsh tone of a vacuum cleaner. Pippin gave a small laugh to lighten the moment. "Oh no. We've worked through all the bugs, I think."

Dr. Baxter pressed her lips together. "Am I your first guest?"

"No, no. Our grand opening is coming up, but we had a soft opening a few weeks ago."

The woman turned her back to Pippin to scan the great room with its welcoming seating area, handmade book-shelves—courtesy of Pippin's brother, Grey—the grand fire-place with its hand-hewn reclaimed wood mantle, and all the other little details Pippin had worked so hard on to make the inn comfortable and welcoming.

"So, you've had other guests, but have none right now?" Dr. Baxter asked, and Pippin thought she detected the tiniest bit of hopefulness in the question.

"We're a small inn. Four rooms total, not including the bunk room on the third floor, which isn't ready yet. You have two of them—the suite. The other two rooms are also currently occupied," she said, channeling industry lingo.

Dr. Baxter heaved a disappointed sigh. "No children, I hope."

She hadn't phrased it as a question, but Pippin answered her anyway. "No, these bookings are child free."

"That's something, anyway."

Pippin ignored the remark. "I'll bring your bags to your room," she said, coming around to the front of the counter. She slid out the handle of the black suitcase and tilted it onto its two wheels while Dr. Baxter picked up a bulky white banker's box. "I can come back for that," Pippin said, but Dr. Baxter marched ahead of her as if she'd been here before and knew exactly where she was going. Her thin red jacket, which added a layer of heat to the already muggy

North Carolina day, was like a beacon for Pippin to follow. "No need. I have it."

Dr. Baxter stopped at the top of the stairs, letting Pippin take the lead. Apparently, her arrogance had a limit. She followed Pippin across the hallway landing that overlooked the great room below. Pippin had worked with Grey to convert the master bedroom into a two-room suite, which could be booked separately or together. Dr. Baxter had taken both rooms. *Breakfast must be served promptly at seven-fifteen and I require privacy for the duration of my stay*, she'd written on the online form when she'd first registered. She didn't seem to mind the additional cost. The inn currently had no vacancy, which was what mattered to Pippin.

Pippin could have used her master key to unlock the door, but Dr. Baxter shoved past her and opened the door with the key she had just received from Pippin.

"Are you here for the dig?" Pippin asked as she wheeled the suitcase across the room, deftly setting it on the luggage rack under the window. Devil's Cove was all agog at the archaeological dig in progress in the dunes at Mariner's Cove on the north side of the island. People expected the fanfare of a dig on Roanoke, but Devil's Cove had escaped the lore of the Lost Colony. Until now. A recent discovery had brought together archaeologists from the Lost Colony Foundation, a North Carolina non-profit wholly committed to multi-disciplinary research into America's beginnings. Their specific focus was on Sir Walter Raleigh's efforts to establish colonies in what was now North Carolina.

"It's a fascinating piece of history," Dr. Baxter said in a way that made it seem like Pippin was a fool for asking. She set her box on the dresser and turned to face Pippin, suddenly asking, "What happened to the Lost Colonists? Where did they go?"

"Oh." The question surprised Pippin. "Well, I know some people believe they were killed by the Native Americans—"

Dr. Baxter cut her off with a dismissive grunt. "Then why isn't there any trace of them? No remains. Very little evidence they were ever here at all. That theory makes *no* sense."

Her words shot out of her mouth with sharp disdain. Pippin drew back as if she'd been slapped. "It's not *my* theory," she said defensively.

Dr. Baxter stared at Pippin with her dark eyes, as if Pippin herself should have the answer to the age-old question. Finally, the woman blinked, as if coming out of a trance. "Of course not. The academics who think they know so much...it infuriates me. They think history is a finite thing, that when someone discovers something and develops the most viable theory, it's put in the history books and that's that."

"But it's not?" Pippin asked—not because she cared that much, but because Dr. Baxter, who was herself an academic, seemed to want her to care.

The woman scoffed. "God no! History is ever-changing. There are too many hidden treasures, secrets, and truths yet to be discovered. The textbooks you had in high school—" She looked at Pippin, narrowing her eyes— "What, ten years ago?"

The guess was close. "Eleven."

She wagged her finger at Pippin. "Let me tell you this. History is most often written from a single perspective, denying all the others that could and should come into play. Take the infamous Drake's Plate of Brass."

Infamous or not, Pippin had never heard of it, so she stayed silent. Dr. Baxter took that as a green light to continue, finger still punctuating her words. "Two female historians—decades apart, mind you—figured out the truth of it. Of course, their theories were buried, taking the real story right along with them."

"But people must know—"

Another scoff. "When those in authority fight to keep the truth hidden, nothing else matters."

The idea of buried truths made Pippin think about her father. He'd fought to keep his research hidden. Her mother had fought to keep the Lane curse hidden. Maybe if they had let more people in, they could have solved the puzzle.

At the same time, it felt risky to share family secrets with people who weren't invested. Even if Cora was right and Morgan Dubhshláine had made a pact with Lir, it was still inexplicable, because how could you explain something magical like that in a world that didn't believe in magic?

Dr. Baxter was still talking. Bitterness seeped from every pore of her being. "People fight to advance their own viewpoint, and if that viewpoint is not the one most widely accepted, it takes a lot of strength to overcome the norm."

Pippin interpreted this to mean Dr. Baxter had a stance about something that differed from whatever was considered accepted history by most others. "But surely people know there are different sides to every story—" she started, but Dr. Baxter cut her off.

"That's a naive perspective. People have killed for less. Different sides or not, those who have something at stake will still fight like hell to promote their own view. *Of course* there are multiple stories. There are multiple versions of every single moment, aren't there? What you see might be completely different than the truth of what's happening. You see things through *your* own lens and based on *your* schema. Your prior knowledge informs your interpretation of things."

A shiver of familiarity wound through Pippin. It was as if Dr. Baxter was talking about bibliomancy. Pippin had to interpret whatever popped out to her in a book, but that interpretation was limited, wasn't it? It was based on what she knew. What she didn't know formed a black hole of possibilities she couldn't fathom.

"There needs to be an ongoing conversation between historians—" She touched her hand to her chest— "and archaeologists to continually expand our understanding of the past," Dr. Baxter continued. "Take this excavation going on. It's practically in your backyard. Do you know what's been discovered?"

Pippin had a déjà vu moment of being back in school, silently praying she wouldn't be called on by the teacher to answer a question about the reading, which Pippin had never been able to finish. The shame and fear that had wound through every single day of her childhood reared its ugly head at the question, brought on by the historian's authoritative tone. She had heard bits and pieces about the discovery at Mariner's Cove, but that was it. She'd been too busy getting the inn ready to learn any more about it. "Artifacts from a long time ago. 18th century, I heard."

Yet another scornful look, this one clearly expressing disappointment at how thick Pippin was to not know more. "That's only part of the story. Back in 1995, evidence of Elizabethan activity was revealed along the nature trail there. Then a team opened up an area where they found human remains from between the 16th and 18th centuries," Dr. Baxter began in a tone normally reserved for educational lectures.

The word *remains* instantly conjured up the unwelcome image of her father's skeleton in the lowest hold of his boat.

Pippin shoved it away, focusing only on what Dr. Baxter was saying.

"Since then, a few random artifacts have been uncovered—until now. What's more, the scientific data revealed through Optical Stimulated Luminescence shows just how long the soil surrounding these artifacts has been hidden away from sunlight. An immense sand intrusion, most likely the Great Chesapeake Hurricane of 1769, covered the site completely. It devastated North Carolina's coast, burying treasures that are just now being discovered. Pottery. Wrought nails. Algonquian tobacco pipes. Things that *seem* to indicate some of the Lost Colonists might have been right here on this island. *I* don't believe it, but some people say the findings support the theory that the bigger group splintered into smaller groups and scattered into the Main."

"The Main?" Pippin asked, her head spinning from everything this historian tossed out with such ease. "Like the mainland?"

Dr. Baxter touched her finger to her nose. With someone else, the action might have come across as a reaffirming. The way Dr. Baxter's eyes rolled up, on the other hand, made it come across as patronizing. "If you've read any of the history on the subject—"

"I haven't," Pippin said, stopping the woman before she could condescend to her more.

Dr. Baxter strode to her suitcase and unzipped the top. She stood there silently for a solid fifteen seconds, then said, "It's *your* history."

Pippin ignored the judgment in her tone. "Well, it's the island's history, but not *my* history—"

At this, Dr. Baxter turned to look at her, eyes narrow. Almost accusing. "So, you're not a native islander?"

Pippin shook her head. "My mother was originally from Oregon."

"Of course. I see," Dr. Baxter said thoughtfully, her harsh voice softening. "One of the teams that helped with a major dig on Roanoke Island came from Oregon. Do you still have family there?"

"Cousins. In Laurel Point. They have an old lighthouse that's been converted into a bookstore. I remember it being pretty cool."

"Full of its own history, I'm sure."

"So, you *are* part of the dig here?" Pippin asked again. It made sense that historians, like Dr. Baxter, would work with archaeologists.

She gave the slightest nod. "As I said, the Lost Colony is a fascinating piece of history." She adjusted her red jacket. "I'm heading over there right now, Ms. Hawthorne. And I need a ride."

Chapter 3

"Respect your curses, for they are the instruments of your destiny."

    ~Joseph Campbell

Ten minutes later Dr. Baxter sat in the passenger seat of Pippin's car. She pointed to the large area of dirt just in front of the pampas grass. "What's that about?" she asked gruffly.

Pippin was quickly learning that the woman's voice held only two tones: *Gruff* and *A Little Less Gruff*. Much as she didn't want to make idle chitchat—whatever level of irritation the cantankerous woman exhibited—it would at least pass the time during the drive to the dig site. She maneuvered out of the driveway, saying, "My dad's boat was dry-docked there for a long time. We had it hauled away not too long ago."

Dr. Baxter glanced over her shoulder, her voice shifting to *A Little Less Gruff*. "It left quite a mark on the ground."

That wasn't the only place the boat had left a mark. Pippin's heart was still healing. Would *always* be healing. "It was there almost twenty years," she said, hiding the hurt behind a conversational tone.

"That's a long time to hold onto a boat you're not using."

"My dad died, and my brother and I went to live with our grandparents in Greenville when we were little. There was nobody to use it."

"And your father, what did he do?"

No *sorry for your loss* or *that must have been awful*. No, Dr. Baxter just charged ahead with whatever question popped into her mind.

"He was a commercial fisherman. He knew these waters like the back of his hand," she said proudly, remembering the maps she and Grey had found, including nautical maps of the area going back hundreds of years.

"A commercial fisherman with an old rum runner's house." So, the exasperating woman had read the *About the Inn* section of the website and knew the history of the house. "And what did your mother do?"

Cassie's only real job had been to keep herself and her children alive. She'd spent every waking minute keeping Pippin and Grey safe. She had protected them from the curse. She'd kept Grey away from the sea and she'd kept Pippin from books. She told Pippin how fortunate she was to have two beautiful children—how it was not supposed to be—but Pippin herself must never risk it. The consequences were too dire. At the time, Pippin had not understood.

The women die in childbirth and the men are swallowed by the sea.

Pippin heard those words over and over in her head. She tried to block them—to switch them around to *I won't die in childbirth* and *Grey will not be swallowed by the sea*. But all she said was, "She worked for a gardening center here on the island."

Dr. Baxter looked taken aback at the triviality of such a job. "A gardener. Interesting. And now you run an inn." Her tone made it sound as if both occupations were hardly worth her time. Still, she pushed the conversation forward. "And do you have siblings?"

"My brother Grey. We're twins." Pippin paused, then added, "He's 73 seconds older than I am."

Pippin glanced over just as Dr. Baxter cracked what Pippin chose to see as a semblance of a smile. It wasn't a full-on expression of mirth, but there was a trace. "Older brothers can be good to have around."

Even ones less than two minutes older, Pippin thought. As she approached Mariner's Cove, she asked, "Do you have one? An older brother?"

She gave a dismissive shrug. "I do, but we don't see each other much."

"Grey lives on island. I don't see him as much as I used to, but we're still close."

"Here's a bit of unsolicited advice. It becomes too easy to have something divide family, and before long a little crack becomes an insurmountable chasm. It comes right back to what we talked about earlier. The truth. If you let the truth be your compass, that's all that matters."

For someone who appeared mostly disinterested in Pippin and her mundane life, Dr. Baxter gave sound advice. "I'll keep that in mind," she said, intrigued by the sudden change of demeanor and passion Dr. Baxter exhibited for that brief moment.

Pippin pulled up to the dig site, instantly captivated by the large area that had been dug down several feet. From there, excavators had created what looked like a chess board with some squares carefully dug out another six or eight inches, the others flattened, as if the earth in those carefully measured squares had been tamped down. The dirt that had been removed was now a hill which sat a few feet away from the patch-worked earth.

Dr. Baxter made no move to leave the car. Instead, she stared straight ahead.

"Are you okay—?" Pippin started to ask, but Dr. Baxter spoke at the same time, her churlish voice cutting her off. "How do you search for something that's been lost to history?"

Pippin didn't think she was supposed to answer, but her own family history surfaced in her mind, so she did. "It's like one of those 3D-illusion sculptures. Perceptual art, I think it's called. You have to be standing in just the right place to see the person or word or object. If you're not in the right place, it's just tangled wires or random objects or pieces of plastic. I think searching for lost history is a lot like that. It's all just bits of information that makes no sense—unless you put it together in just the right way, then suddenly you have this *aha!* moment."

Dr. Baxter turned her head and looked sharply at Pippin. "Interesting analogy," she said. And then she got out of the car and without another word, she strode toward the dig site.

Pippin quickly rolled down the passenger window and leaned toward it, calling, "Dr. Baxter, do you need a ride back later?"

Dr. Baxter didn't break stride, but turned around long enough to say, "I will find my own way back."

"Well, okay," Pippin muttered. That woman was seriously lacking in social skills. Pippin saw a man speak to her, but Dr. Baxter barreled past. A woman moved toward her, but again, Dr. Baxter dodged any engagement and melted into the crowd of excavators, other people who looked like they were part of the dig, and those who Pippin thought were lookie-loos. A few people looked familiar. People she'd seen around town. Island life was small, after all. She waited another few seconds. The red jacket fully vanished into the wooded area beyond the dig and Pippin left the site.

She drove around the bend, stopping for a minute to breathe in the salty air. The small, protected cove connected to an inlet leading to the sound. The water buoyed a handful of kayakers. One bobbed up and down on the lapping water, a fishing line cast out ahead of him. Two others rowed side by side through the inlet. Another man hauled his kayak across the sand toward the water.

Something about him struck her as familiar, but from this distance she couldn't decide what it was. His gait, perhaps? She watched him, then let her gaze backtrack to what she thought was his vehicle. A truck.

Her heart stuttered. Grey's truck.

In a split second, she was out of her Jeep, running, stumbling, catching herself. She hollered as loud as she could. "Grey!"

He didn't turn. Didn't hear her. And the next thing she knew, he was in the water, in the orange kayak, padding toward the inlet with strong, steady strokes that propelled him through the water at a quick clip. "Grey!" she screamed

He didn't turn around. She yelled again and again, until her voice grew hoarse and she gave up. She threw up her hands, frustrated. She'd wait for him. Yes, that's what she'd do. She'd wait for him to come back. She'd pray he *would* come back.

She started to turn back to her car when his upper body

twisted in the kayak. Did he see her? She raised her arm. Would he even be able to tell it was her?

His arm went up in a silent acknowledgement. A long few seconds passed, an invisible connection coursing between them. "What are you doing?" she muttered. In response, he dropped his arm, turned, and resumed his rowing. Her head ached with fear for her twin brother. Why was Grey tempting fate with his reckless disregard for the curse they'd been burdened with?

Chapter 4

"Ah how shameless—the way these mortals blame the gods. From us alone, they say, come all their miseries, yes, but they themselves, with their own reckless ways, compound their pains beyond their proper share."

~Homer

Grey's new business was also his home. In the time it had taken for Pippin to finish decorating Sea Captain's Inn and work out all the details about running the place, he'd converted an old red barn into a workshop, design showroom, and living space. An ancient stone silo stood sentry at the corner of the barn. The history behind the buildings was unknown. All Grey knew was that it was built of glazed hollow blocks in the late 1800s, long before the technology of poured concrete was developed.

Grey hadn't had a chance to pretty up the place, but it had truckloads of character and Pippin knew he'd get there.

He'd hung a handmade, hand-printed sign above the entrance of the barn.

Hawthorne Custom Woodworking

Pippin spotted Grey's truck parked alongside the barn. No sign of that blasted kayak. Good thing, too, or she might have just plowed right over it. Since she couldn't do that, she parked and stomped up to the door. A small sign said BY APPOINTMENT ONLY, but Pippin ignored that, grabbed the handle, and tried to barge in. She was thwarted by the locked door.

She balled one hand into a fist and pounded, throwing her whole body into it. "Grey!"

Nothing.

She pounded again. "Grey Lane Hawthorne, open this door!"

Still nothing.

The sound of a saw or drill or some other power tool buzzed faintly. Aha. That meant he was probably in the back of the barn—in what he designated as *The Shop*—working on one project or another. Pippin strode around the building, resisting the momentary childish temptation to kick dirt right at Grey's truck as she passed by. Since the moment she spotted him in that kayak, worry had settled like an iron weight in her gut. If she and Grey tried to live their lives the way they ached to, they were both doomed. *Of course* she wanted to fall in love. Have kids. Make a family. But she couldn't. She *wouldn't*. Cassie had, and that decision had ended up widowing Leo and leaving her and Grey motherless. She could never knowingly take the risk of that happening to a child.

And even though Leo wasn't a Lane by blood, the curse

had worked on him, too. Grey had to stay away from the water or she knew he'd end up like her grandfather Edgar Lane, her great-grandfather Trevor Lane, or her great-great-grandfather, Artemis Lane. It was their inescapable fate.

Unless they broke the curse.

She balled her fists. Tempting fate like Grey was doing was just plain stupid.

She rounded the next corner and came right up to the open side-by-side barn doors. The buzz of whatever tool Grey had been using cut off abruptly. The thrumming of her heartbeat in her ears ratcheted to a deafening decibel. She was ready to lay into him but stopped short at the sight in front of her. Her breath caught. "What the—?" Disbelief propelled her forward again, a scream climbing from the pit of her stomach to her throat. "Grey!"

He'd just set down the tool he'd been using on a table and now stood with his back to her, his hair covered with a navy bandana. He wore khaki shorts and a t-shirt, and she could see the thin layer of dust covering his arms, his legs, and his work boots. At the sound of her voice, his shoulders stiffened. He turned to look at her, defiance clearly set in his eyes and in his posture. Because right there, cradled in a support that looked quite a lot like the bases Leo had used for his ships in bottles, was a round-bottomed boat.

"What are you doing here, Pip?" he asked, the usual warmth of his voice cooled to tepid.

"What are *you* doing?" she demanded. "That...that's a boat."

He swiveled to look at it. "It is."

She wanted to sob. To slam her fists against his chest. To scream.

Somehow, she kept her voice steady. "Grey, why do you have a boat here?" A boat he was clearly working on. A boat he probably intended to put back in the water at some point.

Grey—who was usually so level-headed, who she'd always been so in-sync with—just sighed. He ran his hand over his forehead, sliding his fingers under the fabric of the bandana and slipping it off his head. His dark hair was matted down, but he clawed his fingers through it until it stood on end. "Why not?" he answered, way too flippantly for her liking.

"Why not," she repeated. "Why not? Why *not*?" She stared him down. "Because, Grey. The men in our family die in the ocean, remember?"

His lips twisted into a mirthless smile and he shrugged as if he didn't have a care in the world. As if his family wasn't cursed. "If that's how I'm going to go, at least I'll have been living my life. I'll die happy."

She gaped at him. A full-on jaw-dropping goggle. "What are you talking about?"

"I've fought it my whole life, but I can't do it anymore." He gave a resigned sigh. "I just can't."

Her heartbeat jerked into an agitated thumping. "You can't protect yourself anymore? Is that what you're saying? So...what—?" She threw up her hands in frustration— "I want to have a child at some point so I should just go get pregnant and forget about the consequences? Forget about the fact that, not only might I die—scratch that, I *will* die— I'll also leave my child motherless and alone to face the curse on their own?"

"It's your life. You need to make your own choices."

"But it's not just my life. It's the life of my child. The curse he or she will bear. And then what about my potential future grandchildren who will also be plagued with it? We have to take this seriously. I can't get pregnant any more than you can *get* someone pregnant. You can't commit your future Lane son or daughter to our fate." She could taste her anger. Her frustration with her brother. She worked to calm her mind. Her voice. "Grey. Where is this coming from?"

The hull of the boat was coated with oysters and barnacles. He lifted one arm and ran his hand over a cluster of them. "I'm talking about boating, Pippin. About fishing. It's in my blood. From Dad. From Mom, too. I don't want to deny it anymore. I don't want to sit here like a coward."

She looked at the boat, its wood planking coated in thick green slime. A power washer sat off to the side. On small portable table sat a collection of scrapers and putty knives. She could see his process. He'd clean what he could with water and use elbow grease to take care of the rest. Then he'd sand it and paint it and get it seaworthy. This was so much worse than seeing him in the kayak.

"The curse is in your blood. You're willing to risk your life so you can fish?"

He gave an embittered sigh. "Is it though? I don't even know if I believe in it."

She balked. "What?"

He looked at the boat. Picked at a barnacle. "It doesn't matter. You don't understand. It's like an ache. An itch I can't scratch. The water...it's like a damn siren, and I don't want to ignore it anymore."

A siren. Like in *The Odyssey*, the book that had led her to the truth about her father. She controlled her breath. In and out. In and out. "But I do understand," she said, her voice low. She felt the same ache. The same itch.

He looked at her, his angry expression disintegrating, replaced by his comprehension of what she meant. "I *know* you want to figure out how to stop this whole thing, but

Peevie, come on. If our parents couldn't do it, what makes you think you can?"

She'd asked herself that question a hundred different ways. She didn't have a satisfactory answer for herself, let alone for Grey. All she could say was, "I have to try."

Chapter 5

"What would you say, if I should let you speak? Villains, for shame you could not beg for grace."

~Shakespeare, *The Tragedy of Titus Andronicus*

"Ms. Hawthorne? Are you up there?" A woman's voice drifted up to the widow's walk. So much for seeing the sunset, or just having a moment's time to think about Grey and his crisis. The questions were followed by the clatter of someone ascending the ladder. Someone who was not as silent as Ruby had been the day before. A head of dark hair appeared, followed by pair of lips set in a thin straight line. A set of dark eyes landed on Pippin.

"There you are. I've been looking all over for you."

"What can I do for you, Ms. Baxter—"

"*Dr.* Baxter," the woman corrected. "I have a PhD. I worked hard for my degree, so please use my title."

"Of course," Pippin said, feeling sufficiently chastised.

She deferred to the academic, though. As a person whose education stopped after high school, she respected the time and effort someone like Monique Baxter had put in to earn her degree.

The woman had only just arrived, but she had already bombarded Pippin with a multitude of questions and demands. *Will there be breakfast in the mornings?* Yes. *Are there deadbolts installed on the doors?* Not yet. *Grumble. What about a safe for valuables?* Yes. *Where is the historical society?* On Beach Street. *Who else is staying here?* There are two other parties, a couple and a single man. *Are they quiet?* Yes. *Take me to the dig site.* Sure thing.

The woman was going to be at Sea Captain's Inn for seven full days. Pippin thought they might be the longest days of her life. "This island doesn't even *know* the secrets it's holding," she'd said to Pippin when she returned from the dig site the day before.

Pippin fully agreed with that. This island held the secret of her father's disappearance for twenty years, only finally releasing it into the wind a few months ago. Whatever other secrets were kept by Devil's Cove, Pippin had no doubt they were doozies. She'd hoped the woman would be more friendly, and more forthcoming about whatever it was she was here to do. Pippin was as intrigued by the mystery surrounding the Lost Colony as every other North Carolinian, especially after their conversation at check in, but the woman was wound tight and didn't appear to be a fan of sharing.

Dr. Baxter climbed all the way onto the widow's walk, wrapped in the same red jacket she seemed to wear everywhere. She caught Pippin's look. It was summer after all. "I get chilled easily," she explained, although Pippin hadn't asked.

"Who are the other guests?" she demanded. "I should have stayed in a hotel, but I thought this might be more private. Now I'm not sure. I saw a man at the end of the hall, and I *heard* him on the phone. Is he here on business? This will not do. I need quiet, Ms. Hawthorne."

Pippin stood straighter, as if a stiff spine could ward off the woman's aggression. "There's a couple coming tomorrow from Florida to celebrate a wedding anniversary. The man at the end of the hall is businessman of some sort. I'm sure he didn't mean to be loud."

She responded with a deep frown. "Is it a young couple? Because they might be too noisy."

"Older, I think," Pippin said, unconvinced that older people, by definition, were quieter than younger people. She thought it depended completely on individual personalities.

"And the businessman? What does he do? How long is he staying?"

"Dr. Baxter—"

She held her palm out, stopping Pippin. "Humor me. I need to know if I should find a hotel instead."

This woman was too much. "He arrived yesterday. Something about antiques, I think," Pippin said, "and he's only here through Wednesday. That's all I can say. I need to honor the guests' privacy."

Dr. Baxter's shoulders relaxed a touch. "I guess that will be okay." She edged around the chimney until she was right next to Pippin. "Beautiful view from up here," she said, her voice going from its standard gruff to the lukewarm, less gruff version. The strain of her attempted smile, though, made it clear that lukewarm wasn't her natural state of being, and the information obtained about the other guests hadn't really eased her mind all that much.

"It is. It's my favorite spot in the house," Pippin said. She'd been escaping to the widow's walk most evenings to watch the sunset. It was just a few minutes each day when she could let everything go and just breathe. She sighed. Pippin hadn't minded Ruby's interruption the other night, but this visit had broken the peacefulness of the moment. "Is there something else, Dr. Baxter?" she asked.

"I'm going to bed now, and I'll be heading out early in the morning. What's happening with this Grand Opening event? You did *not* mention that when I made the reservation."

"It's casual. People will come and go."

Unless the moon shone brightly in the sky, the moment the sun dropped out of sight, darkness fell like a blanket. Tonight, the moon was waning, so no illumination. Pippin had quickly learned that once daylight was snuffed out, making her way back inside could be a hazardous prospect. She flicked on the penlight she brought with her. A small circle of light shone from the tip, illuminating just enough of the floor to guide them to the ladder so they could make it back into the house without incident.

"But it *is* a party? What time? How many people will be here?" Dr. Baxter demanded.

"It's an open house to celebrate the completion of our renovation. It's been a months long project," Pippin said. "It starts at four o'clock. I don't have an exact headcount because it's informal, but I'm anticipating about fifty people, in and out."

The academic harrumphed. "I like my solitude. You did *not* tell me there would be a party," she said again.

Pippin bit back her reply. *The guest is always right*, she told herself. *The guest is always right.* Even this disagreeable woman. Pippin gestured Dr. Baxter forward. The woman didn't descend as gracefully—or quietly—as Ruby had, but she made it down, waiting impatiently at the bottom, tapping one foot, her arms folded like a shield over her chest. Once she was back in the house, Pippin closed the door, shutting off the access to the widow's walk. She turned the lock and tucked the key into her windbreaker's pocket.

"I see you have a deadbolt for *this* door," Mrs. Baxter sniped. "Why are they not also on the room doors?"

Each room had a simple door lock, including the door from the mudroom to the far end of the back deck, but this was the second time Dr. Baxter had mentioned deadbolts. Pippin considered her. "Are you worried about someone breaking into your room?"

"Don't be impertinent. It's just common sense, and common safety."

Pippin realized that every conversation with Dr. Baxter would be like opposing armies facing off on a battlefield. "You're probably right," she said, adding a call to the locksmith to her mental To Do list.

"Probably," Dr. Baxter muttered with a scowl. "More like definitely." Back in the upstairs hallway, she turned on her heel and marched to the master suite. Pippin had moved her room downstairs to what had been her father's study to open another bedroom to rent. The last renovation project Grey had done was to turn the master bedroom into a connecting suite, dividing it into two spaces adjoined by a door. She had no idea why Dr. Baxter needed both rooms. "I'll be down for breakfast at seven-fifteen sharp," she said now, pausing just long enough to drive the message home with an even glare.

And then she slammed the door, leaving Pippin staring openmouthed in the hallway.

Chapter 6

"Secrecy is the element of all goodness; even virtue, even beauty is mysterious."

~Thomas Carlyle

$\mathscr{B}$y early evening the next day, the old house was brimming with people from all over Devil's Cove. Those curious to get a glimpse inside the old pirate's house showed up right at four o'clock and wandered around looking at every detail. Questions flew at Pippin.

Are these the original floors?
Is it true this was a pirate house?
I heard there's a secret room. Can we see it?

SHE GAVE some variation of the same answers over and over and over again:

Yes.
Yes.
Secret room? I'm not sure what you mean.

OF COURSE, the last response was a lie. There *was* a secret room—but it was completely off limits to the guests. That was one of the reasons Pippin had moved her bedroom to her father's study. The hidden entrance to Leo's hidden study was through the bookshelves. She'd put a sign up on the door saying Private, and she kept the room locked. No guest could accidentally wander in.

She didn't go around advertising that the upstairs hideaway actually existed. She didn't want to tempt the curiosity seekers. Only a handful of people knew about the room: herself, of course, Grey, Ruby Monroe and Daisy Santiago—the two childhood friends Pippin had during her younger years in Devil's Cove—, Kyron Washington, Jimmy Gallagher, and Travis Walsh—the three men Grey had hired for the renovations—, old Salty, Hattie Juniper Pickle—who lived across the street—, the local law enforcement in the form of Lieutenant Roy Jacobs, and Jamie McAdams—the owner of The Book Shop.

She trusted Ruby and Daisy not to talk about it. Jamie, too, although he'd probably shared with his grandfather. Pippin was fine with that. The elder Mr. McAdams had known her parents. Not only that, but he'd also tried to help them stop the curse that plagued the Lane family, and he was still trying to help her. Kyron had gone into business with Grey. She trusted him not to share. The others, though, she wasn't quite sure about. Hattie was a talker. She might have inadvertently mentioned it to a neighbor. Jacobs might well have shared with another officer over a pint in The Brewery. And Travis Walsh? He and Salty were both wild cards.

Deny, deny, deny. It was the best she could do. That, and simply keep people out.

For the time-being—hard as it was—she had to put all thoughts about her father's secret room, her parents, her father's murderer, and everything else relating to the Lane family curse out of her head. Without thinking, she touched the necklace she wore—the one she thought had been buried with Cassie. It was a touchstone to both of her parents.

Dropping her hand, she grabbed a plate and a half-full cup of sweet tea, both discarded on one of the side tables in the great room, quickly wiping away the ring the sweating plastic had left on the wood. From the corner of her eye, she spotted Zoe at the registration desk near the front door. Her shaggy nut-brown hair hung to her shoulders. She'd changed from her usual jeans and tee shirt to a striped skirt and solid pink blouse. Zoe was full of energy. She handed a set of keys to the couple checking in. The Lees. The woman leaned back against the counter, smiling and absorbing the energy of the crowd as it shifted through the room. The man, on the other hand, kept his back to the party, his head dipped as if he was studying his shoes.

She knew Zoe would explain the Grand Opening, assuring them that the party would only last a few hours. From the looks of it, Mrs. Lee just might join in the celebration.

Pippin turned and caught a glimpse of movement upstairs. She turned to see a man in a black pants and crisp white shirt slowly making his way across the open hallway. He held his black jacket loosely in one hand. Irritation flooded her. No one should be up there. "Excuse me," she called up. She set the plate and cup back on the table and went after him, pausing long enough to register that the rope and Off Limits sign she'd strung across the stairway were now on the ground.

The man didn't acknowledge her. He lightly jogged down the stairs, passing her at the halfway point. She put her hand on his arm to stop him. "Sir," she said with authority. "The upstairs is private."

He rolled his shoulder, shaking her hand off as he turned to face her. Pippin drew in a sharp breath, stepping back and nearly losing her balance. His eyes were nearly white. Translucent, with pinpoint pupils despite the dim atmospheric lighting. They bore into her. Or maybe they looked right through her, she couldn't actually tell.

She gripped the railing to steady herself, waiting for an acknowledgment from him. No smile. No nod. No nothing, except for the zombie-like stare that made her blood run cold. "The open house is downstairs only," she said, trying to mask the croak lurking in her throat.

Finally, one side of his mouth lifted in a ghost of a smile. The cold stare of his eyes made it impossible for him to appear anything but otherworldly. "Of course," he said, drawing out the last word.

Another shiver slipped through her at his deep cavernous voice. It was slow and southern, sliding out of him like warm syrup.

She felt one of her eyes pinch in response, as if he were the devil himself. She didn't want this man in her house. A vice clamped around her heart, but she pulled herself together. "Can I help you with something?"

"Not right now," he said eerily, "but I'll be in touch, Pippin." And then he moved past her and finished descending the stairs.

She stared after him, spreading one hand across her forehead as she let her breath steady. He said her name as if he knew her. She watched him move through the room, the party guests stepping aside as if they, collectively, were the Red Sea parting. He strolled through with an easy devil-may-care manner, stopping for a moment here or there.

Pippin spotted Zoe amidst the guests and not too far from the eerie man. She waved until at least ten people looked at her. Finally, Zoe was one of them. Her face lit up when she saw her but dropped again as Pippin mimed what she wanted her to do: try to usher that guy out the door.

Zoe sprang into action, zipping through the barricade of guests toward the man. Pippin continued down the stairs, heading straight for Zoe, but by the time she got to the spot where the man and her sole employee had been, they were both gone.

After a long minute, Pippin let the anxiety the man had left in his wake fade away. She'd think about it later. She doubled back to the base of the stairs. The Lees arrived at the same time. She let them pass before reaffixing the rope and straightening the sign. "Please let me know if you need anything," she said.

"Can we come back down to the party?" Mrs. Lee asked.

"Of course! Just slip right past the rope and help yourself to whatever you need."

As they headed up to their room, Pippin turned and caught a flash of something red. Ms. Baxter—no, *Dr.* Baxter. The crowd closed again, swallowing her up.

She caught sight of Mr. Marshall, the guest in the third room. If everyone in the room were to line up, he'd be the one that stuck out like he didn't belong. While everyone else looked fresh, clean, and summery, he was a fifty-something man dressed like a twenty-five-year-old beach bum. His cargo shorts and t-shirt underneath an open button-down shirt all leaned a bit toward the grimy end of the beach attire spectrum. A ball cap covered his thinning hair, his flip flops looked as if they'd seen better days, and a worn backpack was slung over one shoulder. He didn't look like any businessman she'd ever seen.

She caught his attention and gave him a smile and little wave. He forced a smile in return. This grand opening party was clearly the last place he wanted to be. He pointed tentatively toward the front door as if seeking permission to leave. Pippin raised her eyebrows and nodded. He scurried off. All of her guests were accounted for. Sea Captain's Inn officially had no vacancy. The thought made her smile.

"Good turnout," someone said from behind her.

An instant jolt of energy shot through her. Grey. She spun around. "You came."

Grey had taken after their father with his darker hair—not a trace of the strawberry that colored her curls—and square jaw. His eyes were gray-green. While Pippin's had inexplicably grown greener since childhood, like an Irish hill, Grey's had stayed muted—the color of an angry sea, their mother used to say. They were fraternal twins with a deep connection that Pippin hoped would always be there. "Of course, I came," he said.

"I wasn't sure you would," she admitted.

"You think I'd miss your grand opening?" He looked around and gave a little shake of his head. "It looks seriously great, Peevie. You did an amazing job."

She moved her index finger back and forth between them. "*We* did an amazing job."

He shrugged, nonchalantly, as if he hadn't been the one to do every bit of the renovations with his small crew of three. The four men had taken the house from abandoned and decrepit to the showcase it now was. And with Pippin's interior decorating, it now honored their parents, as well as the sea captain who founded Devil's Cove and built the place.

Grey stood there with his hands in his pockets, wearing a slightly chagrinned expression. With him right in front of her, away from his boat and the water, her anger with him settled from a rolling boil to a steady simmer. She lurched forward and hugged him. Just having him in the same room, breathing the same air, gave her an instant infusion of calm, but it didn't take away the unease of the man with the clear eyes. Grey sensed it. He pulled away and put his hands on her shoulders. "Are you okay? Are *we* okay?"

She waved her hand in front of her. "We're fine. It's not that," she said. She'd think of some way to get through to him, but that would have to happen later. "Some man was upstairs and...I don't know. Something's not right."

He looked at the stairs. Noted how they were cordoned off. "What was he doing up there?" he asked, turning back to her.

"I don't know." She glanced around, and then stepped closer to him again so she could whisper in his ear. "Do you think it could be about—" She'd been about to say *the curse,* but amended to— "Mom and Dad?"

Grey might not want to believe in the curse, but he knew as well as she did that there were people out there who were after something their father had kept hidden. Old Salty had proven that. He looked as perplexed as she felt. "Where's the guy now?"

He hadn't answered the question, but she let it go. "Gone, I think."

"Let me know if you see him again."

"I will." Pippin picked up the plate and cup she abandoned earlier and deposited them in the garbage and recycle bin. As she made her rounds through the party, a requirement of the hostess, Grey followed her slowly, stopping to shake hands here and there, to clap a few backs, and to hand out one or two business cards. Pippin smiled at the snippets of praise tossed his way:

I hear you made the dining table. Gorgeous, man, just gorgeous.

That reclaimed wood. My God. Can you make me a mantle like that one?

That hutch! I need one just like it!

He caught her eye with a wink before he settled into what looked like a more serious conversation about a beach-front remodel job and the custom furniture the couple wanted. Good, she thought. Anything that would slow him down with that boat was a good thing.

"Pippin! Oh my gosh, this is amazing!" Daisy's voice rose above the low chatter filling the house, but her petite five-foot two-inch body hadn't yet materialized.

"Daisy! Where are you?"

Pippin saw the flashes of color typical to Daisy's clothes before she saw the pixie-like woman herself. When she finally came into sight, her eyes beamed, and her smile was electrified. "This place. I can't believe you get to live here," she called, still pushing her way forward.

They'd only just reconnected, but Daisy Santiago was Pippin's oldest friend. Their mothers had known each other.

Daisy had old scrapbook photos of the two girls playing before Pippin's life had permanently changed with the death of her mother and then later, from her father's disappearance. Now they were forging a new friendship.

Daisy's cotton jersey sundress, with its vibrant blue background and huge bright flowers in every color, looked a grown-up version of a girls' Hanna Anderson dress. Like the Swedish brand, everything Daisy wore reflected her love of life, her high energy, and the joy kids had—which, even in her late twenties, she still possessed in spades.

She kept her dark—almost, but not quite, black—hair short, though a few long strands hung artfully on either side of her face. She had different colored glasses—one for each day of the week, it seemed. Today her frames were cerulean blue, complementing her dress. She was a sprite, her delicate features, olive skin, hoop earrings, and mile long eyelashes making her adorable and the exact opposite of sophisticated in every way.

She pulled Kyron Washington along behind her. They were a new thing and seemed to be enjoying every second together. Kyron tempered Daisy's exuberance. With his dark skin, tidy neutral clothes, and his black hair cut close to the scalp, he grounded her, the yin to her yang. He was lean and compact, the perfect complement to her five feet two inches.

Finally, they broke through the last cluster of people, her free arm swinging wide and looking for all the world like she was about to burst into a show tune. "Good grief, finally!" she exclaimed. She let go of Kyron's hand and flung both her arms out to the side. "Look at this crowd! Can you believe it? Pippy, the place looks fabulous."

Pippin's brows pinched together. "Pippy?"

Daisy shrugged. "Just came out, but I kinda like it. Whadya think, Ky?"

One side of Kyron's mouth lifted in an indulgent smile. "You do like nicknames."

Daisy took that as approval. She stretched up on her tiptoes and quickly brushed her pink lips over his cheek before turning back to Pippin. "Seriously, though, this is incredible."

"It is."

"Did you expect this good of a turnout?" Kyron asked.

The truth was, she hadn't known what to expect. After too many sleepless nights worrying if she'd made a mistake taking on this venture by herself, she finally felt relaxed. Relieved, even. The three rooms were booked for seventy-five percent of the next two months, and there were already reservations for the days leading up to Halloween, all of Thanksgiving week, and most of December. It turns out people loved the beach, even in the off-season. "I don't know what I expected. The majority of these people are lookie-loos, I think."

"Word of mouth is everything," Ruby said as she sauntered up to them. Tonight her hair was pulled back with a black headband, the strategically highlighted strands almost glowing amidst her dark spirally curls. She wore white jeans and a breezy top that fluttered when she moved.

Pippin looked at her two friends—the women who'd been there to support her after she'd found out her father hadn't left his children but, instead, had been taken from them. Daisy looked like she'd been ripped from the pages of a fairytale. Perfect that she was the head librarian at the Devil's Cove Library. And Ruby. With her statuesque six feet, she could walk any runway in the world. The two were opposites in every way, and Pippin fit somewhere in the middle, in height and in every other way. Where Daisy had olive skin and Ruby's was melanin-rich, Pippin was fair with freckles that mirrored the stars in the night sky. The three of them, side by side, were a study in contrasts, like three women from three different stories. But they worked together. For Pippin, these women were becoming her family.

Her nerves settled again, thanks to being surrounded by friends and support. Maybe the man upstairs had just been snooping through the renovated house. Maybe she was making a big deal out of nothing.

And then someone yelled, "A dog! There's a dog over here!"

Chapter 7

*"If you don't own a dog, at least one, there may not necessarily
be anything wrong with you, but there may be something
wrong with your life."*

~Roger Caras

Pippin spun around, instantly on high alert.
She'd put the rescue Vizsla in her room, for
Sailor's sake, rather than the guests. The noise of the guests
wouldn't bother her, but Sailor was still skittish, and she was
very attuned to body language and gestures. The attention
might freak her out.

The commotion came from the kitchen. Pippin left
Daisy, Kyron, and Ruby, hurrying off to wrangle the dog
before she darted out the back door, over the boardwalk,
and down the shoreline. "Sailor!" she called, knowing full
well the dog couldn't hear her. It didn't matter. Pippin spoke
to her just as she would talk to any other dog, signing at the
same time. Together, they'd learned some basic commands.

A thumbs up meant *good job!* A palm up meant *sit.* A beckoning gesture meant *come.*

Pippin ran around the fireplace that separated the great room from the kitchen and dining area. The combination room was her favorite room in the house. Shiplap dressed up the backside of the fireplace. A farm style hutch, two plush chairs, and a round coffee table at the opposite end of the kitchen creating a cozy reading nook. And then there was the farm table with a reclaimed maple wood top and twelve colorful and mismatched chairs encircling it.

She scanned the room, but there was no sign of Sailor. The French door to the upper deck, however, was wide open. Panic seized her. "Everyone!" she yelled, but only a few people turned to her.

She tried again. "Hey, everyone, I need your attention."

A few more guests turned her way.

There was still no sign of Sailor. Finally, she curled her thumb and middle finger together, pressed them against her tongue, and let out a shrill whistle.

That did the trick. The talking stopped and every face in the kitchen turned toward her. "Someone saw a dog?" Pippin asked. "Where?"

"Over here," a woman called. "And she's just fine."

Pippin recognized the voice and instantly felt relief flood through her. It belonged to Hattie Juniper Pickle, her boisterous and eccentric across the street neighbor. She had become fast friends with Sailor—and with Pippin. Pippin pinpointed the location of Hattie's voice as coming from behind the kitchen island. She waved her hand in the air, telling her party guests, "Carry on!"

"Oh, thank God!" she exclaimed, collapsing to the ground next to Hattie. Sailor lay on the floor, her snout resting on one of Hattie's knees. Pippin bent low to take

Sailor's face in her hands, pressing her nose to the dog's. "You scared me!"

Sailor didn't understand the words, but her tail whipped into a frenzied wag from Pippin's touch.

"Somethin' sure spooked the old girl. She's been shakin' like my old washing machine on spin."

"We didn't mean to scare her!" A little girl, about seven years old and wearing a cotton sundress, and a toddler boy wearing shorts and a Star Wars t-shirt, stood pressed up against the wall. "Our mom told us to be quiet, but we saw her and she's so pretty, so I screamed but I didn't mean to scare her."

"It's okay," Pippin said, giving them a reassuring smile. She touched one of her ears. "She can't hear, is all, so I don't think it was your scream. I bet it's just all the people around that spooked her." She kept one hand on Sailor's head as she beckoned the kids forward. "She's okay now. You can pet her."

Their eyes widened as they inched forward, falling to their knees as soon as they were close enough. The girl stretched her arm out tentatively. "She won't bite?"

Pippin hadn't witnessed a single bit of aggression from Sailor, so she shook her head. "No. Just let her smell your hand first, like this." She demonstrated by holding her own hand out, letting Sailor's pink nose sniff it.

The girl mimicked Pippin, squealing a second later and yanking her hand back. "Her nose is cold!"

The boy took a turn, far more confidently than his sister. Sailor sniffed, touched, then licked his hand. He giggled as he stuck out his other hand, letting the dog repeat the process with it.

A voice rose above the kitchen chatter. The kids turned

to look through the legs of the party guests. "Let's go," the girl said, hopping up.

The little boy frowned but stood up.

"It's time to get Sailor back to her room, anyway," Pippin said, standing.

The kids each gave Sailor a hug before they scampered away. "Bye! Bye, Sailor!"

The dog's tail thunked against the side of the island, her whole backside wriggling with delight.

"Now how in the world did you get out," Pippin asked Sailor, whose only response was more wriggling and more tail thwacking.

"She hasn't grown opposable thumbs, has she?" Hattie suggested, peering at Sailor's front paws as if that were an actual possibility.

"Not as far as I know," Pippin said.

"Well, you never know, do you? Books talk to you, don't they? Magic happens." Hattie waved one hand around, an unlit cigarette clasped between her index and middle fingers. Hattie had told Pippin early on that she'd quit smoking years ago. "Holding the cigarette is the only part of the habit that won't kill me," she'd said.

"Bibliomancy is not quite in the same realm as a four-legged animal developing opposable thumbs," Pippin said. She directed her gaze at Sailor, waving her hand to get the dog's attention. Once Sailor made eye contact, Pippin patted her leg, and then beckoned with one hand. "Come on, let's go," she said, walking slowly so Sailor would follow her.

Out of the kitchen, around the corner, and—

Pippin stopped short. The study...her bedroom... She'd locked it, she knew she had, but the door was now unlocked and ajar. Without those opposable thumbs Hattie had mentioned, Sailor couldn't have opened the door. "How'd you get out, girl?" she asked, the sound of the party behind her fading away. Sailor simply stood by her side, unmoving.

Slowly, Pippin pushed the door in, holding her breath. She jumped back the second it swung all the way open—just in case someone was still in the room.

No one was.

Her visual sweep of the room revealed nothing out of place. The queen bed now sat where her father's desk had been. The cream colored quilt and shams lay undisturbed. Pippin had her own small office in the front of the house, so she hadn't moved a desk into the room. A single nightstand held a lamp, a stack of books, and a box of tissue. A reading chair with a floor lamp behind it on one side sat in the corner behind the door and next to the French doors leading to the enclosed side porch.

Her father's built-in bookshelves were mostly empty. Pippin's interest in books had developed only recently. It was the direct result of discovering her father's remains. She'd turned to bibliomancy to help her make sense of it all. Her father had loved books. Her mother, on the other hand, was a victim of the Lane family curse. She hated the divination of bibliomancy and did everything she could to steer clear of books. If she wasn't around them, they couldn't tell her the future, she'd reasoned.

Leo had kept books only in his study. His most prized books had been housed in the secret study upstairs. Reading had always been a struggle for Pippin. The letters reversed themselves in her mind. They jumped around on the page. They blurred before her eyes. "I believe you probably have a mild form of dyslexia," Jamie had told her. He'd given her some strategies, and slowly, the process of reading was becoming a little less daunting.

She bought local authors and regional books to place on

the built-ins Grey had installed in the great room, but that was as far as she'd gotten. The shelves here in her room were mostly devoid of books.

She let Sailor in, closing the door behind them. Sailor went straight to the plush dog bed Pippin had splurged for. After she first rescued the dog, she'd taken her to the local vet. Dr. Dickens's best guess was that Sailor had been on her own for the better part of a month. She was malnourished, dehydrated, and mangy. Providing a comfy bed seemed the least Pippin could do.

Sailor circled in the bed three times before settling down into a curled-up ball. Once Sailor plonked down, Pippin scanned the room again, but nothing seemed amiss. She strode to the bookshelf, examining the razor-thin vertical line between the beveled groves of the wood. This was the access to Leo's secret study above. Her father at least had the foresight to install a locking mechanism. She'd found the key in his desk before she'd actually found the lock itself, which blended in with the dark stain of the wood. She tugged on the door now, feeling the resistance of the secured lock. She exhaled in relief. At least the secret room was secure.

Whoever had managed to unlock her door, though, was still a mystery.

Chapter 8

"Isn't it astonishing that all these secrets have been preserved for so many years just so we could discover them!"
      ~Orville Wright

Ninety minutes later, bits and crumbs were all that was left of the hors d'oeuvres. The wine bottles had been completely emptied with just a half bottle of rosé left. The three-gallon Mason jar shaped dispensers, with their cork lids and metal and wood handles, sat side by side on the bar. One had been filled with blueberry and mint infused water, one with iced tea, and the third with lemonade, fresh slices of lemons floating on top. All were now down to the dregs. The floor beneath the spigots was wet and sticky.

Quincy Ratherford, reporter for the local Devil's Cove Gazette, waved at Pippin, scurrying toward her. She placed Quincy in his mid-fifties. He'd sprouted a beard since she'd first met him, the ginger hair covering a good part of his ruddy face. With his signature beret, this one in a pale peach lightweight linen, white linen pants, and turquoise and peach striped short sleeved shirt, the man was in a fashion league of his own. Even his sandals were stylish, and his toenails were perfectly pedicured. Pippin was a little jealous. Her nails—toes and fingers—were trimmed short and her cuticles were ragged from all the cleaning solutions and gardening. And a mani-pedi wasn't anywhere in her near future.

"Darling girl, this was amazing! You've outdone yourself."

Pippin brushed off the compliment with a laugh. "But you've never seen anything I've done."

Quincy batted away her words with a wave of one hand. "I don't have to. You have a gift. You and your brother both."

Grey ambled up. "Thanks, man." He held out his hand. "I'm—

Quincy pshaw'd, cutting him off. "I know *exactly* who you are, Grey Hawthorne." He pressed one palm to his chest. "Quincy Ratherford, at your service. I *am* the Devil's Cove Gazette."

When it was clear Quincy didn't plan on shaking his hand, Grey dropped his arm back to his side with an amused smile. "Nice to meet you."

Quincy beamed. "No, no. The pleasure is all mine. Now, I'll preface this by saying that I'm always on duty. So, on the record. I hear you've opened up your own woodworking business. Left your sister here to run the inn on her own?"

It wasn't a slam against Grey. When her brother had told her that he was going to strike out on his own and open Hawthorne Designs with Kyron, it had been an adjustment.

Just like so many twins, they'd grown up together, each of them one half of a whole. They had their own language, their own nicknames for each other, and had been each other's confidants in a family torn apart by secrets and tragedy. They started this project together, inheriting the house and turning it into Sea Captain's Inn, but she couldn't fault him—and she certainly couldn't stop him—from following his own passion.

Grey gave a small grin. "We're out on Old Croatan—"

"Oh, I know exactly where your shop is located," Quincy said with a wink. From anyone else, it might have felt a little creepy, like being stalked, but from the eccentric reporter, it came off as a compliment. "I'll come by and do a profile on you and your business partner."

As if on cue, Daisy and Kyron appeared. Quincy greeted them with a hearty, "Well, hello there! Kyron Washington, I presume?"

"That's right." Like Grey, Kyron held his hand out, dropping it again awkward seconds later.

Quincy looked down at Daisy, "And I know you from the library."

Daisy dipped her chin coyly. "Mr. Ratherford, you know everyone in town."

"I sure do, Daisy Santiago, I sure do. And you call me Quincy. Mr. Ratherford is my father."

Pippin snuck away from the four of them when she caught sight of Jamie, Heidi, and Mathilda McAdams coming in the front door. "Daddy!" Mathilda screeched. "We missed it! It's over!"

Heidi covered her ears dramatically, taking a giant side-step away from her little sister. The two girls were opposites in every way. Mathilda had amber eyes just like her dad's, and her hair was wavy instead of straight like Heidi's. She was six years old, lived in bright colorful dresses, complimented by tights in the winter and bare legged in the summer. She was kind of Daisy's mini-me. Mathilda was a ball energy who clung to her father like velcro.

Heidi was eleven but closing in on adulthood with frightening speed. Her wardrobe usually consisted of jeans, sweaters, and blouses in the cooler months, and, like now, shorts and button up shirts in the warmer months. Most of the time she kept her brown hair pulled into a serious ponytail and her nose in a book. Pippin was three times her age, but Heidi had read a thousand times more books.

"It can't be over if you're here," Pippin said, and Mathilda smiled a toothless grin up at her.

"*Where the Red Fern Grows*," Heidi said, simply throwing out the title of a book as Pippin led them through the great room and into the kitchen.

Another one Pippin had never read. "Nope," she said. One of these days Heidi would name a title she *had* read. The girl would be utterly shocked when Pippin replied with a pleased, "Yes!"

"You just got Sailor, and this one's about a boy and his dogs, so probably not a good one to read for you right now," Heidi said. "What about *The Pearl*? John Steinbeck. It's, like, ninety pages. I'm sure you could read it."

"Heidi," Jamie scolded.

Heidi shrugged. "What? It's short."

Pippin smiled, taking no offense and the innocent truthfulness of the young girl. "You're right, Heidi. Short is better for me right now. Do you have a copy at the bookshop?"

Heidi folded her arms over her chest and harrumphed. "Of course we do, Pippin. Let's make *that* our next selection."

"Okay, then," Pippin said with a serious nod of her head. "*The Pearl* it is."

Jamie often said his older daughter was an old soul stuck in a young girl's body. He was right on the money. Everything was black and white for her and books were like oxygen to her. Ever since she found out Pippin hadn't spent much time reading, she'd made it her life's mission to rectify that travesty. They discussed three books over ice cream at Sprinkles in the past three months. Three books had exhausted Pippin's ability, but to Heidi, it was just the beginning. "We should read twice as many, at least," she proclaimed at least once a week, but it took Pippin at least twice as long to read a book. Their current pace worked just fine for her.

"Books, books, books." Mathilda sighed dramatically. "Daddy, all Heidi talks about is books, and we *did* miss the party!"

Pippin crouched down in front of her and smiled. "I saved some lemonade and a plate of the best appetizers," she said. "You and Heidi being here is the *best* part of the party for me."

The next second, KC and the Sunshine Band blasted through the built-in speakers Grey had installed. Ruby's voice rose above the music. "After party! Dance party!"

Pippin glanced at her watch. They had thirty minutes before she had to shut everything down.

Mathilda's eyes went wide with excitement. She looked hopefully at Heidi. "Dance party!"

"I am *not* dancing," Heidi said, tucking her chin down and looking at her sister as if she was crazy for even thinking it.

"Just go out there with her," Jamie said, nudging his elder daughter. "I'll be there in a minute."

Mathilda kicked off her flip-flops and bounced on her toes. "Yay! Let's go! Let's go!"

Heidi frowned, but Pippin and Jamie knew it was all for show. She let her arms fall to her sides and followed Mathilda to the open area behind the couch. The second they were jumping around to "Boogie Shoes," Pippin spun to face Jamie. "I think someone broke into my bedroom."

His gaze automatically shot in the direction of the open hallway upstairs. "What do you mean, someone broke in?"

"Over here," she said, hitching her thumb toward the study. "I moved downstairs."

He followed toward the kitchen and around the corner. Pippin slipped her bangle keyring from her wrist and unlocked the door, pushing it in. Sailor was still in her plush bed, sound asleep, completely unaware she and Jamie had walked in.

"I didn't know you moved rooms," Jamie stated.

"For such a big house, there are only three bedrooms. Now four since Grey divided the master suite into two. It made sense to make them all guest rooms."

"Right." Jamie stared at the built-in shelf as if he had X-ray vision and could see straight through it to the secret stairs and the room they led to. He nodded toward the hidden door, the question plain on his face.

"It's still locked."

Jamie adjusted his John Lennon glasses before surveying the room. "Was something taken?"

"I don't think so."

"Maybe someone was poking around, opening up closed doors," he suggested.

"Someone was," she said, and she told him about the man with the translucent eyes. "But, Jamie, the door was locked from the inside."

"You're sure it was locked?"

Pippin faltered. She was ninety-nine percent sure, but she followed his gaze to the door and second-guessed herself. The lock wasn't broken, so unless someone had a copy of the key, which was completely impossible, then maybe she only *thought* she'd locked it.

Sailor hadn't moved, but her nose twitched, and her eyes opened. Pippin held one hand out, palm facing the dog, telling her to stay put. She scanned the room again, her gaze landing on the French doors. Had she locked *them*? In three quick steps, she was pushing down the handle, stepping back when it opened.

No, no, no. In all her scurrying around, had she forgotten to lock the French doors? She didn't think so, but...

She scanned the enclosed porch, her finger tapping against her lips. The sky was still light, the sun just beginning its decent to the west. The enclosed space, shadowed from the dark screening, was illuminated by the outdoor lights Grey had strung. She looked beyond the porch to the pampas grass in the yard, starting when she realized a vertical slice of light shone through the mesh. In three strides, she was in front of the torn screen.

Jamie was at her heels. "What is it?"

She slid her fingers through the tear, following it all the way down to the railing. Plenty of room for a person to slip through.

"I *know* I locked the doors. I'm not imagining it," she said. "Someone *was* in there."

"Someone looking for your dad's study," Jamie said matter-of-factly, because that was the only thing that made sense.

Under normal circumstances, she might have thought it

was a crime of opportunity. A break-in by someone hoping to find something valuable.

But her father had kept secrets and her family lived under a curse. These were the furthest things from normal circumstances.

Chapter 9

"Just before they sailed, Drake ceremoniously erected a firm post to which he attached a metal plaque engraved with a formal land claim in the name of Queen Elizabeth for the territory they named Nova Albion."

"What was the secret being concealed? Presented here is the case that Drake's land claim included a vast amount of territory he did not see, and therefore could not have legitimately claimed by the tenants of the time...the latitudes he reached on the west coast of America were not the ones reported in the official record of the claim."

~Melissa Darby, *Thunder Go North: The Hunt for Sir Francis Drake's Fair & Good Bay*

 he dance party had shifted from KC and the Sunshine Band to The Bee Gees to Ariana Grande, the latter at Mathilda's insistence. Despite the lingering anxiety about the man with the crystal eyes and the break in of her room, Pippin felt a surge of contentment in the depths of her heart when she looked at her friends. For a moment, it overwhelmed her. She and Grey had been on their own for so long, depending only on each other. But now they were putting down roots. And these people...these people cared about her.

But her brother was on his way out. "Catch y'all later," Grey said, heading to the front door.

"Wait!" Daisy said. "You have to come with us to the Brewery. It's too early to call it a night."

"No can do. I have an early day tomorrow," Grey said.

They all turned to face him, waiting for more. "Oh yeah?" Pippin asked. Her brother was a genius with wood. Give him a sapling and he could magically turn it into a wooden throne fit for a king. "What's going on?"

"Nothing to get excited about. Potential new client, is all."

"Nah, man," Kyron said. "Totally get excited. He's got a meeting with some folks out of Chapel Hill. They're coming to check out some of our work. They're renovating an old building and want Grey—"

"Us," Grey interrupted.

"Right. They want Hawthorne Designs to do some of the custom furniture."

Daisy's face broadcasted her conflicting emotions. On the one hand, Pippin knew she wanted Hawthorne Designs to land this new client. Small businesses failed more often than they succeeded so Grey and Kyron needed to jump at every opportunity. On the other hand, Pippin knew Daisy wanted Kyron to go out with her to the Brewery. "Are you leaving, too?" she asked him, visibly trying to balance her warring desires.

Kyron's arm slipped around the her pixie waist. "Not yet.

You have me for another hour."

She turned to face him with a smile, her arms encircling his neck. "An hour before you turn into a pumpkin? I'll take it."

Hattie Juniper Pickle nodded her approval at the love-birds. "Take every second of every minute of every hour of... well, you get the idea. In the immortal words of Robin Williams, carpe diem!"

"Actually, by way of Robert Frost and, you know, originally from Horace," Jamie whispered to Pippin.

"Who's Horace?" she whispered back.

"He was a poet during Augustus's rule."

Pippin furrowed her brow. "Ummm..."

"The Roman emperor Cesar Augustus. 23 BCE," he explained.

Before she could ask what BCE was, because she'd always thought it was just BC, Ruby went maternal on the lip-lock of the new couple, spreading her arms and flapping them like a bird trying to fly. "Okay, you two. Children present. That's enough."

As Daisy and Kyron separated, Jamie slipped away to corner his girls. "Let's hit it," he said. "Mom's picking you up at eight sharp and we still have to get you packed."

In pure preteen fashion, Heidi groaned. "That's too early."

"It's Myrtle Beach!" he said, all smiles.

Heidi frowned and almost stomped her foot. "But it's a whole week, Dad."

Jamie prodded her toward the door. "Yeah, a whole *week* at Myrtle *Beach*."

She harrumphed. "I'm bringing ten books."

Mathilda stuck her chin out and waggled her head. "I'm bringing *no* books."

Heidi stared at her. "We own a bookshop, Tilly. How you can *not* like to read is *beyond* me."

"*We* don't own the store. *Daddy* owns the store," Mathilda countered, "and I *do* like to read, sort of. Just not the books *Mommy* wants me to."

"That's why you should pick out one or two you want to bring, dummy. So Mom can't give you something else."

"Heidi," Jamie scolded.

She heaved a sigh. "Sorry."

Jamie scooped Mathilda into his arms and headed for the door. "We'll find you the perfect book to bring, just in case." He turned to everyone with a wave. "Great party. The place'll be a hit, Pippin."

He nudged Heidi. "Thanks," she grumbled.

Mathilda frowned. "Who'll take care of the soldier flowers?"

She was referring to the glazed green pots standing sentry outside the entrance to The Open Door. Toward the end of spring, Pippin had suggested to Jamie and his grandfather that they change the flowers out and add some plants that would drape over the edge of the pots. That had led Pippin and the elder Mr. McAdams to visit Bloom, the island's nursery. Now the pots overflowed with sweet alyssum, petunia, ivy, and a few dahlias for height. Mathilda had taken it upon herself to be the caretaker of those pots, checking for weeds every day. She hauled a watering can that was half as big as she was, the water sloshing over the sides as she carried it from the store's bathroom to the sidewalk, to give them plenty of water.

"I'll take care of them, squirt," Jamie reassured.

Mathilda pursed her lips and angled her head down. "You better, Daddy. They're special flowers. They watch over us. They need loving care."

Jamie nodded, quite serious. "Fear not, Mathilda McAdams. I will give the flowers ample loving care in your absence."

Satisfied, Mathilda waved. "See you next week!" Jamie bounced her once in his arms and she piped up again. "Thank you, Miss Pippin," she said.

A week with their mother, Miranda, sounded like torture. She hoped the girls had fun. "You're welcome! Thanks for coming!" Pippin exclaimed, throwing invisible streams of enthusiastic air kisses at the girls.

Jamie reached for the knob, but stumbled back as the door was forcefully pushed open. A woman burst in, practically knocking the small McAdams family over like so many bowling pins. "Oh my God, I'm so glad you're still open. I got stuck at The Brewery—"

"Which is where we should be right now," Ruby murmured.

"—but I'm here now. Where is she?"

Pippin felt a niggling of familiarity. Had the woman been here earlier? She looked to be somewhere in her mid-fifties, wore an eyelet blouse over pink capris, and styled her blond hair in a boyish cut. "Where's who?" she asked.

"That history lady. She's staying here, isn't she? I need to see her."

"She is, but I haven't seen her in a few hours," Pippin said.

The woman had a cloth bag hung diagonally over her shoulder. She swung it around, dipped both her hands inside like it was a bucket of sand, and brought them back out with something heavy wrapped in a thin blue cloth. "I told her I had a Dare Stone. An authentic one. Of course, she didn't believe me. No one ever does, but she's got a *PhD* so she should *know*. I brought it to prove it to her."

Jamie's entire stance changed and curiosity emanated from him. "A Dare Stone?" he asked.

Ruby piped up, The Brewery apparently forgotten for the moment. "As in a *Roanoke Lost Colonists Virginia Dare* Dare Stone?"

The woman looked affronted. "Is there any other kind?"

Ruby's description knocked something loose in Pippin's brain. Recognition hit. This was Gin White, a native islander who claimed to be a descendant of Eleanor Dare and her daughter, Virginia, and shared her proof with anyone who would listen.

"That's it?" Jamie asked, moving closer, Mathilda still hooked in one of his arms. She had one arm slung around his neck. He needed to get his girls ready for the vacation with their mom, but history threw a wrench in that plan. "Can I see it?"

Gin whipped herself around, moving the heavy bundle in her hands out of Jamie's line of sight. "No! I need to show it to Dr. Baxter. Where is she?"

"I'm right here, Ms. White."

Pippin whirled around. Dr. Baxter appeared out of nowhere. Well, not quite out of *no*where. She'd come from the kitchen reading nook, a book in her hand. How long had she been there?

Gin spun around. "I brought it." She bounced on the balls of her feet, each lift giving her a momentary few inches on Dr. Baxter. "You didn't believe me, but I brought it."

Dr. Baxter narrowed her eyes, not looking nearly as thrilled. Dr. Baxter stared at Gin, eye to eye. "There are forty-seven so-called Dare Stones which have been discredited. The original is believed to be a hoax. What makes you think *yours* is authentic?"

Gin White waggled her head defiantly. "I don't care

about all that stuff. This here, it's the real thing, all right. Wait till you see."

"She's right," Jamie said to Gin, then to Dr. Baxter, he said, "You're right." His eyes practically sparkled with excitement. He released Mathilda, his hands on her back as she slid down his side. "Only the authenticity of the original, found by Louis E. Hammond near the Chowan River, still floats out there. It has never been proven or disproven."

When everyone in the room stared at him, he shrugged sheepishly. "History buff, and this one's right in our backyard."

Gin spun around to face Jamie. "I'm telling you! This is real. Those others, they came out of the woodwork for the reward money. But this one, it was found by my great-great grandfather. Just like you said, he found it on the banks of the Chowan."

"What do you think, Dr. Baxter?" Jamie asked.

Her eyes stirred with life. Reluctantly, Pippin thought, but still... "It's wonderful to talk with someone truly interested in history and the truth, Mr. —"

"McAdams," Jamie said.

"He's being modest," Pippin said. "He's got a Ph.D., too. In Medieval Irish—" She broke off, turning to him. "What's it in?"

"Medieval Irish literature, and one in anthropology, specifically the conquering of the Irish."

Pippin somehow stopped her jaw from dropping open. She didn't know about the second doctorate. The guy was brainiac personified.

Dr. Baxter looked just as surprised. Pippin had the feeling the woman was usually the smartest—or at least the best educated—person in the room. Not so in the company of Jamie McAdams. "My theory, Dr. McAd—"

Jamie shook his head. "Just Jamie's fine. I don't like the pomp that comes with the title."

"You earned it, you should use it," Dr. Baxter countered.

Jamie shrugged it off. "What's your theory?" he asked again. Third time's the charm.

"Yes, yes." Dr. Baxter moved to the couch and sat, sliding forward to the edge. Her irritable demeanor returned. "I don't see how this stone can be any more authentic than the others. My belief is that the same person was behind both Drake's Brass Plate and the original Dare Stone. And perhaps this one." She indicated the bundle Gin still held. Drake's Brass Plate. Dr. Baxter had mentioned the Brass Plate when she'd checked in, and the two women who were discredited when their postulations didn't match the accepted theory.

Jamie sat down across from her and crossed one leg over the other. He leaned his elbow on the arm of the chair and cupped his chin. Dr. Baxter had his full attention. "Go on."

The historian didn't hesitate. She steepled her fingers together as she stated her hypothesis. "Both artifacts were discovered in 1937. They come from the same time period, the late 14th century, and they were both connected to Elizabethan maritime explorers."

"Sir Francis Drake and Sir Walter Raleigh," Jamie said.

"Precisely. But there is a modern common denominator, as well as too many details that don't add up."

"Daddy," Mathilda stood next to him and leaned her head against his shoulder. "I'm tired."

"Not me," Heidi said, listening raptly to the conversation the adults were having. She was standing behind her father, leaning on the back of the chair.

He rubbed Mathilda's back. "We'll go real soon, Squirt.

Give me a few minutes." He pulled her onto his lap and into the crook of his arm. Her eyes drifted closed.

Dr. Baxter picked up where she left off. "In both cases, with Drake's Brass Plate and the original Dare Stone, two historians led the charge in proclaiming their authenticity. Of course, now we know the Brass Plate was a hoax."

Jamie adjusted his glasses. "I've read about that," he said. "Planted by a University of California, Berkeley, professor as a joke for some archaeologist friends to find, right?"

"Precisely," Dr. Baxter said again. "If this stone resembles the first one in any way, the lithic can be tested showing if it came from the east coast, or the west coast."

"I don't know what *lithic* means, but this stone, it's the real deal," Gin blurted.

Dr. Baxter pursed her lips. "I'm not so sure. Louis Hammond was a Californian, out here *vacationing*." She made air quotes around the word. "He just *happens* to be the one person to find the five-hundred-year-old stone? Then he basically *drops* off the map. It's suspect at best. A complete lie at worst."

"Is that why you're here?" Jamie asked. "Are you part of the dig?"

"There is a theory that the colonists were here, but I don't believe it."

Just like everyone educated in North Carolina, Pippin knew the basic story of the Roanoke colonists. They sailed to the shores of what was now called the Outer Banks in the late 1500s. Their leader and governor, John White, had returned to England to replenish supplies. He didn't come back for three years, and by that time, they had disappeared. The story became American Folklore. The Dare Stones were inscribed with messages from Eleanor Dare to her father. Pippin didn't know all but one of the stones found had been discredited. And Dr. Baxter thought *that* one was a hoax?

"Can you tell us anything? What have they found?" Jamie didn't even try to tamp down the excitement in his voice. What was mildly interesting to the average person was, for Jamie, the equivalent of a wreck diver finding a stash of gold coins from the 1700s. Which was to say, he was enthralled.

"I'm afraid not," she said, "It would take time to authenticate anything, and as I said, it's unlikely anything on Devil's Cove is from the colonists. You see, back in early 20th century, two women, independently, I might add, determined it was unlikely that Drake landed where the brass plate was found. Zelia Nuttall's supposition—mind you, this was back in 1915—was that Drake was on the Northwest coast of Oregon or Washington, not off the California coast. Her theory was dismissed and all but forgotten.

"Then in the 30s, Eva Taylor came to the same conclusion. She said Drake had been on the Oregon coast, *not* north of San Francisco. It wasn't until later still, though, that Drake's Brass Plate was deemed a fake. Believe me, the people behind the Brass Plate hoax are the same people behind the forgery of the original Dare Stone. History needs to reflect the findings of these women, and the truth must be accepted once and for all."

Pippin spoke up. "So, if you can prove that whatever is found here came, what, later than the colonists' era, then—" Then what? How would that prove this Dare Stone was also a hoax perpetrated by the same person?

"It is one more piece of evidence that the colonists did not split up into smaller groups and somehow survive."

"But they did," Gin White said. "They did, and my stone will prove it."

Chapter 10

"Does it seem all but incredible to you that intelligence should travel for two thousand miles, along those slender copper lines, far down in the all but fathomless Atlantic; never before penetrated ... save when some foundering vessel has plunged with her hapless company to the eternal silence and darkness of the abyss? Does it seem ... but a miracle ... that the thoughts of living men ... should burn over the cold, green bones of men and women, whose hearts, once as warm as ours, burst as the eternal gulfs closed and roared over them centuries ago?"

~Edward Everett

*T*he next morning, Pippin had breakfast ready at ten minutes past seven, just in case Dr. Baxter came down a few minutes early.

She didn't. Pippin grumbled for a few minutes, debating whether or not she should call the room to let the woman know the breakfast she *demanded* be ready at seven-fifteen was waiting.

In the end, she decided not to. She let Sailor outside—the dog had trained herself and never left the property—coming back inside just as Shan and Genji Lee came down.

"Y'all are up early," Pippin said, directing them to the back porch. She followed them with two heavy white mugs brimming with steaming coffee. She had the mugs custom-made to bear the Sea Captain's Inn logo she designed. It was a simple line drawing of the inn, small flowers and leaves on either side, Sea Captain's Inn was written in a free-flowing cursive font under the picture, and *Devil's Cove, North Carolina* printed and stacked below the name.

She had the same logo made into a cut metal sign. It hung behind the registration desk, and another hung on the wall of the back deck. A few faerie houses and a gathering of succulents in a variety of pots decorated the railings. "These little details make all the difference," Ruby had told her.

"I'm an early bird," Mrs. Lee said. She gave a gentle backhand to her husband. "Shan is not, but we have not had a vacation in, what, ten years?" She looked at her husband, seemingly for confirmation, but didn't actually wait for him to answer. "At least ten years. Maybe more. Shan has a very busy job in pharmaceuticals. They should let him take time off, right? They should. But they don't."

As Mrs. Lee kept talking, Pippin glanced at Shan Lee, noticing the way he darted his eyes to the left, not looking at his wife. He wore a guilty expression and Pippin got the feeling Mrs. Lee talked nonstop. She wondered if Mr. Lee's employer really *didn't* give him time off, or whether Mr. Lee did not *want* to take the time off.

Zoe normally had Sundays and Mondays off, but she'd come in early today to help clean up from the party. By the time Pippin had come down to prepare breakfast, she'd already cleaned the outdoor tables and chairs, wiping away any mist that had gathered overnight. She moved on to wiping down the railing, rearranging the succulents and four cute little frogs. There had been five, but one had fallen and chipped. Zoe had bought some epoxy and glued the broken piece back on. Now it was curing out of the way in the bathroom cupboard upstairs. Pippin thought the heavy cement frog would have won against a battle with the sand, but it had the bad luck to hit the concrete footing.

Pippin held open one of the French doors for the Lees. She caught Zoe's eye, inclining her head toward the kitchen. Zoe gave a final swipe across the wood and scurried away.

Pippin directed the Lees to one of the three bistro tables on the deck. She set down the mugs, vaguely listening to Mrs. Lee say that the walls were thin so she could hear the television and conversations in the other rooms, but she didn't mind too much.

Zoe returned with cutlery and napkins. "It's seven thir-ty," she said in a faux British accent. The young woman slipped into British or Australian or German or French accents whenever the mood struck. She'd missed her calling as an actress. Pippin glanced at her watch. So much for seven-fifteen sharp.

Mrs. Lee was still talking. She'd moved on to ghosts and bumps in the night. She caught Pippin's eyes. "This place isn't haunted, is it?"

Pippin gave a coy little smile. "Well, this house *is* named for a rum runner during middle of the 17th century. His ship, Devil's Rum, wrecked on the shallow shoals, never to be seen again."

Mrs. Lee's hazel eyes were wide. "But I saw signs for wreck diving. Didn't they find it?"

"People say it's in the depths of the Graveyard of the Atlantic, but nobody has ever found it," Pippin said.

"What happened?" Zoe prompted.

Pippin flashed that mysterious smile again. "It is said that two men escaped on a shallop, and managed to navigate through the shoals and into the sound. They ended up in our cove, with bottles of rum strong enough to kill the devil, people say. The island was first called Devil's Rum Cove—"

"And, let me guess, it was shortened to just 'Devil's Cove,'" Mrs. Lee finished. "Amazing. I heard another shipwreck story for another town. A ship was lured to the shore by a lantern hanging from a horse's head on the shore. A *nag's* head," she said. "And that's why the town of Nags Head is called Nags Head."

"You've done your homework," Pippin said.

Mrs. Lee beamed. "I didn't find out anything about this house though."

"Well, one of those two rum runners built it. Captain Hubbard, he was called. He lived and died in this house."

"Are we going to run into *his* ghost?"

"Genji," Mr. Lee said, followed by a clear scolding in what Pippin thought was Mandarin.

Mrs. Lee didn't seem bothered by her husband's admonition. She just shrugged and turned back to Pippin. "So, this house really *is* historical."

"Oh yes. My parents bought it after Captain Hubbard's last descendant, Perry Hubbard, passed." Pippin had heard the story of Perry Hubbard's death from Hattie Juniper Pickle, who seemed to know everyone's secrets on Rum Runner's Lane, and maybe even in the entire town.

Mrs. Lee was enraptured. "Tell me more! I'm a teacher, you know. My students are going to love these stories."

Mr. Lee flashed a bemused look at his wife and sat quietly sipping his coffee.

From the corner of her eye, Pippin saw Zoe slip into the kitchen to finish prepping their breakfast.

"Well," Pippin continued, "There is not much more to say, except that the woman, Perry, became a recluse. She was rarely seen in life, but on a clear night, some people do claim to have seen her ghost on the widow's walk."

Mrs. Lee gasped. She clutched her husband's arm, causing him to slosh his coffee. "It's supposed to be clear tonight!" She turned to Pippin. "We must go up there!"

Pippin hesitated. She didn't want guests to go up to the widow's walk, but she feared Mrs. Lee was used to getting her way and might badger her during the entire stay if she didn't agree. "Just for a few minutes. I'll meet you at the top of the stairs at nine-thirty."

Mrs. Lee clasped her hands together. "We will be there."

"I will *not* be there," Mr. Lee said.

Mrs. Lee didn't miss a beat. "*I* will be there."

Zoe returned carrying a lovely French countryside-style three-tiered stand, the plates rimmed with flute waves. She put two raspberry scones and two small dishes of clotted cream on the bottom tier. In the middle were mini frittatas and quiches, and on the top was an arrangement of vibrant blueberries and strawberries.

Zoe placed it in the center of the table, then laid out the two plates she also brought out.

"Very nice," Mrs. Lee said.

"I'll leave you to it," Pippin said with a smile as Mr. Lee dug in.

"Thank you," he said.

She and Zoe retreated to the kitchen, leaving the Lees to their breakfast. "Will you ever get tired of telling that story?" Zoe asked, sounding a bit like Eliza Doolittle.

Pippin shrugged. "Probably, but I think it's just going to come with the territory."

"You might have to make up some more stories. The sea captain and his long-lost love! The sea captain and his hidden treasure! The sea captain and—"

"Yoo-hoo!"

The glanced at the deck to see Mrs. Lee waving her hand. "Salt?"

"I'll bring it right out," Zoe called. She looked at Pippin, adding, "I'll clean upstairs before we tackle the great room."

"Perfect," Pippin said, grateful she wouldn't be doing all the afterparty work on her own.

Zoe skipped out to the deck with the salt and pepper shakers before disappearing into the mudroom to head up the back staircase. Pippin saw to prepping breakfast for Mr. Marshall. She'd just finished brewing a fresh pot of coffee when the vacuum cleaner blasted from upstairs. No, Zoe. It was too early for that! Mr. Marshall might still be asleep. She started for the great room to get Zoe to cut the noise, but stopped when she caught a flash of a red jacket at the front door. "Mrs. Baxter!" she called. "I have your breakfast!"

The woman paused for a second. She turned slightly. The hood of her jacket was up as if a hurricane roared outside. She threw up a hand. "No time," she said in her gruffest voice, and then she was gone.

Pippin stared after her, flabbergasted. The nerve! That woman had *demanded* an early breakfast. "She isn't too friendly, is she?"

Pippin jumped and pressed her hand to her heart. Mrs. Lee had come into the great room behind her, stealthy as a mouse. "She must have a busy day planned," Pippin answered, walking with them toward the stairs.

"Can't believe she's up so early," Mr. Lee grumbled. "Of

course, with the racket." He looked up, as if he could see through the walls at the vacuum running above.

"I know, I'm sorry. I'll tell Zoe not to run it so early."

"It's fine," Mrs. Lee said. "We heard the woman up late, talking, that's all."

They headed up the stairs to their room. Pippin was right behind them to tell Zoe to keep it quiet. The vacuum stopped and the house fell blissfully quiet. She waited for few seconds to see if it would start up again, but it didn't. Zoe must have realized it was too early.

Pippin headed back to the kitchen. She caught a glimpse of Sailor's tail as the honey-colored dog disappeared into the mudroom. She trailed after her. The door leading to the far end of the back deck was slightly ajar. Her feet crunched on a spattering of sand on the tile floor. Dr. Baxter's sudden appearance the night before shot to her mind. She said she'd been in the kitchen nook. Pippin had seen her leave, but not return. The woman was stealthy and unpredictable, as her sudden departure just now proved. Had she left the party the night before, only to come back into the house through the mudroom, leaving the door open all night? She opened the door and peered outside, as if the sand on the deck that trailed onto the floor of the utility room proved that's exactly what had happened. She locked the door and added *sweep the mudroom* to her To Do list.

Back in the kitchen, she took the scone meant for Dr. Baxter and slathered it with clotted cream, then she cut it in half and divided the rest of the fruit and frittatas on to two plates, one for her and one for Zoe. Together, they'd finish off Dr. Baxter's breakfast.

Chapter 11

"Do not seek death. But do not fear it either. There cannot be life without death, it is inescapable."

~Keisei Tagami

*T*he day of an innkeeper is filled with all the little things that make a stay five-star worthy. Putting out fresh flowers; cleaning guest rooms; cleaning guest bathrooms; wiping down all the doorknobs and other communal spaces; restocking items like soaps, shampoos, and shaving cream. The list went on and on. The bottom line, Pippin knew, was that she had to anticipate a guest's needs.

The Lees had been out exploring in the morning, took a midday nap, then went back out for the afternoon and an early dinner at one of the island's middle of the road seafood restaurants. "We're on a budget," Mr. Lee had reminded his wife when she voted to go to a more upscale establishment.

Pippin wasn't entirely comfortable going into the guest rooms yet, but it was part of the job. Once the Lees were gone again, she threw back her shoulders, used her master key, and went in to straighten the room and turn down the sheets. She never knew what to expect when she entered a guest room, but Mr. Lee's insistence on a less expensive restaurant prepared Pippin for budget-friendly luggage and clothing.

Right on the money. During the decorating phase of the inn, Pippin had placed toile luggage racks in each room to help her guests keep their belongings off the floor. The Lees had them set up along the wall opposite the bed, their ordinary black roller suitcases sitting on top, each closed and zipped up.

The room itself didn't need much straightening up. The quilted bedding had been pulled up. Pippin straightened it and folded down the top four inches. The towels in the bathroom were hung up. She straightened them, pulled the shower curtains closed, and put out a new washcloth, tossing the soiled one on the small housekeeping cart she'd left just outside the door. Back in the bedroom she pulled the quilt tight again, just to feel like she'd done something. She plumped the pillows. Finally, she placed a wrapped chocolate from the Chocolatier on each of the pillows. She left the room quietly, locking the door behind her.

Next up was Paul Marshall's room. As she inserted her master key, her cell phone vibrated in her back pocket. It was Grey. "How'd the appointment go?" she asked, skipping the *hello* and *how are you?*

He made a little noncommittal sound before saying, "Yeah, I think it went okay. They liked my setup and the samples. They said they'll be in touch, so now I just have to wait."

"I hope they know they better snap you up before you're completely booked."

"Ah Peevie, always my biggest fan."

"You know it."

"Listen," he said after a pause. "I think we should talk."

"Okay," she said, but she already felt the dread of their differing views coming up in the conversation. The conflict that might come between them. His refusal of her theories and her opinion of his reckless behavior.

"I'll come to you."

"Great. We can talk in the Burrow."

"The Burrow?" he asked with a wry chuckle. "Is that what you call it now?"

"Leo's Burrow. A nod to Tolkien. Plus, I like the sound of it and it's easier to say that instead of always saying, 'the hidden study,' or 'the regular study,' which, you know, is my bedroom now."

"Right. Makes sense. So..."

"Today? Tomorrow?"

"Tomorrow," he said. "Around three or four?"

"I'll be here."

She tucked her phone into her back pocket and shoved everything about the Lane family, the curse, and Grey out of her mind. She let herself into Paul Marshall's room. He had a speed breakfast—not enjoying his scone and mini quiches near enough, to Pippin's mind—, left a short time later and was still gone.

She opened the door and stopped short on the threshold. She would have pegged Mr. Marshall, with his cargo pants, slightly tattered polo shirt, and worn-out flip-flops, to be a little on the messy side. That was an understatement of epic proportion. His room looked like a tornado had spiraled through it. She picked her way through the man's scattered clothing. His reservation was only for five days, but it looked like he packed for a month. A dirty clothes pile sat in the corner of the room. Several pairs of discarded plaid boxer shorts sat right on top. A short-sleeved casual button-down shirt turned inside-out, and a pair of khaki pants lay halfway off the bed.

"Wow," she said under her breath. She glanced in the bathroom, noticing the puddle of water on the floor. A tornado *and* a hurricane.

The luggage rack for the room was still collapsed and leaning against the wall. Mr. Marshall's suitcase lay open on the floor in front of the window. From the looks of it, most of the contents were strewn around the room. A pair of Tevas, wrinkled t-shirts, rugged shorts, and balled up socks. Even chinos and two button-down short-sleeve shirts were tossed carelessly over the desk chair. A dingy canvas duffle bag sat on one of the chairs, but the backpack he seemed to always haul with him was, of course, gone. She had no idea if the man was on a solo vacation, on a business trip—although there was no business to speak of on-island—, or here for some other reason all together. His belongings gave her no answers.

Pippin popped open the luggage rack, setting it next to the suitcase, and moved the pants and shirt to it. She made the bed, plumping the pillows and turning down the sheets, then added the chocolate.

She tackled the bathroom next, emptying the trash, then mopping up the water with one of the towels Mr. Marshall had discarded. Apparently, he didn't think much about conserving resources by using his towels more than once. Pippin took fresh bath and hand towels from under the cupboard and hung them up, gathered up the damp ones, and took one last look around. The room still looked a disaster, but she'd done the best she could.

She stepped back into the hallway, hesitating before tackling Dr. Baxter's room. It was four o'clock and just like Mr. Marshall, she hadn't returned yet.

The small placard to the left of the door had the inn's logo facing out. Dr. Baxter hadn't flipped it to the Do Not Disturb side, so she figured the coast was clear and the room was empty. Just as she had with the other rooms before barging in, though, she rapped quietly on the door.

No answer.

She tried again, a little louder this time.

Still nothing. The coast was clear for her to enter. She used her master key to unlock the door, reminding herself of her mental note to call a locksmith for deadbolts. She stepped in and looked around. The curtains were closed, making the room dark. Pippin turned on the lamp, leaving the curtains closed in deference to the occupant's preference. The room was not as tidy as the Lee's, but it was not nearly as messy as Paul Marshall's. Dr. Baxter had made the bed. Only the pillow was slightly deflated. Pippin puffed it up, pulled the quilt taut as she'd done in the Lee's room, turned down the sheets, and left a wrapped chocolate on the pillowcase.

She checked the bathroom to see if new towels were needed. Nope. They were all neatly hanging from their hooks. The small trash can was empty. Dr. Baxter had her make up lined up in a row. Her toothbrush and toothpaste lay on an open washcloth. Only the robe, the inn's logo embroidered on the left side, lay folded over the bathtub rather than hanging on the hook behind the door.

Pippin left everything as it was, then ran through the

rest of the evening in her head. She'd do the rest of her chores, make her dinner, show Mrs. Lee the widow's walk, then take Sailor for a stroll before bed. As Mrs. Lee had said, it was going to be a clear evening, perfect for a quick walk to the beach and back.

She managed a twenty-minute lie down around four while Zoe manned the front desk. The phone wasn't ringing off the hook, but it was frequent enough that someone had to be around to answer it when it did. At five o'clock Pippin was back downstairs and turned on the answering machine, the message stating that phone calls would be returned the next day.

Zoe's phone buzzed. "Ooop! My boyfriend's here to pick me up," she said. "Okay if I head out?"

"I didn't even know you had a boyfriend," Pippin said.

"Yeah, for a few years now. Bry's an adventurer. Tonight we're doing...ooo, it'll be dangerous. Kind of an escape room."

"I didn't know we had one of those on Devil's Cove."

"It's kind of a secret. You have to know someone who knows someone."

"Be careful," Pippin said.

"Always." Zoe sang show tunes as she walked down the walkway and slipped into the passenger seat of a four-door navy sedan. Soon, the street was silent, the only sound the distant crash of waves.

The rest of the evening passed quietly enough. She hadn't seen any of the guests again until eight forty-five, at which time Mrs. Lee began pacing back and forth on the landing. Pippin stayed in her room until nine twenty-five. She left Sailor on her bed, grabbed her windbreaker from the mud room at the end of the kitchen's reading nook, and went upstairs.

"It's time!" Mrs. Lee's excited voice seemed to echo through the quiet house. She slapped her hand over her mouth. "So sorry. Shan is always saying I'm too loud and I talk too much. I don't notice."

Pippin swept her arm out to indicate the other rooms. "It only matters after ten o'clock when the other guests might be getting ready for bed."

Mrs. Lee hunched her shoulders and dropped her voice to a loud whisper. "I think we're all night owls. Except Shan, of course."

Pippin smiled. She liked Mrs. Lee. If she'd had a teacher like her when she'd been in school, she might have tried a little harder. At the door to the widow's walk, she put her hand in the pocket to fish out the key she'd put there the other night. It wasn't there.

Pippin spun around, as if it might somehow appear on the floor where they stood. She didn't remember taking it out of her pocket, then again, she'd been so tired these last few days, running around like rabbit being chased by a fox. She did so many things by rote that she had no recollection of doing them at all. "I'll be right back," she said to Mrs. Lee. She took the stairs two at a time, heading for the key rack in the mudroom, but by the time she got to the kitchen she heard Mrs. Lee's booming voice call out down the stairwell, "It's unlocked!"

Pippin frowned. She *knew* she locked the door Friday night when she'd been with Dr. Baxter. So how could it now be unlocked? The only answer, of course, was that someone had found the key in her pocket and used it, not bothering to lock it again afterward and not putting the key back.

The man with the clear eyes flashed in her mind. He'd been upstairs wandering around. But he couldn't have known where her key was, and why would he go up to the widow's walk anyway?

"I'm going up!" Mrs. Lee hollered.

"Wait for me, Mrs. Lee!" Pippin yelled too loudly, but anyone who might have been sleeping had surely already been jolted awake by Mrs. Lee.

She was halfway up the stairs when a scream suddenly shot through the house like a bullet.

Mrs. Lee's voice carried down the narrow steps to the widow's walk. "Oh my!" Then something in Mandarin, followed by, "Lee Shan! Oh my, oh my, are you alright? Oh my, hurry! Please hurry!"

Pippin flew up the rest of the stairs, climbing the ladder to the widow's walk in seconds flat. She ran smack into Mrs. Lee's back. "What's wrong?"

Mrs. Lee turned around, her hand pressed over her mouth, her eyes wide. Pippin glanced over the woman's shoulder. What had spooked her? Surely not an apparition. "Mrs. Lee, I was kidding about the ghosts. Perry Hubbard doesn't haunt this place," she said.

"Look." Mrs. Lee pointed. Her eyes were still wide. Unseeing. "Look look look look look."

Pippin tried to skirt past Mrs. Lee, but the woman blocked the narrow platform around the chimney. Mr. Lee appeared behind Pippin. "What happened?"

Pippin looked back at him. "I don't know."

He practically jumped up the remaining steps, saying something in Mandarin to his wife. She reached for him, managing to squeeze passed Pippin.

Pippin's heart hammered in her chest. She was afraid to look, but she had to do it.

She gripped the railing with one hand as she edged around the chimney.

A little further, then a turn. And then —

She gasped. Slapped her hand over her mouth. Because Dr. Monique Baxter lay in a contorted mass on the floor, a pool of congealed blood under her head.

Pippin's missing key lay next to her hand.

Chapter 12

"One must never set up a murder. They must happen unexpectedly, as in life."
~Alfred Hitchcock

The long day turned into a long night. Once again Sea Captain's Inn was overflowing with people, but this time it wasn't with party guests happily chattering away.

It was crowded with all of Devil's Cove law enforcement, which had come in a pack. Several black SUVs, Devil's Cove Sheriff's Dept. scrawled across the sides in a bold blue with white accents, were parked along the street in front of the house. A group of officers gathered in the upstairs hallway at the base of the ladder to the widow's walk. Lieutenant Roy Jacobs had been the first to examine the scene. He was stocky man with permanent bags under his eyes and a thinning hairline. Before long, his gray hair would be nothing but a memory. He'd overseen the investigation into her father's death, although it was Pippin herself who had been the one to root out the truth of the twenty-year old cold case. Despite the late hour, his navy blue uniform was crisp and the rectangular gold bars on the corners of his shirt collar gleamed.

Now he led a shocked Pippin away from the Lees, Paul Marshall, the officers, and Hattie, who'd flown across the street and barreled her way into the house not ten seconds after the Lieutenant and his posse arrived. Her standard pink lipstick was faded, and her blue and pink hair was mussed like she'd been asleep. "This house ain't haunted," she proclaimed as she burst in. "It's cursed."

Cursed. Cursed. Cursed. The word circled in Pippin's brain. Maybe Hattie was right. Perry Hubbard had been killed here. Cassie had died here. Leo's body had been found here.

Anxiety sprouted inside her, its tentacles creeping through her veins. What had Dr. Baxter been doing on the widow's walk? And who else had been there with her, because there's no way a fall on the wooden floor had bashed in her head.

And the blood.

So much blood.

"Tell me what happened," Jacobs said. The man didn't waste his time with words.

Pippin drew in a deep inhalation, steadying her nerves before giving him a rundown of how Mrs. Lee had discovered the body.

He jotted down what she said in his notepad. "Basically what Mrs. Lee said, but a lot more concise."

A quick snort escaped Pippin. "She is a talker."

The lieutenant was quiet for a beat, then went on with his questions. "When was the last time you saw Dr. Baxter?"

"This morning. The Lees were on the back deck—the one off of the kitchen? They'd come down for breakfast and we were talking. I went back into the kitchen. I saw her leave a little while later."

"Do you know where she was going?"

"She didn't say. But she skipped breakfast, which was surprising because she made a big point of telling me she'd be down at seven-fifteen sharp. And *it better be ready or else* kind of thing."

Jacobs jotted down more notes. "Any other interactions with her?"

"Friday night," Pippin said. "I was on the widow's walk. I try to go up there around sunset to get a few minutes to myself. Look at the stars. Then..."

"Then?" he prompted.

"Then Dr. Baxter came up."

This surprised him. "She climbed the ladder to the widow's walk Friday night?"

"Yeah, suddenly she was just there."

"Did she come to look at the stars, too? Is that an...*amenity* you offer?"

"No...and no. I don't want people up there. It's my private space. I keep the door locked, but..."

"But what?" Jacobs prodded.

Pippin gave a shaky sigh. She cupped her hands over her eyes, the shock of finding a dead body wearing off, her emotions starting to gather. After a few seconds, she resumed. "I thought I put the key in my jacket pocket. But when I went to unlock the door tonight, the key wasn't there, and the door was unlocked."

"There was a key next to her body," he said matter-of-factly. "It fits the door at the base of the ladder. You say you left the key in your jacket?"

"Or maybe I hung it up. I can't remember. I thought I left it in my pocket, though."

"And where do you keep that?"

"On a hook in the mudroom," she said, her words slowing as she remembered something. The night of the party, Dr. Baxter had come into the great room from the kitchen's reading nook. The door to the mudroom was open and the hook where her jacket hangs was visible from there. She very well could have seen Pippin pocket the key that night, then gone back later to take it during the distraction of the party.

Lieutenant Jacobs got there himself without the memory-jog Pippin had. "So, it's possible she saw you put the key in your jacket pocket, figured out where you hang the jacket, and found the key."

"It's possible," she said.

"What about the Lees?" Jacobs asked.

"What about them?"

"You said Mrs. Lee was anxious to see the widow's walk. Any chance she might have gone up there earlier with Dr. Baxter?"

Pippin flinched at the implication. "No! She wanted to see the stars, and also if..." She trailed off, not wanting to make Mrs. Lee sound like a nutter.

But Jacobs wasn't about to let her off the hook now that she'd opened her mouth. "*Also if* what?"

"To see if the ghost stories are real."

He scoffed. "What, that old Mrs. Hubbard haunts the place?"

Pippin gave a little shrug. "She was interested."

He added the information to his notes before looking back at her. "How did she know about the ghost story?"

"We talked about it at breakfast this morning."

"And even though seeing the widow's walk is not an amenity, you let both Dr. Baxter and Mrs. Lee up there?"

Pippin's skin turned cold. It didn't sound good when he put it that way—like she was involved somehow. "I didn't *let* Dr. Baxter up. She came up on her own. And Mrs. Lee was so insistent..."

Jacobs let it go. "Any chance Dr. Baxter could have overheard you talking to Mrs. Lee about the ghosts? Taken the key because she wanted to see if Old Mother Hubbard would show up?"

Pippin fought not to roll her eyes. She'd lay money down that Dr. Baxter was *not* the type to go ghost-hunting. "She couldn't have overheard. We were on the back porch. She didn't come into the kitchen. We would have seen her. Plus, I saw her leaving *after* the conversation with the Lees. Also, she is— she *was* a historian who relished proof and facts. She didn't strike me as someone who believed in the supernatural."

"You never know," he said. "People show you what they want you to see."

"That's true."

"Ms. Hawthorne, is there anything else you can tell me?"

She thought about it but came up blank. "I don't think so."

He handed her a business card, but she held up her hand. "I already have one."

He pocketed it again. "Bad luck to have a dead body at your grand opening," he said blithely.

Yeah, she thought. Bad luck for her business...and worse luck for Dr. Baxter.

Chapter 13

I shall be telling this with a sigh
   Somewhere ages and ages hence:
   Two roads diverged in a wood, and I—
   I took the one less traveled by,
   And that has made all the difference.
   ~Robert Frost, from *The Road Not Taken*

The brick walkway leading from the street to the inn's porch was lined with wide flower beds. Before the opening, Pippin had dug out all the weeds, amended the soil with every mineral rich nutrient she could think of, brought in mulch, and planted a few perennials to build the bones of the beds, adding annuals for color.

Now she was back at it, new flats of petunias and snap dragons to intersperse with what she'd already planted. The beds didn't actually need more flowers, but she needed something to do. A way to keep herself busy. She plunged her wood handled garden trowel into the dirt, created a hole, and plucked a petunia plant from the plastic flat. She took a moment to loosen the roots before depositing it into its new home.

Flower by flower she worked, starting at the top of the bed closest to the front door, moving down the walkway toward the street.

After the night before, her thoughts felt like lines of Tetris blocks combusting and disappearing, only to be replaced by more blocks, each coming faster and faster until she felt as if her head might actually explode. She didn't want to be wrapped up in another murder, not after what happened just a few short months ago. She couldn't make it go away, though. So far, living back in the town of Devil's Cove, in her parents' house wasn't as great as she'd thought it would be. There were positives, sure—Sea Captain's Inn, Grey's business, her friendships with Daisy and Ruby, Hattie Juniper Pickle, The Open Door Bookshop, Jamie and Cyrus McAdams; but there were plenty of negatives, too, like Salty Gallagher, poor Max Lawrence, and, of course, her father, although she was glad to know what actually happened to him.

And now there was Dr. Monique Baxter's death. Another murder. She tried to push it from her mind. Above her, that dratted crow flapped its wings from the porch railing. She waved her arm at it, trying to shoo it away. It flew up then settled itself on the eaves of the house at the highest point, as if it stood sentry.

"Fine," she muttered. "Stay then." She grabbed hold of a weed and yanked it out. It gave no resistance, so the force of the pull knocked her off balance. She careened backward and landed on her backside, her sneakered feet thrust up in the air.

She heard clapping, followed by a hearty, "Bravo!"

Pippin grumbled as she got to her feet and turned. Hattie Juniper Pickle stood smack in the middle of the street, unlit cigarette dangling from between two hot pink lips, her blue hair banded at the crown of her head, wild strands sticking out every which way, and her typical mix and match patterned outfit screaming in all the bright colors of the rainbow. "I bet you couldn't do that again if you tried," she said with a laugh.

"You're probably right," Pippin said.

"Anything new since last night?" Hattie asked.

It was only eight-thirty in the morning, so the odds that Lieutenant Jacobs had discovered any clues were slim, and even if he had, sharing them with Pippin was not part of his procedure. "Nothing."

The sound of a car coming down the street from the east hit them before the vehicle itself came into view. Not a car, but a truck.

Grey's truck. He pulled up in front of the house, cut the engine, and was out the door and halfway up the path before she'd pulled off her gloves. Pippin waved to Hattie. The woman peered at them for another few seconds before she retreated to her purple and teal house.

"I heard what happened," Grey said. "Are you okay?"

"Shaken, but yeah, I'm okay."

As he pulled her in for a bolstering hug, she felt her control slip. She trembled. Tears pricked her eyelids. "A murder," she said, her voice muffled against his shoulder. Finally, she pushed away from him. Ran her fingers under her eyes. She looked at him. "A murder, Grey. You can't say we aren't cursed."

"Ah, Christ. Here we go," he muttered.

"Here we go? What does *that* mean?"

"We're back on the curse. I don't want to talk about it anymore," he said.

Pippin had the sudden feeling of being watched. A shiver raked over her skin. She tossed her gloves down, left her gardening supplies and flowers where they were and started for the porch stairs. "Come inside."

Grey hesitated for a beat, but followed her through the great room, past the kitchen, and into her room. It wasn't until they were in the Burrow that he spoke. "I know you don't understand, but we have to agree to disagree on this, Pippin."

She frowned at his use of Pippin, rather than Peevie. Their truce from Saturday night had faded away. "I don't know if I can do that," she said. "*I* want to stop the curse. *You*, on the other hand, are risking your life in the water kayaking and now you're building a boat—?"

"Repairing and refinishing—"

"Whatever. You have a boat in your workshop. A. Boat. I'm trying to continue Dad's work. *To save us.* But you... you're just pretending it doesn't exist."

He looked at her, never breaking eye contact. "Not even close, Pippin. I'm facing it head on."

She threw up her hands, exasperated. "But you *can't* fight it, Grey, don't you see that? It'll take your life just like it took Mom's and our grandparents and every single Lane person before them. The curse is *always* going to win."

Grey ran his hand down his face then cupped it on the back of his neck. "We're not kids anymore, Pippin. We can't just pretend this isn't happening. Mom's dead. Dad's dead. For all we know Aunt Rose is dead by now, and Cora and Lily, too," he said, referring to their cousins on the other side of the country. "Maybe I can't outrun it, and maybe tempting fate by going in the water isn't the smart thing to do, but I can't do *nothing*."

She took a step toward him. "You can help me—"

Surrounded by their father's books and maps, it seemed possible, but he stayed rooted to the ground. "How? I'm not a bibliomancer. Books don't give me messages."

"Dad was tracing the curse back to our ancestors—"

"Pippin. What good is that going to do? Who cares about Morgan Dubhshláine? How does knowing her name help us?"

"Aunt Rose's letter," Pippin said. "She said Morgan made a deal with a sea god."

"And you believe that? It's bullshit, Pippin." Grey scoffed, pacing in a circle before facing her again. "You actually believe some old Irish god made a pact with our ancestor, cursing us for all eternity?"

Pippin stared at him. At Leo's books. At the floor. She had her doubts. Of course, she did. But now, faced with her brother's question, she knew what she believed. "Yes. I do."

He sighed, long and heavy. "How, Peevie? How could something that happened more than two thousand years ago still affect us now? What if the curse is just a self-fulfilling prophecy? What if we die because we believe it's going to happen?"

"Yeah, because we put ourselves in the position of letting the curse come true, like spending hours in the cove or in the sound? That's not a self-fulfilling prophecy, Grey, it's just stupid."

"So, what, you think the Greek gods were real, too? There's really a tribe of old Irish gods messing with our lives?"

Her resolve faltered. When he put it that way, it sounded

crazy. But... "I'm a bibliomancer. *That's* real, so why not the rest?"

He shoved his hands in the pockets of his khaki shorts and suddenly wouldn't meet her eyes.

"Oh my god." She stared at him. "Oh. My. God. You don't think my bibliomancy is real either?"

He slowly lifted his gaze to hers and she saw it in his eyes. He didn't believe her. "Pippin—" he started, but she took another step closer to him, one palm flat against her chest. "I *am* a bibliomancer, Grey. I can open a book and it'll tell me something. You *know* this."

He sighed again, giving his head a little shake. "I know what Cora and Lily said when we were kids. I know what Dad thought from his research. But is it *really* real?"

She stared at him, disbelief expanding inside of her like a balloon ready to pop. "You've *seen* it," she said again.

He closed his eyes for a beat and hung his head. Once again, his hand went to the back of his neck. "I don't know, Pip."

She didn't know either. She and Grey were twins. They'd spent their childhoods joined at the hip, speaking their own made-up language, each of them a half of the greater whole that was the two of them together. But now... Now everything felt wrong. It was as if they were the two roads in that Robert Frost poem. They'd been on the same path, but now they were at a fork in the road. He was heading down the road everyone else did, forging ahead but willingly wearing blinders to avoid the less accepted truths, while she was taking the road less traveled.

And never had she felt more alone on that road.

Chapter 14

"It's okay to lose. Losing teaches you something. Having to try and going through the trials and tribulations to actually overcome, to get there to win, to triumph, that's what makes life interesting."

~Elizabeth Banks

The Open Door Bookshop sat with its back to Roanoke Sound, its front to Main Street. Pippin paused at the flower-pots housing the soldier flowers outside the entrance, making sure that Jamie hadn't laid the flowers to waste in one day.

He hadn't. The flowers were perky and hydrated, and there was nary a weed in sight. Mathilda would be pleased.

Inside, Pippin spotted the shop's gray longhaired cat. She sprawled across the top of a bookshelf without a care in the world. She cracked an eye open, saw Pippin, and promptly closed it again. Pippin, it seemed, was not worth Miss Havisham's time.

The bookshop was co-owned by Cyrus McAdams, a dapper gentleman from another era, and his grandson Jamie. The McAdams men had divided the store into three sections: new books and used books, plus an entire room for rare books and collectables. They'd created a book lover's haven.

Along with the shelves running the perimeter of the shop, freestanding shelving created rows in the center. There wasn't a single inch of empty wall space. Wherever books could be housed, they were.

In nonfiction, someone interested could find books on any historical subject, every craft and hobby, popular places to travel, as well as things as quirky as the history of cutlery, a compendium on *Friends*, or trivia from *The Babysitters Club* series.

The fiction side was just as diverse, with literary fiction, popular fiction, mysteries, dystopian, plus there was a dedicated section for young adult titles. You name it, The Open Door had it.

And if they didn't, Jamie, who ran the day-to-day operations, would get it.

Pippin had come to appreciate the vast number of stories told in the volumes lining the shelves. Each book allowed a glimpse into the mind of the author. Their thoughts, dreams, wishes, and sometimes the dark crevices hidden away were revealed on the pages.

Pippin breathed in. She was growing accustomed to, and even fond of, the scent of paper, something that had been so unfamiliar to her the first time she stepped foot in the shop. The musty smell of old books had become a comfort. Something to do with the Lane's bibliomancy gift, she supposed. The same gift—or curse—that Grey refused to believe in.

She pushed that rogue thought away. The comfort she

felt in the bookshop certainly hadn't come from a love of books growing up. Her parents had done everything possible to steer her and Grey *away* from reading. That had made the forbidden fruit all that more attractive to her brother, but for her, it had meant a childhood spent trying to hide the fact that she struggled with reading.

When she first returned to Devil's Cove, she'd feared entering the library or the bookstore, but each time she crossed the threshold of either, her trepidation lessened. She had to stop the curse. That meant learning to be a better bibliomancer. Which meant finding a book that could tell her something.

An oscillating fan kept the air circulating. An old-fashioned cash register sat on the checkout counter. Bookish knickknacks lined the shelves behind the counter, tempting every book lover that visited, from Chesapeake Bay to the north and Miami to the south.

The place was a magnet for tourists and locals alike, and with an open archway leading from the bookstore to Devil's Brew, both businesses boomed with customers, even in the off-season. A young couple, that looked a whole lot like newlyweds, smiled at her as they scooted past and went back outside. A mother led her three kids to the children's corner. An older woman wearing a colorful sundress stood at the table of bestsellers, picking up a book, reading the back, opening it to read the first page, then putting it down and choosing another. Jamie had told her that the average customer decided whether or not to buy in about thirty seconds. The cover drew them in, the blurb intrigued them, and page one sealed the deal. Or not.

Watching the woman perusing the book table, it seemed Jamie was one hundred percent spot on. The woman's eyes skipped past several titles, alighting on one at the end of the table. She quickly moved to it, glanced at the back, then opened to page one. And just like that, she closed it, tucked it under her arm, and carried on to the stationery section of the store.

Pippin drew in a deep breath and exhaled, readying herself for the task ahead. "Let's do this," she muttered, and then she propelled herself forward, made a hard right, took a few steps, and stopped. She closed her eyes. Reached her hand out. Grabbed the first book she touched. Pulled it off the shelf.

The Tale of Two Cities, by Charles Dickens.

She mulled over the title. Repeated it in her head. She liked the idea of this book. She didn't know what it was about, but she connected to the title. Her mother had lived in two cities—Laurel Point and Devil's Cove. She and Grey had lived in two cities—Greenville and Devil's Cove. She closed her eyes for a second. If she thought about it in terms of her family, then they'd started in Ireland, and had ended here, in America, in Devil's Cove.

In every scenario there was her island home. What did that mean?

She riffled the pages, opening and closing the book a few times. It was a used copy of the classic, and well-worn. The spine looked like it had been broken in a thousand places. She'd never read it, of course, but by the looks of it, a lot of other people had. How many hands had held this book? How many times had the pages been turned? How many eyes had read the words written by a man who lived almost two hundred years ago?

She crouched down and put the book on its spine. "What can you tell me?" she murmured with her eyes closed. The expression on Grey's face infiltrated her mind. She let the book go and it fell on its side with a quiet thump.

Grey was wrong, she thought. Dead wrong. She *was* a bibliomancer. It *was* real. She took the book up and placed it on its spine again. She chased Grey from her head, closed her eyes, and repeated her question. "What can you tell me?"

This time when she let go, the two sides of the cover fell open. She opened her eyes to see the beginning of the third chapter. Pippin stared at the text, waiting for the letters to turn darker. For the words to peel off the page. For *something* to happen.

The text just stared back at her, unchanging.

Grey's voice sounded in her head. *"I know what Dad thought from his research. But is it really real?"*

She shook her head. She couldn't doubt herself. She had seen it happen, over and over. She didn't just imagine the words lifting from the page, and just because he couldn't see it didn't make it untrue. "It *is* real, Grey," she whispered, then louder, "It's real."

She reached for the book to close it. To try it again, but something was happening. She sank to her knees, staring at the open pages. Slowly, line by line, one section undulated, the letters turning bold. Thickening. Darkening. And then it was as if she were wearing 3-D glasses. The passage seemed to lift until each letter had dimension.

A wonderful fact to reflect upon, that every human creature is constituted to be that profound secret and mystery to every other. A solemn consideration, when I enter a great city by night, that every one of those darkly clustered houses encloses its own secret; that every room in every one of them encloses its own secret; that every beating heart in the hundreds of breasts there, is, in some of its imaginings, a secret to the heart nearest it! Something of the awfulness, even of Death itself, is referable to this.

PIPPIN READ the passage over and over, stumbling over the most challenging words. *Constituted. Solemn. Referable.* Her house—Sea Captain's Inn—held secrets. She knew that, what with her father's hidden study, but this passage said *every* room, but was it was referring to the house, or was it something more?

"What are you doing down there?"

The voice behind her startled her. She leapt up, dropping the book. Jamie stood there holding a single book. His hair was tousled, as if he hadn't paid much attention to it after he'd woken up. His amber-flecked brown eyes were sleepy and red-rimmed under his wire-framed glasses. "Just, you know—" She gestured to the book— "reading."

"Heidi'll be so excited to hear it," he said with a crooked smile. "She'll take full credit for it, you know."

She laughed. "I do know."

"Seriously, though." His voice dropped to a whisper. "Doing some bibliomancy?"

She gave a hesitant shrug. Did Jamie believe her? She didn't dare ask. Not now. "Trying."

He eyed the book on the floor. "What do you have there?"

"*A Tale of Two Cities.*"

"Ah, Dickens. How'd you choose that one?"

"I'm going to go with *it chose me.*"

"Ah. Intriguing. Tell me more," he said.

She could never tell how serious he was being. His words often had a wryly humorous bent to them. She hadn't figured out if that was just the way he was all the time, or if she needed to pay close attention to his tone to figure out what he was thinking. At the moment, she decided to take him at face value. Someone had to believe in her. That someone had always been Grey. For right now, though, she would settle for Jamie. "I closed my eyes and pointed to the shelf. It's the book that jumped out at me."

"Ah, an exercise in precision," he teased. "Not literally, I assume?"

"No," she countered, perhaps a little more tersely than she intended. "Not literally."

His brows drew together behind his horn-rimmed glasses. "You okay?"

She inhaled, then let her frustrations about Grey float away with her exhalation. "Sorry. Yeah, I'm fine."

He shelved the book he'd been holding, then folded his arms over his chest and leaned against one of the shelves. "What are you trying to figure out?" he asked with no trace of his previous teasing manner.

What *wasn't* she trying to figure out? "Who was that man sneaking around the house? Who broke into my bedroom? Who killed Dr. Baxter?"

When she heard herself say it aloud, it *did* sound ridiculous—as if a passage from a random book could simply give her the answers like a Ouija board. But the thoughts dissipated when Jamie tilted his head to one side. His expression was completely serious. "And?"

"According to Dickens, the house has secrets. Which I already knew."

"Can I see?" he asked, pushing off the shelf and striding toward her.

She crouched to retrieve the book, but stopped short when her eyes landed on the open pages—*different* pages

than what she'd been reading a moment ago. A new line
darkened and peeled away from the paper.

*Nothing that we do, is done in vain. I believe, with all my soul,
that we shall see triumph.*

SHE REREAD IT. Was this a message meant to bolster her
confidence? To tell her that her bibliomancy was very
real?

"Pippin?"

Jamie's voice brought her back. She committed the
current page number to memory before she closed the
book, closed her eyes for a split second, and whispered
under her breath, "Show me what you did before."

She let the book fall open and there it was. The first
passage she'd seen darken and rise from the page. Relief.
The book opening to the same page twice reinforced her
belief that her bibliomancy was real.

She moved to stand beside Jamie, pointing to the
passage lifting from the page. He read it silently, then
cupped his chin in his hand as he thought.

"What do you think?" she asked. After all, he was the
scholar, not her. She'd barely managed to graduate from
high school, some of her teachers giving her passing grades
more because of her effort than the actual quality of her
assignments.

"It's basically saying that humans are perpetual
mysteries to each other, never to be fully understood. What
we feel inside is hidden away so deeply that it's inscrutable
to others."

"So, it's not about the house?" she asked. "Because it says, '*those darkly clustered houses encloses its own secret*'."

"I think it's a metaphor for human beings," Jamie said. "Every person encloses his or her own secrets. Let's look at the story. The book is about a doctor imprisoned for years and years. Eighteen, I think. When he's released, he lives with his daughter. The end of this passage is talking about the love he has for his daughter, but it's hidden away inside of him, only revealed when he commits the selfless act of dying for her. That, even the reason behind his death—the depth of his love for Lucie, which nobody understands—is hidden away in his mind. It leaves the reader wondering—or wishing—he'd shown that love during life rather than through death."

Pippin rubbed her forehead with the pads of her fingertips, as if pressing away a budding headache. In reality, she was trying to make sense of the passage and how it could possibly relate to all the questions she wanted answers to. Connecting it to Dr. Baxter was the easiest path to take. If Pippin took the passage and applied it literally to the woman, the message was clear. Monique Baxter had some secret no one knew about. Was her death a selfless act? Had her dying saved someone else?

Maybe that was taking it too far, though. Pippin stuck with the idea that Dr. Baxter had secrets.

She thought about the other passage.

Nothing that we do, is done in vain. I believe, with all my soul, that we shall see triumph.

DID this also apply to Dr. Baxter? That somehow her death also meant her triumph? But she hadn't proved her case about the Dare Stone and the two hoaxes.

Or maybe it was about the strange man in her house. Maybe he'd triumph, finding whatever it was he was after.

The only other interpretation she could make was that it was about herself. That what *she* was trying to accomplish—figuring out why Dr. Baxter died, or even trying to finish her father's work and stop the Lane curse—that in these things she would succeed.

"Pippin," Jamie said. "What is it? What are you thinking?"

She hesitated. Pippin and Grey had lost their parents. They'd grown up trusting their grandparents but discovering they'd kept so much from them had planted doubt into every interaction. Every relationship. She and Grey had only each other—but Jamie was here, believing her, and Grey wasn't. She already trusted him with her deepest secret. He knew about her family's curse, the bibliomancy, about the research her father had been doing, about the ancient artifact Leo had hidden away. She could trust him. She *did* trust him.

She found the page in question and read the line to him, then told him all her thoughts about it.

"'Nothing that we do, is done in vain. I believe, with all my soul, that we shall see triumph,'" he read aloud.

"But I don't know which one is right."

"Maybe it applies to all three."

"It could," she said hesitantly, and then with more assurance, "You're right, it could." She might as well believe that it did until she had a reason not to, right? "I should buy this," she said, taking the book back from him.

"I'm sure Daisy has a copy in the library if you want to get that one instead," Jamie said.

She gave him a wry smile. "You must be the only bookseller alive who tries talking customers *out* of buying a book."

"Good grief, Jamie, my boy. The young lady is right. Don't talk people out of buying our books."

They both turned at the sonorous voice of the elder Mr. McAdams. Every time Pippin saw him, the snowy hair of his receding hairline was brushed back over his head, his goatee was neatly shaved close to the skin, and the puffy half-moons beneath his eyes only enhanced the sparkling blue of his irises. Today he had on crisp denim jeans, loafers, and a black shirt with black embroidered pattern on either side of the buttons. This was dressed down. Casual, yet sophisticated, which was the man's style, but it didn't matter what Cyrus McAdams wore. He was inherently dapper.

"Just trying to help, Granddad," Jamie said, one side of his mouth quirking up.

"I *want* to buy it," Pippin said, rescuing him from Cyrus. "I'm trying to build my collection. Book by book."

"And there you have it, Jamie m'lad," Mr. McAdams said, with a twinkle in his eye. "A woman who knows what she wants."

If he was talking about trying to break the curse plaguing the Lanes or getting better at understanding the messages books sent her, then the man was right. If he was referring to anything else, well, then, he probably knew more than she did.

"Buy your book and join me for a glass of Ruby's iced tea," Mr. McAdams said to her.

She glanced at the clock hanging behind the checkout

counter. Analog, of course. The rest of the world had gone digital, but Jamie McAdams hung on to the past. Sometimes if seemed as if he was born in the wrong century. The wrong *era* even.

Two-fifteen. Zoe was tackling the first of the bathrooms today with her bucket of cleaning supplies. She'd need a break soon, but Pippin had a few minutes. "I'll be right over," she said.

The elder Mr. McAdams gave a single bow of his head. "Excellent."

"Is this an exclusive thing?" Jamie asked.

"You have our bookshop to run," Mr. McAdams said, matching Jamie's droll smile.

Jamie threw up his hands, lips still upturned. "Okay, okay. I know when I'm not wanted."

As the elder Mr. McAdams ambled off, disappearing through the archway between The Open Door and Devil's Brew, Jamie took *The Tale of Two Cities* from Pippin's hand. "Let me ring you up, Pip."

Chapter 15

"For everyone, a book is a search and hopefully a discovery"
~Shelby Foote

Five minutes later, Pippin sat across from Cyrus McAdams, her hands wrapped around a glass of Ruby's iced tea. Cyrus looked at her with his piercing eyes. "How are you holding up, my dear?"

She had to think about how to answer that. The revelation that her family's oldest known ancestor had somehow cursed her descendants and Grey's tempestuousness had her in a tailspin. Add the murder at the inn and it all created a ball of anxiety that lodged in the pit of her stomach and didn't want to budge.

Mr. McAdams had helped her parents trace the Lane family tree all the way back to the first century. He was someone her parents had trusted, which meant he was someone Pippin could trust. She could unload every single thought she had and know that he'd help guide her through the muck, but she didn't want to do that. She didn't want to hoist her troubles on to others to solve. Rather, she felt a need to sort things out on her own. "I'm okay," she finally said. As soon as the words left her lips, she knew they were true. She was a fighter, and if sheer determination were a predictor, she'd win not just the battle, but the entire war.

He considered her for a moment. The horizontal lines marking his forehead crunched together like the bellows of an accordion. "A murdered guest can't be an easy situation with which to deal."

That felt like an understatement. "It's not. It's very unsettling to think that it happened in my house with the guests right there. None of us heard anything. How is that possible?"

"Hmm. A good question. You didn't see anything out of the ordinary?"

If only she had, but she shook her head. "Dr. Baxter was prickly and opinionated, but I can't figure out who would have wanted her dead, or why."

"Tell me what happened," he said.

She recounted the events leading up to Mrs. Lee discovering the body of Dr. Baxter. She ended with, "Her head was bashed in, but there's no murder weapon."

"Premeditated or a crime in a moment of passion?" he mused.

She hadn't even considered that question. She supposed the answer came down to who met the historian on the widow's walk and if it had been pre-arranged. "There was someone..." she started, and she told him about the man with the clear eyes.

Crevices sprouted at Cyrus's temples, deepening as he narrowed his eyes at her. "And you've not seen this man since?"

"No."

"Interesting," he said. "Yes, that's very interesting." He nodded at the Dickens novel she'd pushed to the side of the table. "You're practicing bibliomancy."

It was a statement, not a question, as if he could see inside her and knew exactly what she was doing. "Kind of."

"There is no *kind of*, my dear. Either you are, or you aren't."

He was right about that. She'd gone to The Open Door to find a book that could guide her in the same way *The Odyssey* had. She didn't know if *The Tale of Two Cities* had the answers, but there was no harm in trying. "Then yes," she said. "I am. Practicing, I mean."

"It will take time to master the divination," he said. "It has been neglected too long for it to come easily." She opened her mouth to disagree, but he waved his hand, stopping her. "Not by design on your part, of course. That's not what I mean. Your mother kept the gift from you, and her intentions were pure. She wanted only to protect you from the curse. But now you must face it head on."

Which was exactly what Grey was doing. Only he was approaching it with recklessness.

Cyrus considered her thoughtfully, as if he could see right into her mind. "What has it told you?"

She opened the book and showed him the passage.

A wonderful fact to reflect upon, that every human creature is constituted to be that profound secret and mystery to every other. A solemn consideration, when I enter a great city by night, that every one of those darkly clustered houses encloses its own secret; that every room in every one of them encloses its own secret; that every beating heart in the hundreds of breasts

*there, is, in some of its imaginings, a secret to the heart nearest
it! Something of the awfulness, even of Death itself, is referable
to this.*

He skimmed it quickly, then his eyes moved more slowly as
he read it a second time. "Interesting. It can be interpreted
in many ways," he said.

"I was taking it literally, but Jamie said it could be a
metaphor for people and the secrets they keep hidden from
others."

Mr. McAdams pressed his lips together as he thought.
"Possibly," he said. "Yes, quite possibly that was Mr. Dickens's intent, however, you have a house with secrets, Pippin.
You can read this as a metaphor, like Jamie did, but you also
can take it literally."

"Meaning it *is* about the house?"

"I would venture to say it's about both. Who has secrets
they'll do anything to hide? What else does your house have
to tell you about the past?" He pushed the book back to her.
"And how can Dickens help you?"

Pippin left Devil's Brew and headed home, walking the
same path her mother and father had traveled so many
times before her. It made her feel a little closer to them, the
long ago sounds of their footsteps reverberating beside hers.

The constantly moving water lapped at the edges of the
island. As Main Street turned into Rum Runner's Lane, she
could hear the ghostly echo of Grey and her playing in the
front yard. The old sea captain's house loomed ahead of her,

a house built on stilts, pilings, and piers to protect it from flooding, just like all the Outer Banks beach houses. She walked up the brick path not even registering the flowers she'd left unplanted. It felt like this day might never end.

"There you are, finally!" Zoe's agitated voice broke into her thoughts. She stood at the top of the porch stairs glancing nervously over her shoulder.

Pippin stopped short, one hand gripping the white wood railing as she peered up at her. "What's wrong?"

Zoe looked pointedly at the front door, as if that alone could convey whatever was on her mind.

Pippin waited.

Zoe's response was to raise her eyebrows and tilt her head.

"What?" Pippin demanded. "I don't know what you're trying to say."

"Someone's here," Zoe hissed.

Pippin's first thought was the police. Was Lieutenant Jacobs back with information? She looked back to the street, thinking she must have been so lost in thought that she'd missed seeing his SUV, but no, it wasn't there. A white sedan with a film of dirt was parked in the driveway. The anxiety coiled in her gut tightened. She took the steps two at a time. "Who is it?" she asked, automatically dropping her voice to match Zoe's.

Zoe grabbed her arm. "It's Dr. Baxter's *son*."

Pippin's heart began to beat erratically. She could understand why the dead woman's family would come here wanting answers, but she had none to give. She blew out an audible breath. Zoe held the screen door open for her and she went inside.

A man stood in front of the built-in bookshelves, his back to her.

"Hi," she said from the entryway. "You're Dr. Baxter's son?"

He had wide shoulders and the same dark hair as Monique Baxter, but when he turned around, that was where the similarities ended. The historian's face had had a hardness to it, like she'd seen things that had colored her outlook on life. His mother had come across as calculating. This man's expression was open and, if not quite innocent, at least guileless. "I am. Ron Baxter," he said.

"I'm so sorry for your loss," she said. Her nerves rattled from the different scenarios she imagined. Was he going to sue her for negligence? Would he cry over his dead mother? Would he yell at her for not keeping her safe?

"Thank you," he said.

She exhaled the breath she'd been holding. He was calm. Collected. "Have a seat," she said, gesturing to the sofa and chairs. Zoe followed her, perching on the arm of the couch while Pippin sat on the edge.

Ron Baxter took one of the armchairs. He held onto the book he'd taken from the shelf, absently looking down at it as he turned it in his hands. Pippin placed him in the low end of his thirties. "Are you okay? Can I get you anything?"

His mouth worked, his lips moving in and out, in and out. Finally, he pursed them, raising his eyes first to Zoe, then to her. His nostrils flared as he breathed in, but he still didn't speak.

"Mr. Baxter? Ron?" She nudged Zoe and whispered, "Get some water, please."

As Zoe scurried off, he finally spoke. "I can't believe she's dead. I just saw her, and now...and now she's gone."

"She was...so passionate about her work," Pippin said, wishing Dr. Baxter had talked about her son, too, so she could give the man some comfort.

He didn't seem to notice. Instead, he said, "I talked to one of the detectives..."

"Lieutenant Jacobs? He's in charge."

"He said it's an open investigation, but they don't know anything yet."

"I'm sure he'll keep you informed."

He looked past her for a second. "But can you tell me anything else? Where did it happen? Can I see?"

Pippin's thundering heart had calmed for a few moments, but now it ratcheted up again. "I don't think—"

"She was my—" He broke off. Regrouped. "I *need* to see where she died."

Dr. Baxter's body had been taken away by the coroner, but the floor of the widow's walk hadn't been cleaned yet. "It's not...the area is still..." She couldn't quite bring herself to say that his mother's blood still stained the floor. Finding a service skilled at dealing with blood pathogens was on her To Do list.

He hesitated for a second, as if he was filling in the blanks. His eyes cleared and he seemed to understand what she was trying to say. He stood up and resolutely walked to the stairs. She took that to mean he didn't care what evidence of the killing he might find. "I want to see where she died."

Zoe returned carrying a glass of water, but Pippin was already following Ron Baxter up to the second floor. "Hey! Where are you going?" Zoe called, any trace of accent noticeably absent.

"We'll be right back!" Pippin called over her shoulder. She was pretty sure Zoe had been eavesdropping from the kitchen. A single glass of water didn't take that long to fill. She also imagined her looking crestfallen at not joining them upstairs, but Pippin couldn't help that. Worrying about how Ron Baxter would react to seeing his mother's blood was a much bigger concern. Ron had started jogging, making it to the top before Pippin was even halfway. She had to take the stairs two at a time to catch up. By the time she did, Ron was already at the end of the hallway near the door to the widow's walk.

The opening was crisscrossed with crime scene tape. She'd taken to carrying around the key since the night before. The last thing she wanted was someone else sneaking up the ladder. She stepped in front of Ron, unlocked the door, and stepped back to reveal the ladder.

Ron moved closer and angled his head to peer up. "She was up there?" he asked, pointing.

"That's where she was found."

"Why would she go up there?" He sounded as puzzled as she felt.

"Honestly, I don't know." She pointed to the placard on the door. Private. No Admittance. "Guests aren't allowed."

"Do you think she went to meet someone?"

"I don't know," she said, feeling helpless. She knew nothing that would help this man deal with his mother's murder.

He whirled around suddenly, looking more agitated than he had downstairs. "I need to collect her things," he blurted, turning on his heels and practically sprinting down the hall. He looked at the four guest room doors, one at a time, ending with the two doors side by side. He pointed. "Is that a double? Or a suite?" His eyes found hers. "She'd go for the biggest one. It is, isn't it? Those were her rooms, weren't they?"

The sheriff hadn't put crime scene tape to block off the doors and they were finished with their sweep of the room, so there were no visual clues to tell where Monique Baxter had been staying. But the man apparently knew his mother. "She insisted on the suite," Pippin said. "She wanted her privacy."

"I imagine she would." Ron's voice had calmed down from its frenzied level.

Pippin edged past him and used her master key to unlock the door on the left. Inside, she flipped on a switch which turned on the overhead light and the attached ceiling fan. Pippin knew the room got stuffy under normal conditions. With the door closed and no circulation for the last two days, it felt airless. The cool breeze generated from the fan provided immediate relief.

Ron stood frozen, his gaze the only thing moving around the room. After a long thirty seconds, he asked, "Did the detectives take some of her stuff?"

"You mean the Lieutenant and his people? I don't know that they're really detectives..."

"Whoever," Ron said, his agitation returning. "There's not much here, is there? I mean where are her papers and things?"

Pippin walked around him, taking note of Dr. Baxter's belongings. Her suitcase was on the luggage rack, her belongings tossed all around it. In the bathroom, the makeup had been scattered across the counter. The bedding had been stripped and piled on top of the bed. The Lieutenant's people had searched for clues. It was a messy business, and the mess was left for her to clean up.

Ron strode across the room. He flipped the lid of the black case and rifled through what was left inside. "It's not here," he murmured just loud enough for Pippin to hear.

"What are you looking for?" Pippin asked. "I'll keep an eye out."

Ron turned to scan the room again, his eyes pinching to

keep away the tears. "It's nothing. I was just looking for my mom's research and some artifacts. They were so important to her. I wanted to...

He trailed off, choking on his simmering emotions. "The sheriff may have them," she suggested. "If there was anything here that they thought would help solve your mother's murder, they would have taken it as evidence."

His entire body sagged. "Right," he said. "Of course. I'll ask them."

"Do you want to take the rest of your mother's things?" Pippin asked. It felt more appropriate for Dr. Baxter's son to go through it all than for her to, but he shook his head. "No, no. Not today. I'll come back."

"Sure," Pippin said.

∾

"WHAT DID HE WANT?" Zoe asked, suddenly appearing. "Did he freak out at the blood?"

Pippin blinked. Looked at Zoe's inquisitive face. Snapped back to the present. "Sorry. We didn't go up," she said. "He was looking for her academic papers and things."

"Are you okay?" Zoe asked.

"What? Yeah. Just...upset, I guess."

Zoe put her hand on Pippin's back, leading her to the couch. Across from her on the chair where Ron Baxter had sat lay the book he'd taken from the shelf.

The phone rang. "I'll get it," Zoe said, and she raced to the small reception desk. "Sea Captain's Inn," she said. "How may I help you?"

Her voice faded away as Pippin went to pick up the book. It was her copy of *Homer's The Odyssey*. As she turned the book over in her hand, tendrils of anxiety spread through her body. This book had helped her learn the truth about her father. It felt like a message that it was here in front of her now. Whatever Grey thought, she needed to trust what the Dickens book was telling her. She needed to let the book guide her.

Chapter 16

"You always risk people misunderstanding you when you say anything."

~Phil Lord

The Lees and Paul Marshall had declined breakfast the next morning. With the morning chores done, Pippin took Sailor out early for a walk. Her mind raced, but she knew working with Sailor would focus it. She went out the French doors from the kitchen to the deck, then down the back stairs, barely noting the fairy house or any of the other details that usually made her smile. She didn't use a leash. Sailor never ventured from Pippin's side. They stopped now and then to practice their sign language commands. Pippin made her right hand flat and turned her palm to the sky. "Sit," she said at the same time.

Sailor sat. Pippin took a tiny bit of treat from her pocket

for the dog. "Good girl!" She put her hand on her hip, making sure Sailor saw the movement then said, "Let's go."

They walked another quarter mile side by side. Pippin stopped suddenly and turned to face Sailor. That was the thing about signing with a dog. The dog had to be paying attention to you.

She held her right hand out, palm facing Sailor. "Now stay," she said. She waited a few seconds, repeated the command, then turned and walked away, sneaking a peek to see what the dog was doing.

Sailor sat stone still, her sweet eyes watching. Pippin turned to face Sailor again, counted to ten, and beckoned to her. "Come," she commanded.

Sailor hesitated. She started to stand, but then sat back down.

Pippin took a step forward before she beckoned again. "Come. Come on, pup. Come on, Sailor."

This time, Sailor popped up and trotted across the hard-packed sand straight to Pippin. She gave the dog another treat, giving her extra praise by hugging her and scratching the top of her head. "Good girl!" she said, her mouth pressed against the dog's hair coat. "What a good girl!" She wanted Sailor to feel the vibration of her voice box when she was praised. From the whipping back and forth of her tail, it was evident Sailor understood.

Pippin stood up and held out the first two fingers on her right hand, making an upward motion. "Stand." Sailor obeyed, and Pippin gave her a thumbs up followed by another tiny treat. Once Sailor looked at her again, she placed her right hand on her hip and said, "Let's go," and headed back inside.

It was only when Pippin was halfway up the back stairs, Sailor right behind her, when she remembered the appointment she'd made at The Brewery. She checked the time on her phone. She wasn't late...yet.

Zoe sat at the table making a grocery list. "I forgot about my appointment with Chuck!" Pippin said. She cleaned the sand off her feet, then started on Sailor's.

"I got it." Zoe popped up, grabbed the towel, and took over.

"Oh God, thanks." Pippin had fifteen minutes to get to The Brewery. She knew Chuck Wagner wouldn't mind if she was late, but *she* cared. If she made an appointment, she'd be on time. It was a pet peeve, and a standard she held herself to. She *had* to get her brain back on track. She changed clothes, grabbed the satchel she used for Inn business, and less than ten minutes later, was pedaling toward Main Street. At The Brewery, she waved at Gin White behind the bar and found a seat at a picnic table in the beer garden. She checked her phone again. Right on time.

A minute later, Chuck sidled up to the table wearing a Brewery t-shirt, tan cargo shorts, and flip flops, a glass of pale beer in each hand. His shoulder length dirty blond hair fell in waves. He handed her one as he sat across from her. "Welcome to The Brewery. This one's a Pilsner," he said, cutting right to the chase.

Pippin had been here before, but never on official Sea Captain Inn business. She nodded her thanks for the cold drink. She preferred wine to beer, which is why she'd already contracted with Oak Barrel Winery for special events like the wedding the inn was hosting in September. But other people liked beer, so here she was. She took a sip, her upper lip curling at the dry, bitter flavor.

Chuck watched her, cracking a smile. "So, not a Pilsner girl."

Not a Pilsner *woman*, she thought, but she kept it to

herself because she knew Chuck didn't mean anything by it. From his laidback attitude, suntanned and sun-spotted skin, and his slow, easy drawl, she figured he'd probably spent his youth surfing and smoking pot. Now, somewhere in his forties, he owned the microbrewery and looked like a happy camper. "I suppose not," she said.

"They are kind of hoppy. Good in the summer, though."

Probably the same way a lovely rosé was crisp and fresh on a hot day and the perfect wine to compliment light summer food.

Chuck asked her a series of questions to discern her beer needs. Finally, she said, "I want an array, I guess." She told him about the fall wedding, the groom's preference for IPAs, and his father's love of stouts.

Chuck moved his head in a slow nod. "Not a problem. I can bring out a flight if you want to sample a few." She raised her eyebrows in a question, and he continued. "It just means small servings of a few beers to give you the full experience of our craft brews."

She waved her hand. "I'm good," she said. "I trust you."

He grinned and his sun-drenched face broke into an array of happy wrinkles. "Good deal. September, you said."

"Right."

Chuck didn't have any paperwork on him. Just as Pippin was about to ask about a contract, because she wanted everything buttoned up, a woman appeared carrying a manilla file folder. She slid onto the picnic table bench next to Chuck and flipped the folder open. "I'm January," she said.

Chuck draped an arm around her shoulders. "My wife. Ain't I a lucky guy?"

Aha. January must be the business side of the operation. She smiled at them. "Nice to meet you. Pippin."

"Oh, I know who you are. I think *everybody* on island knows who you are." January's vowels dripped with her North Carolina accent.

"I hear that a lot," Pippin said.

"I bet you do." After a few minutes of chitchat, January opened the folder and slid it across the table to Pippin. "The terms are straight-forward. You just need to let us know as early as possible about any gig you want us to provide our craft beer for. It'll always be on a net-30. If you cancel at least forty-eight hours prior to the event, there is no penalty. If you cancel within that forty-eight-hour window, there's a two-hundred-dollar cancellation fee. We'll start this weekend with the order for that discussion group."

Pippin didn't blame her for not attempting to say *Synkéntrosi.* It was a group Jamie was part of. They'd be in the great room of the inn for Saturday night, a three-hour booking during which a group of men would have intellectual discussions about whatever was on the docket for the month. The contract with The Brewery supported the local business and ensured the men had the libations they wanted to guarantee a second—or maybe ongoing—booking with the inn. Fingers crossed. "Perfect," she said.

Pippin read the contract through once, then again. Then she picked up the pen January had placed on the table and signed on the dotted line.

January disappeared for a few minutes, returning with a duplicate folder. She handed one to Pippin. "We'll keep the original. This is your copy."

Chuck had sat, quietly sipping his beer. "A pleasure doing business with you," he said when the deal was done.

Pippin smiled. "Same."

January relaxed, her business façade softening. She pulled her shoulder length brown hair back into a stubby ponytail. "Such a tragedy about that lady dying at your place."

"Yeah." There wasn't much more to say.

A man wandered out to the beer garden. He looked hot and tired, a trail of sweat running down the center back of his t-shirt. Chuck left his half full mug of Pilsner on the table and extricated himself from the picnic table. A second later, he pumped the man's hand with unrestrained enthusiasm. "Dr. Bligh, the archaeology guy! Good to see you again, my man."

Pippin's ears pricked. Dr. Bligh the archaeology guy. From the dig?

Chuck glanced around. "Did you bring your crew again? That was a full house last night. Appreciate it, man. Really do."

"They'll be along, and we'll need a couple of pitchers. It's looking more and more like we're on the wrong track."

"No lost colonists here?" Chuck asked.

Dr. Bligh shook his head. "It's too early to tell for sure, but I'd lay money down that what's been found is much more recent than the late sixteenth century."

So, Dr. Baxter had been right! January's voice brought her back to the table, splitting her attention. "I hope they figure out what happened, for her sake, and for yours. Was she here on vacation?"

"No, no. She was part of the archaeology dig," Pippin said. "She was studying the Lost Colony."

The words had scarcely left her mouth when Dr. Bligh asked, "What's that?"

"Dr. Monique Baxter," Pippin said. "The woman who just died. She was here for the dig."

The man wiped his sweaty forehead with a napkin and frowned. "Not *my* dig."

Pippin frowned. "Oh. But—"

Dr. Bligh pocketed his damp napkin. "I know everyone on the dig. There's no Dr. Baxter involved in it."

Pippin let the words circle through her mind. That didn't make any sense. "But she told me she was. I even dropped her off there last Friday."

Dr. Bligh gave her a *sorry to disappoint you* look with a slight shrug of his shoulder. "I don't know why she'd say that because she wasn't."

Chuck clapped one hand against Dr. Bligh's back. "He's the main man, so he oughta know."

Pippin looked down at her intertwining fingers, trying to recall her conversation with Dr. Baxter the morning she drove her to Mariner's Cove. She distinctly remembered asking if she was part of the dig. That's when Dr. Baxter had said she was heading there and needed a ride. But—

Pippin started. Dr. Baxter had never actually answered her question, had she? Pippin had just assumed the answer was yes. She left The Brewery with a single question circling in her mind.

If she hadn't been part of the dig, why had Dr. Baxter been in Devil's Cove?

Chapter 17

"The greatest discoveries all start with the question 'Why?'"
~Robert Ballard

*T*wenty-four hours later, Pippin stood in her downstairs bedroom, arms akimbo. She'd spent thirty minutes scouring every nook and cranny for the contract with The Brewery. Nothing.

She'd run her hand across every bookshelf, most of which were still empty. Nothing.

Searched under the bed. Between the mattresses. Nothing.

Looked under the single armchair. Nothing.

She'd been so distracted lately. Could she have put it in her father's old safe and just not remember? She didn't think so—they belonged in her office, which is where she thought she'd left the folder, but rote tasks were done without any conscious intention, therefore forgettable. So maybe.

The safe sat on a shelf in the small closet downstairs in her bedroom. During the renovations, she and Grey had discovered it behind a piece of drywall, protected all the years the house had been vacant. They had tried for a to open it for a solid month, spinning the dial, trying different combinations of important numbers to Leo.

They had no luck until she found a clue. Leo had written a series of numbers and symbols on the inside flap of a copy of *Treasure Island*. They didn't immediately put together that the scribblings were a clue to the combination. It was the number 73 that drew her in first. The number of seconds between her birth and Grey's. It took them another two weeks to decipher the rest, but they finally succeeded. When they'd opened it, they'd found a collection of photographs Leo had kept of their family before Cassie had died. A personal treasure valuable to no one but them.

She'd bet against the fact that she'd put the papers in the small safe, but she opened it, hoping the envelope would magically be there. It wasn't. Everything else was in order. A file with her social security number, the bank information for her personal account, a copy of her father's will.

She closed the door and scrambled the combination. Leaning her back against the shelf, she sighed. It irritated her that she'd been careless enough to misplace it.

She surveyed her room. After her search, it looked messy in the same way Dr. Baxter's room had looked. Her thoughts drifted. Dr. Baxter hadn't seemed herself she plowed out the door Sunday morning. She'd been in a hurry. Carrying her box.

Where had she been going?

Pippin pressed her hands to her head, her fingers bending as they clawed into her scalp. Strands of hair pulled from her already loose bun. Dr. Baxter kept popping up, but she needed to leave her death to Lieutenant Jacobs. She came back to The Brewery contract. She'd checked her office once already, to no avail. Five minutes later, she'd completed an exhaustive second search of her office. The room was small and not populated with much furniture. There was no place else to look.

"Hello?" Zoe's voice boomed from the entryway. The front door closed behind her.

"In here," Pippin called.

Zoe stopped short in the threshold. "Wow. You don't look so great. You okay?"

Pippin looked up and sighed. Zoe had only her usual Southern accent at the moment, so Pippin must really look bad. "I'm fine. Just tired."

"Aw, I'm sorry. Anything I can do? I can go clean the bathrooms. I can do the Turn Down service tonight. I can—"

"It's nothing like that, Zoe. I just can't find the envelope I brought home from The Brewery the other day. It has the new agreement between us—?

She stopped suddenly. "What?" Zoe asked, looking at her, alarmed.

Pippin jumped up. The only place she hadn't looked was the guest safe.

"Why would you put it in the guest safe?" Zoe asked.

It was a good question. Pippin couldn't imagine why it would be in there anymore than it would have been in her father's safe, but she was driving herself crazy at this point. "I don't know, but I've looked everywhere else."

"I'll go check for you," Zoe said, but Pippin was already skirting by her. She'd had the safe installed in the mudroom so it was tucked away where guests didn't go. A minute later, she pressed numbers onto the keypad. The lever inside clicked. With Zoe by her side, both of them holding their breath, Pippin pulled the door open.

And then she heaved a frustrated sigh. No folder.

Her eyes narrowed. There was, however, an object wrapped in a thin gray cloth. "What's that?"

"What's wha—" Zoe broke off. Her hands flew to either side of her face and her mouth dropped open. "Oh my God, I forgot!"

"What is it?"

"I don't know. Oh my God. I don't know whose it is. I mean someone at the party the other night asked if we had a safe. When I told him we did, he handed it to me. He said it was—" All the color drained from her skin. Her voice dropped to a hoarse whisper. "He said to put it in there for safekeeping."

"It was a man?"

Zoe looked up to the ceiling for a second before nodding. "Yes."

"A guest? Mr. Marshall? Mr. Lee?"

"N-nooo."

Pippin stared at her. "Someone from town? An islander?"

Zoe shook her head, her face still pallid. "I don't know."

"Why would you put something in the safe that doesn't belong to one of our guests?"

Zoe's lower lip trembled. "I-I'm sorry. I shouldn't h-have..."

"What did he look like?" Pippin asked.

"I...I didn't recognize him, but..."

"But what?"

Zoe hesitated. Finally, she confessed, "He's the one you wanted me to get to *leave*. You know, the one with the eyes?"

Pippin's body went cold. "What about them?"

"They were white. Or maybe clear. So light. It was like they were laser beams or something. Alien."

That was exactly what Pippin had felt looking into them. Haunted. "He's the man who gave you that?"

Her shaggy hair flew in front of her face as she nodded. "At the party, and then he left."

But she'd seen him walk down the stairs. He hadn't been carrying anything. And then it hit her. He'd had his jacket off. Whatever he'd given to Zoe...whatever was in the safe in front of them right now...he'd carried it *under* his jacket.

Pippin took the object from the safe. Slowly and carefully, she unwrapped the gray cloth. In her hands rested what looked like the hilt of a dagger or sword. The handle was short. It was tarnished—perhaps bronze or silver. But no. That was impossible. It would have been much heavier than it was if it was pure bronze or silver. Plated, then. She studied at the base of it, where the blade would have been. Maybe it was wood underneath.

A series of grooves had been carved into the handle, and several other markings that weren't readily discernible.

"That looks *so* old," Zoe said. The tone of her voice communicated her lack of interest. "I thought it might be some jewels, or something cool like that."

"You should have told me, Zoe," Pippin scolded.

"I'm sorry," Zoe murmured, her voice tremulous.

After a minute, Pippin put a reassuring hand on Zoe's shoulder. "It's okay." Everyone was distracted by the murder. She could hardly blame Zoe for forgetting when she'd lost track of a simple folder.

She looked at the hilt again. It *did* look ancient. And something about it made Pippin's head spin. She wrapped it back up, left Zoe to close the safe with her still trembling hands, and went into her room. She locked the door behind her, opened the bookshelf door, and slipped up to Leo's Burrow.

PIPPIN HAD THOUGHT LONG and hard about how to broach the subject of the sword hilt with the inn's guests. Of course, it stood to reason that the artifact had belonged to Dr. Baxter—and that it may have had something to do with her death. She was a historian, after all, so it seemed well within the scope of her job and interests, but Pippin had to eliminate the others before she went full speed ahead with that theory.

She went to the Lees first, catching them after Zoe had cleared their breakfast dishes. "Where are you off to today?"

"To the beach!" Mrs. Lee proclaimed with forced enthusiasm.

"We have plenty of those," Pippin said. Then nonchalantly, she asked, "Have you seen the museum?"

Mrs. Lee shook her head. "Mr. Lee is not a museum person," she said, ignoring the cocked eyebrow her husband gave her, which seemed to say, *Me? I'm not the museum person?*

Pippin pressed on, "It is fascinating, though. All the history of the island is there, all the way back to the rum runners and theories about the Lost Colony. There are artifacts for sale—"

Mrs. Lee brushed away the very idea by slicing her hand through the air. "I collect hippopotami figurines and such, but that's it. I can't think at all, not after seeing that poor woman. Not that you have to think at a museum, but you have to read and appreciate the artifacts and such, and I'm just not in the mood for that anymore. No, the beach. That's all that's on our agenda today. And maybe a stroll through town. Mr. Lee wants to see about a boat charter for tomorrow, and I want to check out that olive oil shop."

If she took them at face value, that was that. Hippopotami, but not ancient artifacts. She crossed them off the list.

Paul Marshall had yet to take advantage of the inn's breakfast. So far it was hit or miss whether Pippin saw him coming or going, but he was checking out today. She made a point of loitering in the great room, dusting the shelves and straightening the spattering of books and maritime knick-knacks she'd placed on them. Finally, at eleven o'clock, she heard his door close. A few seconds later, he descended the stairs hauling his duffel, suitcase, and backpack. He wore his signature cargo shorts, an open button down over a t-shirt, flip flops, and a ball cap. Pippin had seen other clothing strewn about his room, but these seemed to be his Go-To clothes. She smiled at him. "Good morning, Mr. Marshall. Thank you for staying with us. It was really unfortunate..." She trailed off.

He adjusted the backpack he had slung over his shoulder. "Poor woman," he said gravely. "I hope they find whoever did it."

Pippin paused for a moment out of respect for the dead. She took Mr. Marshall's proffered room key. "Did you have a chance to see the museum? It's fascinat—"

"Nope. Not interested," he said, cutting her off before she could mention some of the highlights.

"Got it. Not a history buff," she said.

A beat passed before he said, "Right."

"I hope your stay has been good," Pippin said. "Not including the...the..."

"Poor woman," he said gravely. He gave a very slight

smile in what Pippin was sure was a huge effort to be friendly. It didn't come naturally to him. "But don't worry. I'll be back in a few months. I like to get away to the Outer Banks every few months, and Devil's Cove is my favorite island."

"Great," she said, waving him off.

He planned to be a return guest, and he had no interest in history. And he'd left without claiming anything had been stolen from his room. That seemed to eliminate him as the owner of the hilt.

The only other scenario was that the man with the eyes had stolen the artifact from Dr. Baxter.

Her mind churned with questions. *Why* did the historian have it? Did it have something to do with the Lost Colony dig? *Why* had the man with the eyes stolen it from upstairs? And *why* leave it behind in the inn's safe?

The front door opened, and Mrs. Lee appeared. "I forgot my hat; can you believe it?"

Every one of Pippin's questions left her brain when she spotted something red in Mrs. Lee's hands. She knew what it was before she said, "And I found this under the porch steps."

Pippin's heart skipped a beat. Mrs. Lee held Dr. Baxter's missing red jacket.

Chapter 18

"A man who tells secrets or stories must think of who is hearing or reading, for a story has as many versions as it has readers. Everyone takes what he wants or can from it and thus changes it to his measure. Some pick out parts and reject the rest, some strain the story through their mesh of prejudice, some paint it with their own delight."

~John Steinbeck, from *The Winter of our Discontent*

*P*ippin paced the short length of the Burrow. Sailor lay on her bed in the corner, watching every move. Five steps. Stop. Turn around. Five steps back. The space was small. The room usually made her feel like she was wrapped up in a warm blanket, giving her solace she didn't experience anywhere else. But right now, on the heels of a murder and the discovery of the object in the safe, and Dr. Baxter's jacket mysteriously under the front porch, not even the feeling of her dad's presence comforted her.

The room was compact with just the two chairs, a small

occasional table, and their father's desk. And the built-in bookshelves, of course. Finding it had been pure luck, yet Pippin felt that, somehow, Leo had led them to it. He'd *wanted* them to find it. To continue what he'd started.

She'd called Grey first. He showed up an hour later, grimy from working in his shop. Pippin sent Zoe to start a load of laundry, grabbed Grey's hand, and raced into her bedroom, through the hidden door, and into the Burrow. She handed him a pair of cotton gloves, then reverently passed him the bundle of gray cloth.

"It was in the safe?" he repeated after she told him about it.

"Yes." He set it down, removed his gloves and leaned against the bookshelves. "It doesn't make sense," he said.

"Ha. Which part?"

The question was rhetorical, but Grey gave a suppressed little laugh. "All of it?" He went on to list his thoughts. "Who would have this? Is it valuable? If so, how valuable? You said none of the guests are archaeologists. Dr. Baxter was a historian, so it makes sense that it was hers? You said she was upset there were no deadbolts, so why would she keep it in her room? Why wouldn't *she* have asked to put it in the safe? And that just touches the surface of my questions. If this guy with the eyes *did* steal it, first of all, why? Second of all, how did he know it was here? And third, why give it to Zoe to put in the safe here? If he stole it, he's playing a game that only he knows the rules to."

He'd voiced nearly all of her questions. She posed the lingering ones. "What do we do with it? Keep it in the safe?" Mr. Marshall was gone. If it was his and missing, surely, he would have reported it. But she could ask the Lees if it was theirs. Or she could give it to Jacobs.

She moved next to him, no idea what to do with it. They

mirrored each other standing side by side, backs against the shelves, arms folded on their chests, staring at the hilt.

JAMIE MCADAMS WAS the only history buff Pippin knew, and he was far more than just that. He was a scholar. She'd called him twenty minutes ago, and now here he stood looking like a fox in a hen house. At the moment, he was less concerned with how Pippin had come into possession of the artifact—because according to him it definitely *was* an artifact—and more with what it actually was. "You're right," he said, cradling it in his gloved hands. "It's definitely the hilt from a sword."

"Not a dagger? You're sure?" Grey asked.

Jamie used his thumb to nudge his glasses up. "Those words are pretty much interchangeable. The blade was probably about twenty-five inches. Shorter and wider than earlier versions. It probably had a tapered point."

"What year?" Pippin asked.

Jamie cracked a smile. "There is no way to tell the year. We might—well, not *we*—" he corrected, circling his finger to incorporate the three of them— "but, you know, archaeologists might be able to get to a ballpark on the general era, give or take a century or two."

Pippin frowned. "That doesn't sound very precise."

"Without proper authentication, it would be hard to even identify the era. You know, back then—in the 1st and 2nd centuries, for sure—soldiers weren't outfitted with standardized weapons. Mostly, they would have been responsible for bringing their own armor and weapons. That's a lot of potential variety in weaponry. And that variety makes it hard to accurately date them. I don't think there's even a true evolutionary timeline for Roman swords."

"But it is Roman, though?" Grey asked.

"Oh yeah. One hundred percent."

Pippin peered at it wishing she could see what he did. "How can you tell *that*?"

"The Irish sort of, mmm, decorated the hilts of their swords. They elaborately adorned them with gold. Gems." As he spoke, he gestured with one loosely fisted hand, like a professor lecturing to a rapt room of students. "But a Roman geographer named Solinus—from the 3rd century, if I'm not mistaken— was the first to note that the most prevalent decoration the Irish used was actually the teeth of sea animals. And Seahorses."

Pippin flinched. "Seahorses? Seriously?"

"Ancient times," Jamie said with a shrug. His gaze travelled to the book sitting on the table between the armchairs. "Any luck with that?"

She followed his gaze to the copy of *The Tale of Two Cities* she'd brought up. Honestly, she hadn't had much time to think about the secrets this house might hold, or Jamie's interpretation that the quote was a metaphor for the secrets people kept. Except—she looked at the hilt. "That's a secret revealed, isn't it?"

"What are you talking—?" Grey started but stopped when he saw the book. He picked it up, turning it over in his hands. "Ah. Book magic."

Pippin hadn't told him about the passages the book revealed to her. She told him now, turning to the first passage about secrets in a house, briefly going over the possible interpretations, and then showing him the second passage about triumph

"*Nothing that we do, is done in vain. I believe, with all my soul, that we shall see triumph,*" Grey read aloud after she'd turned to that page. He looked up at her. "Well. I believe you could interpret that to mean that *I* will be triumphant against the sea."

She rolled her eyes. "I don't think that's what it's telling me. I feel like I'm missing important information."

Grey held the book out to her. "Let's try it."

She stared at him. "Let's try what?"

"Bibliomancy. Book magic. Let's see if Dickens has anything to say about the hilt. How do you do it? Is it like a Ouija Board? You ask something and it gives you the answer?"

"Greevie, you know how it works," she said. "*You're* the one who told me that *I* assign the meaning to whatever a book shows me."

"But I haven't seen it in action," he said. "I haven't *seen* you do it."

She hadn't realized that, but it was true. Her first several attempts had been almost accidental, and they'd been in the presence of Daisy, Ruby, and Jamie. But not Grey. There was no rhyme or reason as to why, but bibliomancy was a gift for the female Lane descendants, not for the males. Grey had never said he wished he had the gift. They'd never actually talked about it, but now Pippin felt his hidden desire, thin and weightless like a cobweb. It would have given him the power to *do* something. To be proactive. To try to solve the mystery of the curse. The fact that he didn't have the gift left him powerless. And reckless.

The Dickens quote. Jamie and Cyrus were both right in their interpretation, she realized. It *was* literal. The house had revealed a secret—the sword hilt. But it was *also* a metaphor because *Grey* concealed a secret, too.

Now that the thought entered her brain, she knew it was

true. He didn't harbor bitterness, but her ability to do book magic created a chasm between them. It was something *she* had that he never could. But now he wanted to see how it worked. It felt like a step in the right direction.

She took the preferred book and sat cross-legged on the floor in the center of the small room. Jamie had done this with her before. He sat in front of her to the left. Grey took the final spot, the three of them forming a triangle. Pippin placed the Dickens book down between them. Grey was silent while Pippin folded her hands in her lap, interlacing her fingers, and explained. "First I set the book on its spine and let the pages fall open."

His nostrils flared as he inhaled, processing. "And...? What happens next?"

"I'll just show you." She put the book on its spine, holding it closed. "What can you tell me?" she asked, as if she were speaking to the universe rather than to the tangible object in her hands.

She let go. The book split, the front and back covers falling away from each other, the pages fluttering before they finally settled. Pippin opened her eyes. Instantly, she saw a passage blacken, as if it had been printed in boldface. "It's the same page as before," she said. The beginning of chapter three.

Grey tapped his lips with one finger. "So, since you already used this book, that's it? You're done with it?"

Jamie adjusted his glasses. He shook his head. "No. No, I don't think so. Is that the same question you asked last time?"

Pippin nodded. "*What can you tell me?*"

"Try something else."

Grey forced a laugh. "Like asking who killed Dr. Baxter?"

Jamie gave a *why not* shrug. "Can't hurt to try."

Pippin thought it was highly unlikely the book would reveal the name of a killer. Still, she reset the book on its spine and tried again, posing her request in a way she thought might work. "Help me figure out who killed Dr. Baxter." She let the sides of the book fall open, and once again, the pages fluttered to an early chapter, settling. She saw the darkening letters right away, undulating then peeling away from the page.

It was like the last feeble echo of a sound made long and long ago. So entirely had it lost the life and resonance of the human voice, that it affected the senses like a once beautiful color faded away into a poor weak stain. So sunken and suppressed it was, that it was like a voice underground.

THEY SAT in silence for a long thirty seconds. "Read it aloud," she said, pushing the book to Grey and pointing to the passage.

He did, then looked at her, still skeptical. "Any ideas how this can help ID a killer?"

She'd asked for help figuring out who had killed Monique Baxter. She hadn't expected the killer's name to be revealed, but the message was finally becoming clear. The hilt of the sword—buried so long ago and revealed during an archeological dig. It was a concrete metaphor for the human voice that had been silenced through death. It was the voice underground. Literally.

She moved across the room to stand in front of the life-sized family tree Leo had created. It hung next to the map pinned to the beige bulletin board. She traced her finger over the yellow sticky notes at the very top. Leo had left the spaces blank, but Pippin had added the names *Morgan Dubhshláine* and *Titus*. Their ancestors. Aunt Rose had written about a pact with an Irish god. This, this was where the Lane curse began.

Perhaps the hilt of this Roman sword had belonged to Titus.

Chapter 19

"An open foe may prove a curse, but a pretended friend is worse."

~John Gay

The inn's phone rang. A second later, Zoe hollered, "Daisy's on the line for you!"

Pippin headed to the registration counter, secretly thankful the Lees weren't in sight. Zoe lacked common sense sometimes, like running the vacuum too early in the morning. "Zoe. Next time put whoever is on the phone on hold and come get me or use the intercom."

The phone system Pippin had set up had a built-in intercom system for just this reason. It was less intrusive to the guests to buzz her through one of the remote stations compared to hollering through the house.

Zoe looked properly chagrinned. "Sorry."

Pippin took the phone from her. "Hey Daisy—"

She'd barely gotten the words out before Daisy interrupted with, "There's a man here and he wants to see you!"

The urgency in Daisy's voice made Pippin's spine crackle. "At the library? What man?"

Daisy dropped her voice to a croaking whisper. "At the library. He didn't give his name, but Pippy, he's freaky."

Pippin didn't even crack a smile at Daisy's nickname. She immediately turned her back to Zoe and walked out the front door. "What do you mean, freaky?"

Daisy cleared her throat and seemed to cup her hand around the phone's speaker. "It's his eyes."

Daisy didn't have to utter another word. Pippin's stomach dropped. She knew exactly what man had asked for her.

The front door opened behind her. Pippin turned to see Zoe poke her head out. "Everything okay?" she mouthed.

The girl had major Fear of Missing Out syndrome— FOMO—desperate to know what was happening at all times, and if she should or could be involved. Pippin forced a smile and waved her away. She waited until Zoe grudgingly closed the door again before she spoke again. "What's he doing?"

"Harold just set him up with the microfilm reader. Pippin," she said, her voice dropping even lower. "He looks like a Bond villain."

Pippin bit back a nervous laugh. That was precisely what the man looked like.

"Are you going to come?"

"I'm on my way," Pippin said, hanging up before Daisy could respond. She burst back into the Inn and handed the phone to Zoe. "I'll be back in a little while."

Zoe's eyes bugged, clamoring for more information. "Crisis at the library?"

Instead of answering, Pippin called over her shoulder, "Hold down the fort." She raced to the garage, which was really more of a storage shed underneath the raised house. When a hurricane hit the island, the small space would be flooded. She didn't keep anything valuable stored there, except the coral Electra Townie bike her grandmother had bought for her after high school, and even that wasn't worth more than a few hundred dollars.

She loved it, though, and not for the first time, gave a silent thank you to her grandmother. The town of Devil's Cove had been planned with pedestrian and bicycles in mind. Pippin could get to most of the places she needed to through either means, including the library.

She straddled the bike and set off. Less than ten minutes later, she parked the bike on the side of the pale blue clapboard house. The city had expanded it in the back to make it large enough to hold the library's book collection, but the facade maintained its quaintness. The sign hanging over the porch announced it as the LIBRARY. There were both steps and a wheelchair accessible ramp, as well as a local government sign at the edge of the property showing a figure holding a book.

The earthy smell was the first thing that hit her every time she stepped inside the old building. A byproduct of living on the Carolina coast was the ever-present dampness. It manifested in the library as a woodsy scent mixed with earthy undertones. She took a deep breath in, filling her lungs with the comforting musty smell.

Inside, Daisy stood behind the circulation desk. Her dark hair was held back with a hair clip, a few careless strands framing her pixie face. With her ever-present hoop earrings, colorful glasses—teal and cat-eyed today—, olive skin dusted with a luminescent glitter, and her pale pink lips, she appeared more faery then human. The second Daisy's gaze landed on Pippin, she propped her forearms on the desk, leaning forward as if she were ready to tell a secret. "What does he want?" she half-said, half-breathed.

"I have no idea." Pippin looked around. People browsed and a few kids sat on pillows in a reading corner. Months ago, when Pippin had come to dig through the microfilm, Harold had taken her to a back corner where a CPU was set up for just that purpose. Now she looked in that general direction. "Back there?"

Daisy pointed and nodded.

She turned on her heels and headed toward the back corner leaving Daisy behind. A few seconds later, the man came into view. Pippin had expected to see him sitting down, his back to her as she approached. Instead, he perched on the edge of the table, his legs extended out in front of him. His arms were folded across his chest and one side of his mouth lifted in a slight—very slight—grin. "Ah, Pippin Lane Hawthorne, we meet again. Thank you for coming."

Pippin slowed her heart rate, taking a moment to think. She hadn't had time to come up with of a plan of action. He'd summoned her and she'd come. But she suspected him of stealing the sword hilt from Dr. Baxter. Had he also murdered the woman? Anything was possible.

This was a public place, though, so she didn't feel in imminent danger. That fact emboldened her. Sarcasm tinted her words. "How did you know I'd show up? Why not just come back to the house if you wanted to talk to me. You know the address."

"I like the predictability of human nature. From our encounter, I knew you were curious. That ensured your presence."

The man spoke with what Pippin thought was a well-educated syntax. A lot like Jamie, she thought, but without the youthful charm.

"Well, I'm here," she said. She slid her hands into her back pockets to stop them from fidgeting.

The man's black slacks and white shirt could have been the very same ones he'd worn Saturday night, still crisp and clean. He laced his fingers, remaining still otherwise. "And I suspect you have several questions to ask me."

She did, the first being: *What game was he playing, and was he a friend or foe?*

Instead, she started with the most obvious one. "Who are you?" Her tone was more peevish than she'd intended.

The man's mouth quirked up on one side. "That's not really important."

"It is to me," she replied.

"I'm here to help you. Let's leave it at that."

Needles pricked inside her head. She suddenly felt this wasn't about Dr. Baxter at all. "Help me with what?"

"Shall I call you Pippin?" he asked, blatantly not answering her question.

"Sure. What should I call you?"

"Call me...Hugh."

The way he said it made it clear that it wasn't his real name. "That's not *actually* your name."

He shrugged. "But it'll do."

She didn't think it would do at all, but she let it go. "You said you wanted to talk to me."

"We have a common ancestor."

Whatever she thought he *might* say, it wasn't that. "Wh-aat?"

His smile quirked up on one side. "We have a common ancestor."

Her bones suddenly felt made of rubber, but she kept her eyes glued to Hugh and her voice steady. "And who would that be?"

He tilted his head to one side. "Come now, Pippin, surely you must have a guess."

The answer came to her like the water of a hurricane crashing against the shoreline. "Titus," she said, her voice nothing more than a breath.

He nodded, his face breaking into a smile, but with his crystalline eyes, it didn't make him look any less formidable. "Very good."

"So, it's true?" she asked. "Morgan and Titus?"

She touched her mother's necklace and immediately thought of the fragment of parchment in the Burrow. Jamie's translation had been correct.

"We share *one* common ancestor," he said again, correcting her assumption.

Her mind raced and the answer came to her. "Not Morgan, then. Titus."

"Indeed. He left my mother in Rome, pregnant with a child. That is my lineage."

Pippin's head pounded, conflicting thoughts crashing around. She'd thought the love affair between Morgan and Titus was romantic. The beginning of a legacy. But if he had a family in Rome, that changed things. The pact with Lir shot to her mind. Morgan had been betrayed by the man she loved and she unwittingly cursed her descendants for the affections of a man who had another family. "What did you mean when you said you were here to help me?"

"Cut to the chase. I like that about you, Pippin. Titus entrusted something with Morgan."

A shiver danced over her skin. She'd been right. The hilt *did* belong to Titus. "How do you know that?"

"The how isn't important."

She clenched her jaw and schooled her face. This man said he was here to help her, but she didn't believe that for a second. He angled his head to one side, considering her. She made her mind blank, letting that translate to her expression. "Of course, it is. How could you *possibly* know that Titus gave something to Morgan more than two thousand years ago, or that he gave her something at all? And that you're even a descendant? That's impossible."

That last word—impossible—lingered in her mind. She was a bibliomancer. The Lane family was cursed. Nothing was impossible.

"Historians can be relentless with their research. Nothing is impossible," he said, echoing her thoughts. He watched her with an intensity she'd never felt before. It was as if his translucent eyes radiated beams that could penetrate the surface of her skin and see inside. Her nerves ratcheted up, fueling her resolve to find out what this man really wanted. "You knew Dr. Baxter had it," she said.

"Correct. And I'm not alone. Others suspected she found it, as well. And there are people who have traced the ancestry of this...treasure...to you," Hugh said.

A scratch of alarm lodged in Pippin's throat. It all felt very cloak-and-dagger. "What people?" she asked.

"People who are *not* your friends."

Implying that he *was* her friend. A shiver wound through her. He felt like the furthest thing from a friend. His words echoed in her head. "How did you know her?" she asked.

"Dr. Baxter? There's a group. History buffs, you could say. Treasure hunters..."

Pippin grimaced. Like Salty Gallagher. "And you're both part of this group?" she asked.

"I am. She was."

Pippin had thought Dr. Baxter's death had something to with the Lost Colony dig with Dr. Bligh, but Hugh was pushing her in a different direction. Needles pricked her eyelids. "She was killed because of what she found."

Hugh pressed his thin lips together for a second. "It's possible."

She shoved away the realization that Dr. Baxter's death was connected to her. To the Lane family.

"I don't understand why you're telling me this."

"Because what Titus gave to Morgan rightfully belongs to you and your brother."

Her gut constricted at the mention of Grey. "How do you know—?" She broke off, immediately realizing that if the man knew a two-thousand-year-old artifact belonged to their shared ancestor, surely, he knew she had a brother. "But if you're Titus's descendant, then it belongs to you as much as it belongs to us."

"Because it was Titus's, yes. But he gave it to Morgan, so I relinquish my claim to it."

"Was Dr. Baxter planning on giving it to us?"

"Doubtful," Hugh said.

That explained why he'd taken it from Dr. Baxter and ensured it was placed in the inn's safe. Still, she didn't trust this man.

Pippin threw her hands up in exasperation. "Then what was she doing here? And what do *you* want?" she demanded. Before he could answer, her breath stuttered. The question of whether *he* had been the one to kill Dr. Baxter raced through her mind again. Dr. Baxter could have discovered the theft, summoned him to meet her on the widow's walk, and confronted him. "Did you kill her?" she blurted, immediately chastising herself. What a stupid question.

He gave a slightly mocking laugh. "Pippin, Pippin, Pippin. Why would I do such a thing?"

"Because she—"

His laser eyes bored into her. "She what?"

"She didn't want us to have the artifact."

He didn't speak for a few seconds. After an audible exhale, he finally said, "I am telling you in all honesty, I did not kill her. Trust me, Pippin."

She bit back a mirthless laugh. She'd trust him as much as a hen would trust a wolf in the coop. "What do you want from me?" she asked.

"You know the old adage; one person's trash is another's treasure? It's true. There are many types of treasures. Ancient weaponry. Old armor. Roman coins. Or—" He paused. "Old letters."

She froze. Swallowed her reaction. Carefully schooled her expression. Could he know about the letter she and Jamie found hidden in Leo's study? She drew in a bolstering breath then asked, "You think there's more? Something else Titus gave to Morgan?"

"Something *else*?"

She tried not to shrink under his scrutiny. He'd found the hilt. Giving it to her had simply been a way to gain her trust. This was the game, then. He was after something bigger. Something more valuable. Something he had yet to find. "You said coins or armor."

His spine seemed to crackle. He was on high alert. "Have you found anything like that? Something your parents kept secret or hidden?"

She pressed her lips together. Dug her fingernails into her palm. Anything so he wouldn't see her nerves rattling.

Slowly, she shook her head. "My grandparents had all my parents' thing taken out of the house. When we took possession, there was nothing left but the house itself."

Finally, he released her from his gaze. "That's unfortunate."

Pippin itched to leave this room. To get on her bike and pedal around the island until she couldn't think anymore. But she had one more question for Hugh. "Why didn't you talk to me at the open house? Why did you wait four days before contacting me?"

"Dr. Baxter was alive at that point. I had planned to speak with her about her finding. We had a similar goal."

"Finding Titus's treasure."

"At that point, there was no reason for me to believe you were in danger."

A cold shiver danced over her skin. "But you do now?"

He looked at her as he stood, trying his best to appear earnest, something wholly impossible given his other-worldly eyes. "I wouldn't want anything to happen to you..."

He trailed off, leaving the idea that she was in danger hanging between them like a sugarcoated threat. It hit home. "You think I'm in danger?"

"I don't know," he said. Pippin felt the intensity of his gaze on her, and a touch of whiplash when he changed subjects. "Your mother was from Oregon. Came out here to forge a new path for herself."

Neither one of those sentences were questions. She watched his back as he returned to the computer. "You seem to know a lot about my family, Hugh."

"I am a student of humanity—"

"As well as a history buff—"

He shrugged. "They go hand in hand—"

"And a treasure-hunter."

He glanced at the computer. Pippin couldn't tell what the article was about, but she saw a photograph of her house. Of Sea Captain's Inn.

He reached over and pressed a button. The monitor went black. "The Lane Curse," he said. "It's an intriguing bit of Irish lore."

For the first time, she thought she heard a slight lilt in his voice, but it was the words themselves that turned her blood cold. "What do you know about it?"

He looked back at her with his icy eyes, that infernal ghost of a smile on his lips. "I know enough, Ms. Lane," he said. "I know enough."

Chapter 20

"Memory is the treasure house of the mind wherein the monuments thereof are kept and preserved."
~Thomas Fuller

I know enough. The words went round and round in Pippin's head like vultures circling their prey. She'd been swamped with work the moment she returned to the Inn. Now, well after eight o'clock, she was in her room, her mind rehashing everything Hugh had said. Finally, she had time to sit down and actually *think*.

She summed up what she learned about Hugh. Next to nothing, she realized. But he knew plenty about her. She ticked items off on her fingers.

- *He'd asked to see her.*
- *Hugh was certainly not his real name.*
- *He'd known Dr. Baxter personally, and he'd known she had the hilt Titus had given to Morgan.*

- *He was a self-proclaimed history buff and student of humanity, whatever that meant.*
- *He knew she had a brother—and about Cassie being from Oregon.*
- *And he knew about the curse.*

Another chill washed over her when she recalled the way he'd stared at her when he mentioned old letters. She thought again about someone breaking into her room. Whoever it was could have been after the hilt, or it could have been Hugh, looking for the fragment of parchment. Something he deemed more valuable.

There were far too many unanswerable questions.

Before she left the library, she'd asked Daisy to find the article Hugh had been reading. Of course, Daisy had come through. Pippin had shoved it in her back pocket for the bike ride home, but now she flattened the creases with her hands. Why had Hugh been reading it? Had he intended for her to see it? To lure her into getting her own copy of it? The more she thought about it, the more she knew it had been calculated. Everything Hugh did was with careful intention.

Sailor made a faint sound as she stretched, then settled back to sleep in her bed. Keeping her room locked up during the long summer days meant it was a stuffy sauna by dark. The evening was cool, so Pippin opened the French doors to let in some air, and took the article out to the rocking chair on the screened-in side porch. The wall-mounted sconce didn't provide enough light to read by, so she pulled up the flashlight feature on her phone.

The article was about the death of Perry Hubbard more than thirty years ago. Perry Hubbard, the last descendant of the Sea Captain himself. The woman had fallen from the back decking of the house. Pippin held her breath as she read a quote by Deputy Ron Bosworth. "The woman was pushed to her death by a treasure-hunter searching for his pot of gold." The article went on to say that Perry Hubbard's death was a tragic end to a woman who'd had a lonely life.

Pippin swallowed the rush of emotions that rose inside her and kept reading. Perry Hubbard was the subject of the article, but equal printed space was given to the old sea captain's house and the man who built it. It was all information Pippin already knew. It was the same story she told the Lees the previous Sunday morning.

She reread the article, blinking away the letters that reversed themselves, or flipped upside down. Reading was becoming easier, but when she was tired, her eyes skipped over words and they blurred under her gaze. She read the article until she couldn't read it anymore.

As she rested her eyes, she heard Hugh calling her Ms. Lane. His voice in her head and those white eyes sent a fresh shiver through her. Pippin had so many questions. Too many questions to sit still on her side porch. She checked on Sailor, locked up her room again, and hightailed it across the street. A few minutes later, she was knocking on the front door of Hattie Juniper Pickle, and a few minutes after that, the two of them sat on the new rocking chairs Hattie had bought and painted to match the teal trim of her house. Hattie peered at the printed article through her bright-pink-framed readers. After yet another few minutes, she looked over the rims at Pippin. "Your mama and me, we discovered Perry Hubbard's body, you know."

Pippin gawped. "You never told me that."

Hattie gave a toothy grin. "I figured it'd come up eventually, and look, now it has."

"How did you happen to discover Mrs. Hubbard's body?" Pippin asked.

Hattie's elbow rested on the arm of her chair, her ever-present unlit cigarette between two fingers. "Your mama, she got concerned when she never did see Perry out and about. Something made her think trouble was brewing. Now what was it?" She tapped her chin, but tsk'd and finally gave up. "My memory ain't what it used to be. Anyway, she thought something was wrong, and sure enough, she was right."

Pippin touched her mother's necklace. It was as if each story she heard about Cassie could be captured like a tuft from a cloud, then imbued into the metal. Each bit helped create a fuller picture of the woman she didn't get the chance to know.

"Do you think there's still treasure hidden in the house?" Pippin asked, because if anyone would know, it was Hattie Juniper Pickle.

"Well, I can't give you a direct answer to that, darlin'. I told your mama 'bout it long time ago, though."

"Told her about what?"

Hattie pushed out her bright pink lips and knitted her brows together, a look that clearly said Pippin needed to pay closer attention. "The treasure, o' course."

"But you just said—"

"Now listen." Hattie waggled her cigarette hand. In the darkness, her smile looked more like she was baring her teeth. "Most people think Cap'n Hubbard's rum was the treasure he brought to the island, but other folks, they thought there was something more. Most the treasure hunters dive to the wrecks, but there've always been folks who believe there's something more to the story, something that hasn't yet been revealed. The legend of the Sea Captain, you know."

Pippin leaned forward, her elbows resting on her thighs,

her fingers interlaced under her chin. "So, you told my mother about the *legend*?"

"Sure," Hattie said with a snort. "Plenty of people have come to search that house for it. It might exist. But it might not. If it does, it might never be found. This island holds more secrets than my key drawer has keys."

Pippin had seen that endless stash of keys. During the decades Hattie had lived in her house, neighbors and friends had given her house keys to keep for emergency or back up. Hattie never got rid of a single one. God knows how she ever managed to figure out what key went to what house.

"Do *you* think the sea captain left a treasure in the house? Could it still be there?" Pippin asked, coming back around to her initial question.

Hattie's cigarette dangled precariously from her fingers. Thank God the woman didn't actually smoke anymore, or Pippin felt sure she'd accidentally light her house on fire. Hattie tilted her head this way and that, her lips moving from pursed to pressed together, pursed to pressed together. Finally, she said, "If you really want me to take a stand on that question, I have to go with *no*."

"No treasure." Pippin exhaled with relief.

"Now just wait a minute. You asked if I thought there was a treasure from old Cap'n Hubbard. To that, I say no. I could be wrong, o' course, but I still say no. I think he probably had his rum, and that was good enough for him. But that don't mean there's not treasure hidden away in that house. Secrets, remember? There's the secret room, for starters. Leo, that dad o' yours, he was a clever one. And your mama's history, well, it's possible they hid something there, but I'm not sayin' yes or no. I'm sayin' *maybe*. I'd be completely confuzzled if something from Cap'n Hubbard showed up. He built that house goin' on one hundred and seventy-five years ago. Course it stayed in the Hubbard family till Perry died, then your folks bought it. It was a short-lived resurrection of life in it, 'course, 'cause then your mama died, and your daddy disappeared. Only the old ghosts and that old crow were rattlin' around in there till you showed up again. That house has a few secrets left I reckon." She wagged her unlit cigarette. "Probably not from that old sailor, but yeah, I think the old house is holding onto a mystery or two."

"More secrets from my parents," Pippin muttered, but it was the idea of a treasure that sat in the pit of her stomach. If Hattie thought it was true, it very well could be. The hilt was something Dr. Baxter had brought into the house, but what if Hugh's story was true and Cassie had some two-thousand-year-old treasure passed to her from her parents, something she'd hidden away between the walls or under the floorboards?

She looked back at the photograph in the article. It was a black and white picture, and captured several details of the house that weren't there anymore: the wrought iron fence; flowers running up either side of the brick walkway; curtains closing the inside off to the world.

The photo showed the old sea captain's house standing just as strong and proud as it was again now. Grey had covered the exposed pilings and stilts the house sat on with lattice. A tourist sign in Manteo showed just how high the water had risen during Hurricane Irene. The storm churned up water from Shallowbag Bay, bringing the sea level in the town to seven feet, eleven inches. Living on the North Carolina coast was not for the faint of heart. Neither was ferreting out the truth about a two-thousand-year-old story.

Pippin peered closer at the grainy photo. Her eye traveled to the roof. She squinted at a dark smudge, then shined the beam of light from her phone's flashlight directly at it. It wasn't an ink mark. It was a black crow, and it was perched right on the edge of the widow's walk. A shiver wound through her.

Hattie bent close and followed her line of sight to the crow. "People think they symbolize bad luck and death, but that's not really true. That ol' crow hung around every day your mama was in that house. She thought it was a bad omen, but I disagreed because the crow is a misunderstood creature. They're watchful. They symbolize intelligence. Transformation. Change. It was a powerful protector for Cassie, there to help her fight against her destiny, but that curse got her just the same."

Pippin jumped when Hattie's hand clamped around her knee. "That crow's back, Pippin. It's gonna protect you, too, but it ain't enough. You gotta stop the curse. And you can do it, too. Oh yes, lovey, you can do it."

Chapter 21

"The value of identity of course is that so often with it comes purpose."

~ Richard Grant

*P*ippin jolted upright in bed. She felt disoriented for a moment. Hugh's veiled threat, warning her she was in danger, circled in her mind. She shook her head as if she could erase the thought like shaking an Etch-a-Sketch that dissolved whatever had been drawn there. It was still dark outside. Far too early to start the day. She lay back down and squeezed her eyes shut, but sleep eluded her.

Out of nowhere, Ron Baxter's face loomed in and out of her consciousness. His mother's jacket. She'd draped it over the arm of her sitting chair. Of course! That's why he came to mind. She needed to return it to him. She kicked herself. Why hadn't she thought to get the man's contact information?

Sunrise was still an hour off, but she was wide awake.

She swung herself out of bed, left her room, and padded through the kitchen and great room, unlocking her office door with the key she brought with her. She grabbed her laptop and hurried back. Sailor, asleep in her bed, hadn't budged.

Pippin sat cross-legged on her bed, her laptop open in front of her, the search engine pulled up. First, she typed in Dr. Monique Baxter. She scanned the entries on her, just as she had before. Her bio, as well as other academic information about her, was listed on various sites, but none of it mentioned her family. She spent nearly thirty minutes opening links, scanning for biographical information, closing it again, and moving on to the next one.

That's when it hit her. Dr. Baxter had led on that she was an historian, but the more Pippin drilled down, searching for information on her, the more she realized that while history was the umbrella, the doctor's specialty was, indeed, archaeology.

So, she probably *had* been here for the dig, whether or not she was officially part of it. If Pippin went back to the theory that Dr. Baxter was killed because of something connected to the Lost Colony, then she, herself, wasn't in danger. That, at least, was potentially one mystery solved.

Finally, she gave up the search for Dr. Baxter's personal information. That was getting her nowhere. Next, she typed in Ron Baxter, then Ronald Baxter. An accomplished jazz saxophonist filled the first several pages. Then came a random mention of a basketball player with the same name, but that was it. No connection at all to historian Monique Baxter. The woman kept her private life private.

After another fifteen minutes of searching, Pippin's eyelids finally drooped, sleepiness overtaking her again. She set the laptop aside and drifted off.

When she awoke again, an idea was fully formed in her mind. It was still early, though, so she went through her morning routine of walking Sailor, preparing breakfast for the inn's guests—now just the Lees, and cleaning up. She didn't have the luxury of leaving dirty dishes in the sink, or things out on the counter, left to air dry. She put the kitchen in order, leaving it just how Zoe had left it the afternoon before, tidy and clean.

She checked her watch for the tenth time, giving a silent cheer when it read ten oh five. Finally, she was done with her chores and the university would be open. She holed up in her bedroom, bringing up Dr. Baxter's bio on her university's website. The building in which her office was housed, along with the mailing address, phone number, fax number, and department email were listed in the left sidebar. Pippin was betting that the phone number belonged, not to Dr. Baxter herself, but to the department's central line.

After three rings, a man answered with a clipped, "Hello."

"Oh, hello!" Pippin made her voice warm and friendly. "I'm calling about Dr. Monique Baxter—"

He interrupted her. "She's no longer at the university."

"Oh right, I know," Pippin said before he could hang up on her. "I'm, um, she was staying at my inn when she died."

He was silent on the other end of the line for a few seconds, then said, "Right. How can I help you?"

"I'm trying to reach her son, actually. He came to collect some of her things, and I have her jacket for him—"

The man cleared his throat, stopping her. "Miss, Dr. Baxter didn't have a son."

Pippin started, cupping her hand over her forehead. Her brain felt like it was ready to explode. "I'm sorry, what?"

"Dr. Baxter didn't have children."

"Are you sure? Ron—"

"I'm quite sure. She was married to her work. Is there anything else?" he asked.

"No. Thank you." She hung up and muttered the words the man had spoken. "Dr. Baxter was married to her work. She didn't have children."

She slammed her laptop closed. Then who the hell was the man who claimed to be Ron Baxter?

A possible answer came to her in a blast. He could be one of those people Hugh referred to. Someone after the hilt. Someone willing to kill for a two-thousand-year-old Roman artifact, or whatever other treasure Dr. Baxter might have had. What if Ron Baxter—or whatever his name was— had somehow snuck in—or prearranged—to meet Dr. Baxter at the widow's walk expecting her to have the hilt? But she *didn't* have it because Hugh had already taken it by that point. Had he killed her because of that? Maybe they'd struggled and he'd smashed her head in to stop her from fighting him.

What if he then left her there and went to search of her room? It would have been fruitless, though, because Hugh had already stolen the hilt by that point. Of course, Ron Baxter wouldn't have known that, hence his visit to the Inn to ask about his so-called *mother's* belongings.

It was a better scenario than, say Dr. Bligh, who might have an interest in the hilt from an academic standpoint, but had not been seen in or around the inn and had no stake in anything but his dig.

Somehow, it wasn't comforting, though, because now the idea that she was in danger resurrected itself. And Ron Baxter could be the enemy.

Chapter 22

"Vision is the art of seeing what is invisible to others."
~Jonathan Swift

*P*ippin walked into the bookshop expecting to see Jamie behind the counter. Instead, a beanpole thin woman with thin gray hair and curious eyes stood there. "Hello there," she said with the slightest lilt in her voice. "Looking for something in particular or just browsing?"

"Just browsing," Pippin said. She put her palm to her chest. "I'm Pippin Hawthorne. I'm a friend of Jamie's—"

"Oh my goodness, yes! Of course! I know exactly who you are, and you're even lovelier than I expected."

Pippin lowered her head, looking at the woman through her lashes. "I am?"

The woman walked out from behind the counter on spindly legs, her arms extended. For a second, Pippin thought she was going to be pulled into a bear hug by this thin woman who she might actually be able to snap in two. Thankfully, her arms came together as she clasped one of Pippin's hands in hers. "I'm sure that sounded strange, given that I'm a veritable stranger. I'm Erin. Erin McAdams," she said. "I'm Jamie's mother."

Pippin's puzzlement vanished and she could instantly see likeness between the two, and even into Heidi and Mathilda. "It's so nice to meet you!" she exclaimed—because it was. All Jamie had told her was that his mother was Irish and had beaten breast cancer. And now here she was in the flesh—what little of it there was.

"Likewise. Jamie and Cyrus are out doing God knows what," she said, answering Pippin's unasked question. "I'm sure you know the two of them are thick as thieves."

Pippin had witnessed Jamie's bond with his grandfather firsthand. They were close, co-owned The Open Book, and had an easy, light rapport with one another. She knew next to nothing, though, about his parents. His father had walked out when he was a toddler, and his mother had raised him. That's all he'd ever revealed, except to say that Cyrus was the only real father he'd ever known.

"Are you visiting?" Pippin asked, tamping down her disappointment in not being able to tell Jamie everything about her meeting with Hugh and her revelation about Ron Baxter.

Erin McAdams gave a nonchalant shrug followed by a mischievous grin. "Visiting. Passing through. Staying indefinitely. Who knows?"

Pippin didn't quite know what to say to that. They were three entirely different responses. She got the feeling Erin didn't quite know what the answer was, either, and that she was just fine with that.

Erin waved her hand in front of her and waggling her

head. "I'm just kidding. Good grief, but Jamie would have a fit if I didn't come with a specific plan. He's a rule follower, that one. Goodness knows he didn't get that from me. I'll take up two parking spaces, say 'it's grand!' about near everything, and I have a habit of saying yes when I mean no, maybe when I mean yes, and no when I mean maybe. It's an Irish thing."

Pippin grinned at Erin's charm and vivacity. "And Jamie didn't inherit those Irish traits?"

"Ah, he's grand—see?" She slipped into a full-fledged Irish brogue when she said, "He's just grand. Irish runs deep in him, like you, but he only needs one parking space, the lad."

Pippin laughed. From what she'd seen, that was true. He was very good at slipping a car into the space between two painted white lines.

Erin wasn't done singing her son's praises. "I'd go so far to say that Jamie is as good as they come. He's a devoted father to those sweet girls." She glanced over her shoulder as if someone had slipped into the shop, unseen, and might be standing right behind her. "I would never say this to him, and certainly not to my darlins', Heidi or Mathilda, but he escaped a life of torture when that wife of his left. It was a blessing in disguise, it was. The only good things she's *ever* done was bring those girls into the world, then leave them to Jamie to raise."

"He loves them. From what I've seen, he's an amazing dad," she said, hoping that conveyed to Erin McAdams that she shouldn't tell her the details of her son's marriage. If Jamie ever chose to share her his marriage story, that was one thing, but becoming privy to his life without his knowledge, that was something else entirely.

But Erin didn't notice, and she seemed to be lacking in

boundaries. She was mid-story and Pippin got the feeling she was going to finish no matter what. "She's a dancer, that one. As high on her mighty horse as a person can get. Jamie, on the other hand, well he's a lot closer to the ground. With both feet rooted to this place and to his girls. At some point Miranda decided Jamie wasn't good enough and being a mother didn't fit her image or the lifestyle she wanted."

Despite her misgivings, Pippin listened with rapt attention. That explained the animosity Pippin had witnessed between them when Miranda had come to the store to drop off Mathilda. "But she has them for a week. Will she be okay with them?" she asked, biting her lip the second the question floated off, wishing she could pull it back. It wasn't her business. Still, she'd come to care for the girls and didn't want them unhappy.

Erin pressed her lips into a grimace. "Their custody agreement says she'll take them a few times a year for vacations. Other than that, they don't see her much. They'll be okay. They have each other."

Pippin had seen that in them. Heidi watched out for Mathilda, and Mathilda looked up to her big sister. They were a lot like her and Grey, in fact. They might run into some bumps in the road along the way, but they'd always have each other.

Erin was still talking. "You have a brother, I hear," she said, as if she'd read Pippin's thoughts.

She told her about Grey. Erin clapped her hands and laughed. "Seventy-three seconds apart! Oh my goodness. That's grand."

"It is," she agreed. She still didn't know what to do to stop him from getting in the water, but she couldn't worry about that right now.

"Look at me, I've been talking your ear off. Are you here

for a book?" She spread her arms out wide. "I can definitely help you with that!"

Pippin had come to see Jamie, but she didn't feel that she should leave empty-handed, not with Erin McAdams looking at her so expectantly. "I'm not really sure what I'm looking for." Which was true. She was still learning the intricacies of bibliomancy. Was a book always supposed to come to her with some reason? Some connection to whatever she was trying to understand, or would any book do?

She looked at the rows and rows of shelves. At the myriad stories told, the multitude of lives lived in the volumes tucked tightly next to each other. How was she supposed to choose the right one?

Erin broke into her thoughts. "Let the book choose you."

Pippin started. Did Erin know about her bibliomancy? About the curse? About her father? Had Jamie told his mother about Pippin, but no—she shook her head slightly —no, she didn't think he would tell *that* particular secret. At least not yet.

But the way Erin looked at her made her question if she was right. It was as if the woman knew that picking a book is personal, but for Pippin it was more so. She didn't say anything else, though, just let Pippin wander, hoping a book would, in fact, make itself known to her. She moved slowly up and down the aisles, letting her fingertips trail over the uneven line of the book spines. She's started with poetry, moved to self-help, then the other nonfiction sections. In fiction, she started with mystery, moved to romance, westerns, classics. Up and down the rows, looking at each shelf.

And then she felt it and her heartbeat ratcheted up. The spine of a single book stuck out farther than the rest in the row. She stopped and spun to face the shelf, grabbing the hardcover book by the top of the spine, pulling it out. It was blue with white crisscrossed lines that reminded her of a clothesline holding kites and flags. "*Gulliver's Travels*," she murmured.

She'd heard of it, of course, in the same way she'd heard of *The Tale of Two Cities* but, like the Dickens book, she didn't know much about the Jonathan Swift story. Something about a giant living amongst a society of tiny people. Lili...Lila...Lilliputians. That was it. There was a movie with Jack Black playing Gulliver. Maybe she'd rent it, she thought, but quickly dismissed the idea. Heidi would be disappointed if she found out Pippin had watched a movie about a book before actually reading the words in print. It was one of the girl's hard and fast rules and it was beginning to rub off on Pippin. Of course, that might limit Pippin's movie adventures because she read at a snail's pace compared to the preteen.

"You found one!" Erin's voice sing-songed from where she stood back behind the front counter.

Pippin held it up for her to see. "I did. Have you read it?"

Erin snorted. "*Gulliver's Travels*? No. Reading is Jamie and Cyrus's thing. That's not to say I can't read, or that I don't enjoy a book now and again. But I'm more visual. What I do know is that there are several movie versions and I've seen at least a few of them." She held a finger to her lips. "But shhh. Don't you dare tell Heidi that. I'll never hear the end of it."

Pippin laughed. "Your secret is safe with me. I just told myself I'd better read the book before watching the movie for the very same reason."

Erin sighed out her granddaughter's name. "Ah, sweet lass. She's one of a kind."

Pippin paid for the book, thanked Erin McAdams, and scooted out the door before the woman could reel her back in with another story.

Chapter 23

"In archaeology, context is everything. Objects allow us to reconstruct the past. Taking artifacts from a temple or an ancient private house is like emptying out a time capsule."

~Sarah Parcak

*P*ippin pedaled up to the inn, *Gulliver's Travels* in the basket of her bike, just as the Lees backed out of the driveway. Mrs. Lee rolled down the driver's side window. "We're off to see Cape Hatteras and the Graveyard of the Atlantic Museum," she said.

Pippin put one leg down to support herself and the bike while they chatted. "I'm so glad you're feeling better," she said, and she was. The spark had been reignited in Mrs. Lee's eyes. "You'll love the lighthouse. It's a tough climb to the top, but worth it."

Mr. Lee grimaced from the passenger seat. "I'll just tip my head back and look up at it."

Mrs. Lee batted his arm with the back of her hand. "You can wait for me, then, because I'm doing it."

"There's great history there. Did you know the colors of a lighthouse's stripes and the rhythm of a lighthouse's flashing lights helps orient sailors..." She trailed off when Mr. Lee brought his phone to life. He seemed to be just along for the ride while his wife relished adventuring and exploring new sights and places.

"There's also a good bookstore in Buxton," she suggested.

This got Mr. Lee's attention. "That I'll do, and we're going to find crab cakes."

Pippin smiled. "Plenty of places for those."

Pippin found Zoe on the back deck sweeping away the cobwebs and brushing away the thin layer of sand from the planks and from around the little cement frogs on the railing. The fifth one was back, the chip repaired and not even visible. The kitchen was clean and the grocery list written. "I'll clean the Lee's room after I'm done here," Zoe said.

Australian again. Pippin smiled. "Perfect." That would leave her a few minutes to do a little book magic with *Gulliver's Travels*. She headed toward her office, stopping when Zoe blurted, "Oh! I almost forgot. The lieutenant called."

Pippin stopped in her tracks. She didn't want to talk to Jacobs. She knew she was in a gray area by not turning in the sword hilt, and she didn't want to lie to his face. She turned around. "What did he want?"

Zoe held the broom out with one hand as if she were a wizard and it was her staff. "He didn't say."

Pippin gave Zoe a pointed look. "You didn't say anything about the thing in the safe, did you?"

Zoe pulled a face, looking more like a sulky teenager

than the young woman she was. "Of course not." Her expression cleared. "Did you find out anything about it?"

"Only that it's really old," she said.

As Zoe rolled her eyes. "I could have told you that," she muttered. Armed with her broom, she headed back to the deck. Pippin closed herself up in her office and fanned out the pages of *Gulliver's Travels* before placing the spine of hardcover on her desk. She closed her eyes for a few seconds, repeating her question several times in her mind before finally opening them again and saying it aloud. "What do you have to tell me?"

She let the book fall open. Once the pages settled, she looked down at it. Instantly, the words of a single passage darkened and lifted—just barely—off the page.

There was a society of men among us, bred up from their youth in the art of proving, by words multiplied for the purpose, that white is black, and black is white, according as they are paid. To this society all the rest of the people are slaves.

SHE READ and reread the two sentences. "White is black, and black is white," she said softly, but speaking it didn't help her understand it any better because black was not white, and white was not black. They were two different things, so why would anyone try to prove otherwise?

But an idea tickled at the edge of her mind. According to Dr. Bligh the Archaeology Guy, Dr. Baxter didn't have anything to do with the excavation. She recalled the conversation she had with Dr. Baxter when they'd first met, and then the conversation with Jamie about authenticating the

Dare Stone. She had never actually *said* she was an historian, and now Pippin knew she wasn't.

Yet she required a ride to the dig site on island. Nothing was black and white with Dr. Baxter. She replayed the scene in her mind's eye. She'd dropped Dr. Baxter off and watched her talk with someone at the dig. Then she'd melted into the crowd on the edge of the woods. There had been familiar people amidst the dig crowd, Pippin remembered.

A crazy idea surfaced. What if she'd been meeting someone there? Mr. White Eyes? But no, the man had actually stolen the dagger hilt from Dr. Baxter, giving it to Zoe so it would end up in Pippin's hands. Why would he meet Dr. Baxter at Mariner's Cove?

Then who? Gin White? That was a possibility. The woman had said she had talked to Dr. Baxter before showing up at the Inn the night of the open house. Gin White was, in fact, trying to convince Dr. Baxter that black was white—the last name White!—just like in the quote. She was trying to convince Dr. Baxter that her Dare Stone was the real deal, but Dr. Baxter didn't believe it.

But why go to Dr. Baxter, who apparently wasn't part of the dig, when an entire team was on-site and looking for real proof of the Lost Colony?

Pippin stretched her arm toward the floor where Sailor lay next to her chair. As she absently scratched the dog's head, she remembered something else. The night of the inn's open house, when Gin White had shown up with her Dare Stone, Jamie had asked Dr Baxter if she was here for the dig.

Once again, the woman hadn't answered directly. Instead, her response had been something about her theory that the colonists had never actually been on Devil's Cove.

The woman was a study in contradictions and distractions.

Pippin pushed *Gulliver's Travels* aside and popped open her laptop. Once it powered on, she opened a browser page and typed **Dr. Monique Baxter** in the search bar just as she had in the wee hours of that morning. She sifted through the results, then clicked on the link to her university bio.

Pippin stared at the screen, reading slowly, forcing her eyes to focus despite the twisted letters. She reread to make sure she understood. Finally, with her heart in her throat, she pulled out her cellphone and dialed Jamie's number hoping he wasn't tied up with Cyrus. He answered on the third ring. "Hey, Pip—"

There was chatter in the background, but she interrupted and jumped straight to the point of the call. "She wasn't a historian. She had a doctorate in Medieval History and Archaeology."

"What?" he asked, distracted.

"Jamie," she said, more slowly this time. "I'm talking about Dr. Baxter. She wasn't a *historian*. She was an *archaeologist*." Emphasis on the last word.

There was a weighty pause before he said, "Hang on, Pippin." His voice was muffled for a second, then he said to someone, "Come take over for me for a sec." So, he was back at the shop, probably calling on his mom to help out. A few seconds later, he was on the line with her again. "Sorry, we're swamped. I kid you not, a hundred people just swarmed the shop."

"That's a good problem to have," she said.

"It is, but I only have a minute. What were you saying?"

Pippin repeated what she'd just discovered about Dr. Monique Baxter. "She had nothing to do with the Mariner's

Cove excavation. She was an archaeologist with a focus on human remains in ancient Ireland."

Those five words left a chasm of silence between them for a heavy moment. She broke it by repeating, *"Jamie, she studied human remains in ancient Ireland."*

He let out a low whistle.

"There's more," Pippin said, looking back at her computer screen. "I found an article about a lecture given at the Centre for Scottish and Celtic Studies at the University of Glasgow. A professor of Celtic Archaeology at University College Dublin talked about the Neolithic period and stone axe production in, like, 3000 BC, in a place called Lambay."

"Right. I know about that. It was the island of Reachrú, but now it's known as Lambay. Its strategic position made it key in controlling sea routes and access to Dublin during the medieval and early modern periods."

She knew Jamie would have some commentary on what she'd found. "Listen to this," she read directly from the article, telling him about the construction of the inner harbor wall during the 1920s. "Burial sites were discovered, along with Romano-British objects from the Ist century. This professor connects all that with a prom—"

She stumbled over the word. "Promontory," Jamie supplied. "It's a rock projecting into the water."

"Well, that rock fort at Drumanagh—"

"Riiight," he said, as if he was putting something together. "It's a headland north-east of Dublin. That fort *did* produce Roman artifacts."

"Like the sword hilt?" she asked.

"Could be."

"Like *our* sword hilt?"

He hesitated for a moment before he said, "I don't know, Pippin. How would it have gotten from the artifact collection in Lambay to Devil's Cove, North Carolina, in *your* safe?"

"I wondered that, too." She pulled up another article she'd found about a theft from the Drumanagh collection. "Listen. It says, 'only one item was stolen, the hilt of a Roman sword believed to be from the 1st century, a rare find supporting the idea that while Romans did not conquer Ireland, they did, in fact, have a presence there.'"

Jamie gave another low whistle. "You missed your calling as a researcher," he said.

She swelled at the compliment. "So, it could be our sword hilt?"

This time Jamie didn't hesitate. "Is there a photograph?"

"Not so far."

"Keep looking."

"Oh, I will," she said. The very idea that something Morgan had held in her hands 2000 years ago was now in Pippin's possession was mind-boggling. She was going to get to the bottom of this mystery.

The chatter in the background rose a decibel. "I have to go, Pippin, but send me the links you found, would you?"

She did, right then and there. After hanging up, she made up her mind on her next steps. It was only after she hung up that she realized she forgot to tell him about Hugh and Ron Baxter.

Chapter 24

"The world is not fair, and often fools, cowards, liars and the selfish hide in high places."

~Bryant H. McGill

*H*aving Zoe as the sole employee of Sea Captain's Inn was a godsend. Pippin's chores were piling up, but she had to prioritize and right now, and talking to Gin White was at the top of the list. She texted Ruby, who knew everyone and everything about Devil's Cove, and cut to the chase. Do you know anything about Gin White?

It took a solid thirteen long minutes before Ruby responded. Devil's Brew was probably just as busy as The Open Door. Just as Pippin was about to add a question mark, Ruby replied with, *With the Dare Stone from the end of your party? Sure. Works at The Brewery. Kinda cray-cray.*

That's right! Pippin had seen her at The Brewery. Her

thumbs flew over the texting keyboard. *Do you know if she's working today?*

Don't think so, Ruby texted. *She stopped in for a lemonade a while ago. She just left...mmm...maybe ten minutes ago?*

Pippin typed, *Where does she live?*

This time Ruby responded right away with: *Somewhere off of Buccaneer, I think.*

Another text from Ruby came through. *She said she was heading back home.*

The three little dots on Pippin's phone flashed indicating Ruby was sending another text. They stopped for a second, started again, then the message popped up in gray on the left side of her screen. *Swamped. Gotta go.*

Thanks, Pippin typed.

Buccaneer was an offshoot of Main Street. Heading north, Main Street turned into Rum Runner's Lane, but veering left a little way after The Taco Shop took you onto Buccaneer Lane. Hattie Juniper Pickle's house backed up to it, but there was no direct way for Pippin to get there unless she walked back toward town, then did an about face at the intersecting streets.

Pippin didn't waste any time. She found Sailor and harnessed her up, told Zoe she'd be back in a while, and practically ran out the door, dragging a groggy Sailor behind her. Zoe's voice—and Zoe herself—flew up behind her. She called out from the top of the porch when Pippin was halfway down the steps. "Okay, but where are you going?!"

FOMO again. "Just taking Sailor for a quick walk," she said, barely slowing down to answer.

"You're in a big hurry for a walk," Zoe muttered just loud enough for Pippin to hear. The girl was perceptive.

This time Pippin slowed down long enough to look over her shoulder. "Lots to do today," she said. "I want to get this girl some exercise while I have the time." She locked eyes with Sailor, made her index and middle fingers on one hand go back and forth, and said, "Walkies!"

The harness had already started to knock the sleepiness out of Sailor, but the eye contact and seeing the sign for taking a walk sent her tail wagging, her hindquarters moving right along with it. Pippin threw up her arm in a wave. "We'll be back in a bit."

Zoe frowned, but nodded. Pippin felt the girl's eyes on her as she hurried down the street but ignored it. Zoe couldn't be part of everything, much as she wanted to, and Pippin certainly didn't want her mixed up in Dr. Baxter's murder or the Lane family lore. Some things she just had to do alone.

At the corner, Pippin made a hard right turn, heading back the way she'd come, but at an angle and on Buccaneer Lane. She hurried along in what amounted to a jog keeping her eyes peeled for the woman. After a few minutes, she was heading northwest, Buccaneer getting farther and farther away from Rum Runner's Lane. The houses grew smaller and were closer together. A figure appeared in the distance and Pippin sped up. As she got closer, though, she could see it was a man.

After a few more minutes, three teenagers sauntered along at a snail's pace on the opposite side of the street. They slowed when they saw Sailor, oohing and awing. On a different day Pippin would have stopped and let them cross over to give the dog some love, but not today. She gave a friendly wave to them and hurried on.

Another person appeared in the distance. Pippin narrowed her eyes and peered at the figure, but from this distance, she couldn't tell if it was Gin White or not. She caught Sailor's eyes and made her fingers do the walking motion again, speeding up so her gait was somewhere between a jog and a full-on run.

She grew closer. It was a woman.

After another minute, she thought the figure was familiar. The curve of the shoulders. The angle of the head. "Ms. White!" she called, catching her breath in between the two words. The woman didn't turn, so she tried again, louder this time, "Gin White!"

The woman stopped and looked over her shoulder. And waited. By the time Pippin caught up to her, both she and Sailor were panting. Gin didn't say anything. She tilted her head and watched with careful eyes as Pippin bent at the waist and pressed her hands to her legs above her knees and caught her breath.

"I'm so glad...I caught you," Pippin said. "I'm Pippin—"

"I know who you are. I came to your house," Gin said. "And everyone on the island knows who you are."

Pippin drew in a final bolstering breath before standing straight again. If she only had a dollar for every time someone said they knew exactly who she was. "Right."

Gin looked at Sailor. "Who's this pretty thing?"

Pippin looked at Sailor and made her hand go up and down like the waves in the ocean. It was the symbol she'd come up with for the dog's name. "This is Sailor," she answered.

"She's deaf?"

"She is."

Gin swung her crossbody bag around to her back, which by the way it looked, still held her precious Dare Stone. She hitched at the waist to get her face closer to Sailor's. "A rescue?"

"She is," Pippin said again.

Gin took Sailor's face between both hands and spoke

right to her as if Pippin hadn't just confirmed that the dog couldn't hear. "You sweet thing. You have a loving home."

It didn't matter that Sailor couldn't hear a word Gin said. Her backside wriggled and her tail wagged double-time. Gin scratched Sailor's cheeks one more time before standing up. "She's a beauty."

She was. Golden hair that shone in the sunlight. Coppery eyes that saw everything. And a disposition as sweet as saltwater taffy.

Gin started walking again and Pippin fell into step next to her, Sailor behind them both. "I was wondering if I could ask you a question," Pippin said.

Gin gave her a suspicious glance. Pippin wasn't really surprised by it. Gin had a reputation as being on the fringe. For all she knew, Pippin was going to chastise her about bursting into the Inn so late Saturday night. Gin peered at Pippin. "About what?"

"It's about Dr. Baxter—" Pippin started, but Gin stopped short and interrupted her with a curt, "I don't want to talk about her."

"Why is that?" Pippin asked.

Gin shrugged. "I just don't," she said, then suddenly she was walking again.

Pippin wasn't going to be brushed off that quickly. She gestured to Sailor and fell back into step with Gin. "I'm just trying to make sense of what happened."

Gin gave Pippin a sidelong look. "I guess I can see why."

"Right. Because she died on my property. I don't want *that* to be the reputation of the inn."

"Well, I can't help you with that. I met the woman twice, and frankly, I didn't care for her much."

That was a sentiment Pippin shared, though she kept it

to herself. "I dropped her at the dig the day she checked in, but apparently she wasn't actually part of it."

Gin balked. "Of course she was! That's where I met her."

"I met Dr. Bligh. He's the one in charge. He said he didn't even know Dr. Baxter."

Gin's mouth pulled into a deep frown. "She *looked* like she was part of it when I saw her there. I thought she was somebody important. That's why I asked her about my stone."

Dr. Baxter had carried herself with a certain aloofness that clearly communicated that she was a step above everyone else. "I can see why you thought that about her."

Gin suddenly turned and walked across a dirt yard. Pippin stopped abruptly, course corrected, and came up behind her just as she climbed the steps to the porch and let herself into the house. Gin left the door open, but Pippin hesitated at the threshold, unsure of her welcome.

Gin slipped her bag over her shoulder and set it aside. "Come on. You can come in."

"I can't leave Sailor alone out here."

Gin came back to the door and crouched on her haunches. "Do you wanna come in?" she cooed. "You do? I know you do." She patted her thighs, but Sailor didn't budge. Gin looked up at Pippin for guidance.

"Use both hands and beckon to her. Make sure she's looking at you," Pippin said.

Gin did as Pippin had told her, catching Sailor's attention by waving one arm, then using her fingers to coax her inside. Sailor's tail wagged as she stepped into the house. "Praise her," Pippin said, giving the leash slack.

Gin crouched again and took Sailor's head in her hands, bending nose to nose with her. "You're a good girl. Such a good girl."

Sailor's tail whipped excitedly, but as soon as Gin let her go, Pippin stepped forward, got the dog's attention, and flipped her open palm to face the ceiling. "Sit," she said.

Sailor did.

"I've never met a deaf dog," Gin said.

"I hadn't either till I met Sailor," Pippin said.

"Hattie said she was hiding out around your house."

"She was. Covered with fleas and scared, but she's doing great now. You know Hattie?"

"Doesn't everyone?" Gin said as she walked through the hallway to the kitchen. Pippin quickly got Sailor's attention again and signed for her to stand, and then to come with her.

The kitchen was small but tidy. Pippin had scarcely stepped one foot onto the linoleum flooring when Gin turned around with a frown. "I don't have much. Do you want some water?"

As thin as Gin White was, it wouldn't have surprised Pippin if the cupboards were completely bare. The woman was a rail with bones that looked like they might crack right in half under the weight of her bag. "I'm fine," she said, "but maybe some for Sailor?"

Gin found a plastic bowl. A few seconds later, Sailor lapped noisily. "I don't know anything else about Dr. Baxter."

Pippin wanted to ask her point blank, *Did you murder her? Hit her with your Dare Stone?* Instead, she said, "I'm just curious how you met her."

Sailor laid down near the table and Gin sat in a chair next to her. If she wasn't a killer and Pippin needed a dog sitter, Gin might be first in line.

"These digs," Gin said. "They happen periodically, you know, but mostly the archaeologists don't give me the time of day. I wasn't even going to try this time—at least not right away—but then I saw Dr. Baxter and, like I said, she seemed like she was somebody important. I almost talked myself out of approaching her, but I thought, why not? The worst she could say is that she wasn't interested in taking a look."

"But she was interested?"

Gin blew a raspberry. "Evidently not. You heard her."

Dr. Baxter had seemed *a little bit* interested, but she hadn't necessarily agreed with Gin's belief that her Dare Stone was authentic.

"Did you ask Dr. Bligh to take a look at the stone?"

"Is he the one in charge of the dig? The tall drink of water?" she asked.

Pippin held in a laugh. That was an expression she'd only heard in old movies. "Dr. Bligh the Archaeology Guy," she said, which was now the only way she seemed able to think of the man. "Yes."

Gin's eyes lit up at the prospect, but the light quickly faded. "It wouldn't matter. He'll probably say the same thing, that the stone is a fake."

"But don't you want to have him look at it? Maybe he can tell you for sure—"

"Dr. Baxter agreed to see it, but she didn't take it seriously. She was a liar. They're all liars."

Pippin couldn't get past the several problems with the idea of Gin being a murderer. First, she was half as big as Dr. Baxter. It would have taken the element of surprise to sneak up on her on the widow's walk. Ruby had come up the ladder silently, but most people didn't have such a light touch.

Second, the stone looked heavy. As well as needing the element of surprise, it would have taken strength to clobber someone in the head with it. Maybe Gin was stronger than she looked. But maybe not.

People have killed for less. Those words circled in her mind. She felt sure Dr. Baxter's death was connected to the Lane family, but she wanted to eliminate Gin White and the Lost Colony link once and for all.

"Can I see it?" Pippin asked. "The stone?"

Gin jumped up and raced out of the kitchen. She was back in seconds, hauling the stone from her bag. Pippin didn't look at the uneven words carved into the stone. She flipped it over, studying both sides for signs of blood, because there would be some if it was the murder weapon, wouldn't there?

There wasn't.

Which, to her mind, meant Gin White was as innocent as hurricane season is long.

Chapter 25

"Truth is mysterious, elusive, always to be conquered. Liberty is dangerous, as hard to live with as it is elating. We must march toward these two goals, painfully but resolutely, certain in advance of our failings on so long a road."
~Albert Camus

*P*ippin rushed into The Open Door bookshop with its creamy white wainscoting, pale yellow walls, and endless shelves of books. She looked for Jamie, but only saw Noah, the high school kid Jamie employed. He was lanky and tall and had Air Pods positioned in each ear. "I'm going up to see Mr. McAdams," she said.

He glanced at her and nodded, quickly returning his attention to the laptop computer open on the counter in front of him.

She glanced down the hallway to the closed door of Jamie's office. She suspected he was already holed up researching the sword hilt. If he was, she didn't want to disturb him. At the moment, she wanted to see Cyrus. She opened the door to the stairwell leading to the second-floor apartment where the elder Mr. McAdams lived. He opened the door to her before she had the chance to knock. "I've been expecting you," he said, his voice deep and warm.

She cocked her head at this. She hadn't given him any warning about her visit, but he seemed to have a sixth sense about her. "Have you?"

He gave a solemn nod of affirmation, then stood back to let her enter. Puffy half-moons cradled his eyes. Lines marked his forehead below his receding hairline. He dressed neatly, even when in the privacy of his own home. He was dapper. Distinguished. Wise. Everything about him filled her with a sense of calm. The ocean breeze scent of him. His slicked back silver hair and neatly trimmed goatee. The smooth tenor of his voice.

Just being in his presence made her feel hopeful. She'd get to the truth eventually. And she'd figure out how to break the curse, one way or another.

Mr. McAdams led her into the large living room. Everything was black, gray, and white. Modern and sleek. She sat on one of the low-profile white chairs. "Why were you expecting me?"

He sat in an identical chair opposite her, answering her question in his typical way, with a statement of his own. "Jamie told me about the discovery in your safe. A sword hilt from the first century."

Which meant he'd known she'd come to him to discuss it. Her parents had trusted him with their secrets. With the curse. She'd come to trust him, too. She clasped her hands, her thumbs under her chin, her index fingers pressed together in front of her mouth. "It's Roman."

"So Jamie told me. Interesting that it turned up in your inn."

That seemed like a massive understatement. "Did he tell you about the theft in Ireland?"

He cocked his head with curiosity. "He did not."

So, he hadn't talked with his granddad since their phone call. Pippin told Cyrus about her research and the stolen sword hilt. "If I take Hugh at face value, he wanted me to have it."

"I question if you should take him at face value," Cyrus said.

It was a fair point, and one Pippin had been grappling with. "I don't trust him, but even people who lie sometimes tell the truth."

"If he wanted you to have it, why wouldn't he have handed it over to you himself?" Cyrus posed.

That was a good question, and one Pippin didn't have a good answer to. "He said there were too many people around."

Mr. McAdams dipped his chin thoughtfully.

A voice from the door said, "Or because a particular person was there."

Pippin turned to see Jamie at the door. He strode across the room and perched on the edge of the gray sofa. From the sparkle in his eyes, she could see he'd made some discovery.

Cyrus's eyes illuminated with satisfaction. "Well done, my boy."

Pippin looked from grandson to grandfather. "You mean Dr. Baxter," she said, "but she wasn't at the party."

Jamie wagged his finger. "Not necessarily. Just because you didn't see her doesn't mean she wasn't there."

That was true. Dr. Baxter had suddenly appeared when Gin White arrived looking for her. Pippin had seen her leave through the front door earlier but hadn't seen her return. Then again, she'd also been distracted by Hugh, Sailor, the Lees, and everything else. It was entirely possible Dr. Baxter had been the one to cut the screen and sneak into Pippin's room through the French doors, then exit through the regular door, leaving it ajar just enough for Sailor to escape.

"Dr. Baxter was in Ireland around the time of the theft," Jamie continued.

Pippin stared at him. Her mind processed the implication. "Does that mean—"

"That she was the thief in Lambay? It's probable. I found a photo of the stolen artifact. It appears to match the one from your safe." Jamie paused a moment before saying, "Pip, it needs to be returned."

She bit the inside of her cheek. She didn't want to return it, not yet. Still, she nodded.

Cyrus sat back in his chair, one arm folded over his chest, the other cocked at the elbow, his index finger tapping lightly against his lips. "Very interesting indeed."

Questions circled in Pippin's mind. *Why would Dr. Baxter have stolen the hilt? What made her connect it to Pippin and the Lane family? How did Hugh know about it? Who else was after it?*

"It's clear Dr. Baxter was not here for the Lost Colony dig. She was part of some history group, same as Hugh. So, it's not a coincidence she was at Sea Captain's Inn with a stolen artifact from the first century. When she asked me about my family, she was either digging herself or confirming what she thought she already knew about me. She connected that hilt to my family just like Hugh did."

Mr. McAdams cleared his throat. "It seems both the house *and* the man have revealed a bit of a mystery to you," he said, circling back to their previous conversation at

Devil's Brew regarding the quote from *The Tale of Two Cities*. He had a way of speaking that made him seem like a wise old owl—simultaneously thoughtful and thought-provoking.

That passage was about profound secrets and mysteries. Pippin hadn't made the connection, but he was right. The house had held the secret, quite literally in the safe, and Dr. Baxter, it seemed, had plenty of mysteries she'd been keeping under her belt, right alongside Hugh.

And then there were the broader mysteries held by the house and the Lane family. Morgan Dubhshláine and her pact with Lir. The bibliomancy. The Burrow. The curse of her family. And now the stolen hilt. It was a puzzle with too many missing pieces.

She hadn't told Cyrus about the second passage *A Tale of Two Cities* had shown her. She recited it now.

It was like the last feeble echo of a sound made long and long ago. So entirely had it lost the life and resonance of the human voice, that it affected the senses like a once beautiful color faded away into a poor weak stain. So sunken and suppressed it was, that it was like a voice underground.

"It's about the sword hilt," she said, telling him her interpretation of the text. "It was *literally* underground."

"A metaphorical voice," Jamie added.

Cyrus nodded, looking both contemplative and pleased. "It seems your practice is paying off, my dear. Well done."

Chapter 26

"A man may learn wisdom even from a foe."
~Aristophanes

After an hour of aimless wonderings, Pippin still didn't know how to find the man who'd claimed to be Monique Baxter's son. She didn't know how to find Hugh, again. Yet they were the people who could provide more information about Dr. Baxter's connection to the Lane family, and why she'd come to Devil's Cove in the first place. What she knew about the curse that plagued her own family, and who else might know about it, was limited.

She needed mindless work so she could think. She stood at the kitchen counter refilling the saltshaker. The Lees liked their food salty, so much so that the shaker was already down by almost a third. She had a small funnel in the neck of the shaker. That word. Salty. It triggered her. Sent a slice of anxiety through her.

"Pippin!"

She blinked at hearing Zoe's voice. "Oh!" The salt was overflowing, creating a circle around the shaker. She jerked, stopping the flow.

"You were miles away," she said, a stack of neatly folded bath towels cradled in her arms.

"Yeah," Pippin said, but her mind was still processing her thoughts. Salty. He might be able to give her some answers.

She cleaned up the salt and left Zoe to finish the laundry and take phone calls and reservation. Fifteen minutes later Pippin was on her way to the Dare County Detention Center.

Visiting a prison wasn't on the top of her list of Things To Do and visiting the person responsible for killing her father was even less so. She almost talked herself out of it during the drive, but she knew she had to do it. There was a bigger picture here she didn't yet understand. Salty had been on his own treasure hunt, but she'd never gotten to the bottom of the *how* or the *why*. Maybe he would have answers to some of her questions.

The process of getting on the approved visitor list hadn't been particularly easy. It wasn't as simple as showing up at the facility, signing in, and *Bam!*, there you were, talking with your inmate. No, the inmate himself had to send you a visitor form, which you then had to fill out, submit, and wait for it to be processed.

When Salty had first been arrested for the twenty-year-old murder of Leo Hawthorne, Pippin had gone to Cyrus McAdams for guidance on getting visitor access. He'd tilted his head to one side as he considered her, finally asking, "Are you sure about this?"

That was a loaded question without an easy answer. "No.

I don't want to see him now, but I think there will come a time when I want to get the truth from him."

Cyrus hadn't asked any more questions, and the next thing she knew, she was on the approved list for Shannon 'Salty' Gallagher.

The man had been held, awaiting trial, for several months. She hadn't been able to bring herself to pay him a visit...until now.

She went through the check-in process, having no choice but to succumb to a light pat and frisk by a female officer, and finally was led into the visitation room. She sat on one side of a small rectangular table, legs crossed, one foot nervously tapping the air. She rehearsed what she planned to say, but by the time the man was escorted in wearing the standard orange prison jumpsuit, her thoughts were scrambled. He sat down across from her, appearing none the worse for wear given the time he'd spent here.

He looked almost the same as he had the last time she'd seen him, with the exception of the eye patch he now wore over one eye. She'd hurled a book at him, the corner of the hardcover catching him smack in the eye. She hadn't realized then that it might cause permanent damage, but maybe it had. She couldn't say she was sorry.

He was grizzled with a white beard and bushy mustache, though his facial hair did look a bit neater compared to when she'd first met him. The vertical divots on the end of his bulbous nose highlighted his decades of sun exposure. She thought he actually looked a tiny bit healthier now, too. His face had filled out, softening the weathered wrinkles lining his face, the byproduct of a life spent on the open seas.

The only other thing distinctly different was the fact that his tattoos weren't visible. The woman in a bikini top and grass skirt, the rope and anchor, the circle with a face, cradled by a V shape, the ship with billowing sails—they were all hidden under the long sleeves of the jumpsuit. When she'd first met him, she'd thought he looked like a character straight out of a Popeye comic. Now he looked like Billy Bob Thornton playing an incarcerated, slightly menacing, cookie-deprived version of Santa Claus.

Pippin didn't waste time on small talk. She had no interest in learning about Salty's life in the North Carolina incarceration system. She didn't care how his trial preparation was going. There was no innocent until proven guilty in her mind. He could rot in here for what he did to her father for all she cared.

"Well, well, well." He leaned back in his chair, stretching his legs out in front of him, crossing them at the ankles. "Pippin Lane Hawthorne. Has Hell done froze over?"

He spoke slowly and with an Eastern Carolina accent, still heavy with Cockney from back when the British settlers had called the state Virginia. It made him sound friendly, even when she knew the vitriol lurking just underneath the long vowels was just waiting to be unleashed.

"All blue skies and heavenly outside," she said, forcing a small smile that she was pretty sure looked more like a smirk.

He leaned forward, resting his crossed forearms on the table. "I look at ya and I see Cassie," he said. "You're the spittin' image."

So she'd been told. Her mother's hair had been darker, but they shared the same freckled complexion and strawberry-hued locks. She didn't like that Salty had fixated on Pippin's similarities to her mother. She shuddered, mentally wiping away the trail of filth his words left behind. She gathered up her gumption and stared straight into his one good eye. "Do you miss the wide-open space of the ocean, Salty?"

His mouth twisted into a scowl. "Don't ya worry none. I'll be seein' it again. I never thought I'd be seein' ya here, though. Surprised the hell outta me."

"That makes two of us."

He glowered, the bitterness of his imprisonment outweighing the fun and distraction of having a visitor. "Spit it out, girl. What do ya want?"

"I'm looking for someone I thought you might know," she said.

"An' if I do, why would I tell ya a damn thing? You put me in this hellhole."

She was prepared for this question. She leaned forward, looked him square in the eye, and gave a sad smile. "Because you loved my mother."

The response caught him by surprise. It was the truth, but from the surprise on his face, he hadn't thought she'd be so forthright about it. "That I did, little lady. That I did."

She got right down to it, not wanting to spend a second more with Salty Gallagher than she had to. "I met a man the other day—"

"And you came all this way to tell me about it. What a lass."

She ignored both what he said and the snide undertones of the comment. She moved slowly, making sure he watched her hand as it touched her neck. As she took hold of the white gold chain she wore. As she clutched the uneven circle of the pendant between her thumb and forefinger, angling it toward Salty. It was a reminder of Cassie.

The nostrils of Salty's bulbous nose flared, but he remained silent.

She held it higher, giving him a solid view of the faded

Fleur de Lis on the front. His good eye twitched, his upper lip lifting to match. "You're playin' with fire, love."

She schooled her expression into one of innocence. "What do you mean?"

His eyes flicked to the pendant and his hands clenched into fists. "What'd'ya want?"

She let the pendant fall against her skin, never letting her gaze falter. "As I was saying, I met a man the other day. He told me about a group of history buffs. Treasure hunters, he said."

His good eye pinched slightly in the corner, but he shrugged with indifference. "What does that have to do with me."

She inhaled silently, bolstering her resolve from the inside out. "*You* are a treasure hunter, right?"

His eye skimmed over Cassie's necklace. "That there's the only treasure I want. A reminder of the woman I loved."

"Oh Salty, you're such a romantic," she said, the sarcasm heavy in her tone.

"You said it."

She grabbed the pendant again. Held it out. Spoke through clenched teeth. "You killed my father over this."

He grinned. "Got yer goat, eh?"

He had. She let the pendant hang loosely again, then stared down at her lap for a few seconds. Once her nerves were collected, she looked at him again. "That night you were arrested, you said something about a legend. What do you know about it?"

He barked out a derisive laugh. "You're like a cavefish, swimming around in the dark."

"Am I though?" she asked. "I know there's an ancient treasure people are after."

She thought his eye twitched again, but he crossed his

arms and stared at her. Defiance shot out of every pore in his body. "You don't know anythin', girl."

She looked at him with steely eyes. "Why don't you tell me, then?"

"Where's the fun in that?"

"If you loved my mother—"

One of his gnarled hands shot up, stopping Pippin in her tracks. "Listen here. I *did* love Cassie. Sure as the sky's blue, I loved her. She coulda loved me back and we'd'a gotten rich together."

She didn't react to his comments about her mother but pressed on. "What do you mean, gotten rich?"

"Them Lane family secrets go deeper than the Atlantic's graveyard. Yer daddy, he was on ta somethin'. Damn shame he died when he did."

Pippin breaths came fast. Furious. The full force of her hatred for this man bubbled over. She leaned toward him and leveled her gaze. Somehow, she kept her voice low and controlled. "You took our father from us, Salty Gallagher. You made us orphans. It *is* a damn shame he died, and I hope you sit in prison and rot because of it."

"Ah. Now we're gettin' down to it."

In that moment, Pippin realized that she was at his mercy. He could slap the table with his palm to get the guard's attention and be out of the room in seconds flat. He'd do it, too, cutting off their little chat just like he'd cut her father out of her life. She had to cut to the chase. She gritted her teeth, steeling herself to press on, to ignore that this man was her father's killer. The stolen sword hilt. That man pretending to be Dr. Baxter's son. Hugh. It all added up to something. She just didn't know what that something was. "Salty, what legend were you talking about?"

"Ya think I'm goin' to just spill my guts to ya because ya

ask real nice? Not even real nice, come ta think of it. Uh-uh. No way."

Pippin pulled out the only card she had—the letter from her Aunt Rose. "Let me tell you what I know."

Salty's eyelid fell to half-mast. If he dipped his chin to his chest, he'd probably fall asleep. He looked like he didn't have a care in the world. Like he wasn't locked up awaiting trial for the murder of Leo Hawthorne. Like his son wasn't locked up and awaiting trial for the murder of Maxwell Lawrence, a professor who'd become collateral damage in this...this *battle*.

"I heard a story once about a Roman soldier named Titus who was in love with an Irish woman named Morgan Dubhshláine."

She kept her eyes glued on Salty, gauging his reaction. She thought his upper lip twitched, but it was so quick and minuscule that she wondered if she'd imagined it.

"It's said that Titus gave Morgan something. Here's where it gets interesting. There are people who think whatever he gave her still exists today, more than two thousand years later."

His lip twitched again, and this time there was no doubt it was in response to her words. He might look like he was about to drift off into slumber, but Pippin knew he was listening to every word she said and watching her with as much scrutiny as she was watching him.

"Here's the thing, Salty." She interlaced her fingers. "I think a woman was killed because she was hunting for this treasure."

She'd kept some of her cards close to the vest. She wasn't about to reveal that she and her aunt Rose both had fragments of a letter written in the first century. If Salty was working with anyone else besides his son Jimmy, and the letter proved to be important, revealing that tidbit would only put herself in more danger. She hadn't mentioned her cousins Cora or Lily, or her great aunt Rose, but guilt spread tendrils through her insides anyway. By talking to Salty, she hoped she wasn't putting any of them in danger.

Salty still reclined in his chair, looking carefree rather than incarcerated. "Sounds like you answered your own question, love."

That word—him calling her *love*—grated on her last nerve. She snapped. "My mother never even liked you. She hated you."

Salty's jaw tensed. His good eye flew open, and he jerked upright, crashing his forearms against the table. "If ya think Jimmy'n me are the only ones prowlin' 'round your family tree, you'd be mistaken. That woman who was killed—she ain't the only one, you know. There *are* other people who know, you're right about that, and you best watch your back, 'cause people show ya what they want ya to see. No more, no less. And one of 'em'll find what they're after."

She couldn't tell if that was a warning or a threat. A dark chill slithered down her spine. Could he be talking about the dagger? She dropped a lure, hoping he'd bite. "The man I met, the one with the clear eyes—"

A spasm seemed to shoot through Salty. "What's that?"

"The man who came to the house. He looks very ordinary—except for his eyes."

Salty pushed back, the legs of his chair scraping against the floor. "He was at your mama's house?"

She pressed one hand to her chest. "It's my house now. And yes."

Pippin jerked at the hard thump of Salty pounding the table with his fist. He barked at the guard. "We're done."

The guard strolled toward them, but Pippin jumped up. "No! Wait."

The guard stopped short, his hand instantly clutching his baton. "Sit down, miss."

Pippin put both hands flat on the table and lowered herself back into the chair. She looked at her father's killer. "Give me another minute." She gritted her teeth as she added, "Please."

Salty hesitated for a few seconds, but finally nodded at the guard, who backed up again.

"Who is he?" Pippin asked.

Salty collapsed into his chair. He wagged a finger at her. "I did love your mother, ya know. I'm sayin' this for Cassie. You get yourself 'round folks you can trust, and that's it. 'Cause there are people out there who're nothin' more'n pirates, only out for themselves."

Her gaze shot to his arm. Didn't he have a pirate tattoo? Did Hugh? "Pirates like you?"

He shrugged. "Sure. Like me. Like Jimmy."

So, she'd been right. Hugh was not to be trusted. She'd spent enough time with Salty Gallagher. She wished she could scrub every trace of him from her mind. She settled with asking him the one question she thought might evoke some real emotion from the man. "How's Jimmy holding up?"

His nostrils flared. He slapped the table with an open palm. "Guard," he barked. "We're done."

Chapter 27

"Enemies make you stronger, allies make you weaker."
~Frank Herbert

*P*ippin leaned against the built-in bookshelf in Leo's secret study. "Salty told me to surround myself with people I can trust because there are pirates out there who are only out for themselves."

Jamie nudged up his horn-rimmed glasses. "You know what they say. It takes one to know one."

Salty was, indeed, like a modern-day pirate, from his leathery skin to his eyepatch. "He definitely knows who Hugh is, so if they're part of this same treasure hunting group, he knows about Titus and Morgan. The legend says that he gave something to her that's been passed down through God knows how many generations." She looked at the hilt of the sword Jamie held in his hands. "Salty was definitely warning me about Hugh. So why would Hugh make sure I got that?"

"This can't be the two-thousand-year-old treasure Titus gave to Morgan, Pip." Jamie turned the relic over in his hand. "It's valuable, but not *that* valuable. Not worth killing over."

She'd thought the same thing. Monique Baxter had brazenly stolen it from a dig site, but then she'd brought it here in her suitcase; and Hugh had just as brazenly stolen it from Dr. Baxter's room and handed it off in the middle of a party to put in the inn's safe. If it were valuable enough to kill over, would either of them have handled it so casually? Pippin collapsed into one of the club chairs.

"What would a soldier give the woman he loved before leaving her for the open seas?" Jamie murmured.

"Could it be the letter?" Pippin asked. "Is *that* valuable?"

Jamie set the hilt on the cloth he'd unwrapped it from. "Anything's possible," he said after a few seconds. "But it doesn't seem likely. How would anyone know about the letter? Plus, it's ripped apart, and aside from talking about the deal with the sea god, there's not much in it."

They stared at the hilt. At the clock where the letter was hidden. At each other. Despite knowing the hilt had belonged to Titus; despite the knowledge that there were historians and treasure hunters who knew about the Lane family and were looking for something; despite the fact that Pippin now thought Dr. Baxter had been killed because of whatever she knew or had been in possession of; despite it all, she was no closer to finding the killer or stopping the curse.

～

PIPPIN SPENT the next hour holed up in the Burrow. She'd practiced bibliomancy in a variety of ways—standing, the book on a table or desk in front of her; sitting at said table or desk; letting a book fall open on her lap; but she was most comfortable when she sat cross legged on the floor, the book in front of her. And while the book magic could happen anywhere, right here in her father's secret study felt the most natural. It was as if he was here with her, his presence wrapping itself around her like a cocoon.

Sailor stretched out by her side. She was relaxed, but not asleep. Her eyes watched Pippin and every time Pippin reached out to pet her or scratch her stomach, Sailor's tail wagged, hitting the floor with a light *thump thump thump*.

Pippin had been unwittingly developing a ritual, of sorts, each time she practiced bibliomancy. She riffled the pages, loosening them up, then held the book against her chest and closed her eyes. It almost felt as if she was offering up a prayer, but that wasn't it at all. She slowed her breathing and chased all her thoughts away. Her only focus was on the book and the questions she planned to ask.

Then she placed *Gulliver's Travels* on its spine on the floor in front of her and quietly asked the question she had come to pose each time she started. "What do you have to tell me?"

She let go. The front and back covers fell to either side and the book settled open. She picked up the open book. Her eyes quickly scanned the words, looking for the anomaly. For the printed lines that would become bolder and lift off the page. She saw them immediately.

He shall be our ally against our enemies in the island of Blefescu, and do his utmost to destroy their fleet, which is now preparing to invade us.

SHE STARED AT THE PASSAGE, rereading it two—three—four times. It didn't leave much to interpretation. She cupped her hand across her forehead and rubbed her temples. If only she knew who her enemy was and who was truly her ally.

Chapter 28

"People should always have a good bottle of extra virgin olive oil, a packet of pasta, tinned tomatoes and a good cheese somewhere in their fridge."

~Gino D'Acampo

he idea of allies and enemies circled in Pippin's head as she rode her bike to town to run her last-minute errands. She started at Olive's Oil, purchasing two bottles of oil—one robust Spanish and one wood smoked. After that came The Barkery where she picked up a bag of treats for Sailor. With her purchases safely wrapped and tucked into the basket attached to the bike's handlebars, she debated her next stop. She needed both chocolate and cheese for a short reception she was hosting at the inn for a local women's club over the weekend. This event was particularly important because it was the first booking for the Devil's Cove Women's Club. She was hoping that it would go well, just like the men's discussion group, and there would be many more bookings to follow.

She went to Charcuterie first, locking up her bike and taking her olive oil and dog treats with her into the store. Colette de Maurin, the cheesemonger who'd opened the shop only a few years ago, greeted her from behind the counter. "Pippin Hawthorne, right?"

Pippin hadn't been into the cheese shop since she'd been back to Devil's Cove, but just like she knew her own reputation preceded her, so did Colette's. The French woman had fallen in love with an American in Europe. Together, they came to the United States and now they carried on her family's tradition of cheesemaking in the form of this cheese shop.

"That's right."

"Colette de Maurin," the woman said, looking just as French as she sounded. Three words immediately came to Pippin's mind: timeless; chic; sophisticated. Whatever makeup the woman wore, it was minimal, with just a hint of color to highlight the shape of her lips and the hollows of her cheeks. She wore a gray t-shirt tucked into jeans, a gold belt cinching them at the waist. A lightweight white blazer finished the outfit. Even her jewelry was understated. Colette de Maurin looked to be in her mid-fifties, and she also looked like she'd never go out of style.

"Nice to meet you," Pippin said. She stood just inside the threshold, taking in the details of the shop. There were too many cheese varieties to even count, the collection filling a series of long deli cases along one side of the space. Across from the array of cheeses were shelves with pale blue and cream colored linen aprons, locally sourced honey, hard salami, jams to accompany the cheeses, a variety of crackers, charcuterie boards, and cheese serving sets. Another shelf held t-shirts and hats with the Charcuterie logo—an imperfect double lined circle with Charcuterie written inside of it in all caps, a wedge of cheese above it, and the words *LOCAL. HANDMADE,* and *ARTISANAL* along the inner top edge of the circle. It was as classic at Colette herself.

"Would you like to do a tasting?" Colette asked.

"Definitely," Pippin said. She set her packages on a small round table just inside the entrance and stepped up to the counter.

Colette placed a small, thin board in front of her, proceeding to place chunks of cheese from a variety of wedges and wheels onto it. "I've arranged these horizontally from mildest to strongest. We do this for your palate, so you do not get overwhelmed by eating something strong, a blue cheese, for example, early on. Because then you cannot taste anything, *n'est-ce pas?*"

"Makes sense," Pippin said, hoping she answered the question.

"I have also selected only North Carolina cheeses for you. I find it is interesting to arrange it this way. You get cheese from the same place, but it represents different styles. Now, to properly taste, first you must look at the cheese. Notice the exterior—the type of crust, the mold, and then focus on the inside. Most cheese, you see, ripens from the outside in. This is why the color is not uniform. The eyes, or holes, also help characterize it.

"Next, you touch it. Lift it. Is it light? Rubbery? Fragile? Hard? Soft? These are the things which give us a clue about how it will taste. Finally, you breathe in the aroma of the cheese. Take it in your hands and break it apart to smell the inside. Is it floral or grassy? Fruity or nutty? Spicy, or even it can smell as a barnyard," Colette said with a smile. "Finally, you taste. Try to detect the different flavors."

She led Pippin through the soft, bloomy cheese covered with a white, downy rind, all the way to the most pungent blue. Colette talked about each one in turn, giving highlights to each of the creameries and dairies they came from.

"You sold me," Pippin said after she'd tried them all. She picked out a charcuterie board, a serving set, a jar of fig jam, crackers, capers, salami and prosciutto, ending with far more cheese than she'd need for the women's club meeting.

Colette arched a brow as she looked out the shop's front window. "Are you taking all of this on your bike?"

Pippin did a mental head slap. She'd been so wrapped up in the tasting that she'd forgotten her mode of transportation. "I'll have to go home to get my car," she said, tucking her credit card back into her change purse.

"Very good idea," Colette said. She laid her hand on the bundle. "I will keep this all for you until you return."

Pippin retrieved her olive oils and dog treats, mounted her bike, and pedaled down Main Street toward Rum Runner's Lane to trade in the Electra Townie for her old Jeep. As she approached Devil's Brew, she saw Ruby locking up, her back to the street. It was barely three o'clock, far too early for her friend to close up the cafe. She was about to call out when Ruby put her cell phone to her ear and ducked back inside. Pippin rode on, concern for her friend like static on the ends of her nerves. Something Ruby had said to her before Dr. Baxter died resurfaced—God, it felt like such a long time ago, but it hadn't even been a week. Ruby had talked about the struggles of owning a small business, the hundreds of daily decisions that could wear you down, and the fact that she needed a vacation. For the second time, she wondered if there was something besides the responsibility of running Devil's Brew behind Ruby's weariness.

She pedaled on, spotting the familiar figure of Cyrus McAdams walking alongside a woman. As she drew closer, she recognized Erin McAdams, his daughter-in-law. Pippin turned her head to wave as she passed them by. Erin's brows suddenly rose in alarm. She pointed and yelped. "Watch out!"

Pippin whipped her head around. Looming a mere yard ahead of her was the back of an illegally parked car she hadn't noticed while lost in her thoughts. She registered the sound of traffic behind her and reacted, jerking her bike's handlebars to the right. Her front tire hit the low curb at an angle and popped up on the sidewalk. The bike wobbled as the back tire jumped up. She held tight to the handlebars, working hard to straighten them out, at the same moment seeing two pedestrians, a few yards apart from one another, walking toward her. Pippin didn't have time to stop, so she gripped her hands more tightly and wove around them, first Gin White, who stopped and stared like a deer in the head-lights, then...was that...Ron Baxter?

Pippin came to the point where Main Street turned into Rum Runner's Lane and the sidewalk ended. She bounced off the curb, immediately clamping the brakes, bringing the bike to a jerky stop. She kept it steady under her straddled legs as she turned her upper body and yelled. "Hey!"

Gin still stared at her, hands on her heart. "Who, me?"

Pippin waved her away with one hand. "Hey! Mr. Baxter!" she yelled again, but Ron Baxter ignored her. He'd started running, then jumped into the passenger side of the car she'd almost hit. It roared to life. For the first time, Pippin realized someone was already in the driver's seat. A man, but she couldn't see him. A second later, the car flipped a U-turn and zoomed off, leaving Pippin, Gin White,

Cyrus, and Erin staring after him. Something about the driver was familiar, but Pippin couldn't place how or why.

Cyrus and Erin rushed to her, and Gin continued to stare, spooked by the entire incident. "My dear, are you alright?" Cyrus asked.

Pippin put her palm to her chest, pausing to catch her breath. "That...that man," she said finally, pointing in the general direction the car had gone. "He said he's Monique Baxter's son, but—"

"But what, darlin'?" Erin prodded.

"But I talked to somebody from the college she worked at. Monique Baxter never had any children." She suddenly spun to look past Gin...past the break in the road where Main Street ended and Rum Runner's Lane started...past the row of houses lining the street. Had he come from *her* house? From Sea Captain's Inn?

Her heartbeat ratcheted up again, her body pumping with adrenaline. "I have to go," she said.

Cyrus and Erin objected, trying to make sure she was all right. "I am," she said, not revealing just how shaken up she really was. "I'll be fine."

And then she was off, following her hunch that the man who was calling himself Ron Baxter had been back at the scene of the crime.

The question was, why?

Chapter 29

"Curses are like processions. They return to the place from which they came."

~Giovanni Ruffini

$\mathcal{P}$ippin flew off her bike and grabbed the packaged olive oil and dog treats that had miraculously survived her near crash. The porch steps were split at the base, one set leading up from the right, the other from the left. They converged on a landing, which then went straight up to the porch. Pippin sprinted up one side of them, turning and charging up the rest. She yanked open the screen door, flung open the front door, and hurried inside.

She rounded the registration desk to put her things down but stopped short. She gasped. Right there on the floor, tucked under the counter, was the box Dr. Baxter had carried up to her room when she checked in.

She dropped her packages. As she crouched down, she hollered at the top of her lungs. "Zoe!"

The girl appeared like magic. "You're back early—" she started, stopping when she saw Pippin appear from behind the counter, the box in her hands.

"Was Ron Baxter here?" Pippin demanded.

Zoe's skin turned pallid, already reacting to Pippin's tone. "Ummm...what—?"

Pippin didn't let her finish. "Was Ron Baxter here? I just saw him."

Zoe's eyes went wide. "If he was here, I didn't see him."

Pippin looked at the box again. Just because Zoe hadn't seen him didn't mean he hadn't been here. The front door was unlocked during business hours. The only explanation was that he'd passed himself off as Dr. Baxter's son at the sheriff station and had taken possession of her belongings. But why bring the box back here?

She answered her own question two seconds later. Because he wasn't actually her son, he was done with it, so better not to have it in his possession in case his ruse was ever found out.

Zoe's lips trembled. "I'm s-sorry. If he was here, I d-didn't see him!"

"It's okay." Pippin pulled Zoe into a hug, holding her tight until her nerves calmed. "You didn't know."

Pippin let her go when the front door opened and a young man walked in, tattoos filling in every space on one arm, with one or two on his other arm. The start of a new sleeve. He looked at Pippin, then Zoe, hesitating as if he sensed something was amiss. "Hey, uh, I can come back—"

"It's fine! I got it," Zoe said. She dragged the back of her hand under her nose and pulled herself together. "Hello! Welcome to Sea Captain's Inn."

The young man smiled awkwardly. "Uh, hello."

"Is this your first time in? The front desk will be closing soon. You got here *just* in time."

Closing soon. "Oh no!" Pippin glanced at her watch. Four forty-five. The cheese shop closed in fifteen minutes. She practically threw the box in her office and locked the door. She wanted time to examine its contents, but that would have to wait. She figured anything important had already been discovered by the police whenever they'd recovered it, and by "Ron Baxter" when he'd taken it into his possession. Still, it was worth a shot.

Zoe had the young man enthralled by the story of the sea captain. Pippin caught her eye. "I have to run back out for a few minutes."

Zoe still looked pale, but she smiled and carried on, telling the man how Captain Hubbard and his rum had survived a shipwreck. He was in good hands.

Seven minutes later, Pippin was back at Charcuterie. "You look—what is the English word? Oh yes, frazzled," Collette de Maurin said.

Pippin patted her head, letting her hand move around to feel the wild strands of hair that had come loose from her frenzied bike ride home. "I almost crashed into a car," she said.

Collette threw her shoulders back and tsk'd. "*Mon Dieu!*" She rushed out from behind the counter and went straight to one of the little square tables against the window. "Come. Sit."

As Collette disappeared into the shop's back room, Pippin sank onto the wooden chair, grateful for a moment to think. Was the supposed Ron Baxter searching for the sword hilt? It's the only thing that made sense, but Jamie had said it wasn't that valuable. And if Ron *had* killed Dr. Baxter, perhaps furious that she no longer had it, there had to be a very good reason to return to the scene of the crime.

But Pippin had no idea what that reason could be.

Collette returned, carrying a round charcuterie paddle board by its marbled epoxy handle. On the hardwood portion was a selection of cheeses, salami that had been folded into flowery shapes, olives, a few cherries and straw-berries, several pieces of whole grain crackers, a spattering of walnuts, and even a sprig of rosemary. In her other hand she cradled two glasses of wine. Before Pippin could even stand to help her, she'd slid the charcuterie board onto the table, took one of the wine glasses into her free hand, and held the other one out for Pippin.

"It is a rosé from Oak Barrel," she said.

Oak Barrel Winery had a tasting room on Devil's Cove, but the vineyard itself was an hour west of the island along the Scuppernong River. Pippin took the proffered glass. "You didn't have to do this," she said, feeling too windblown and distracted by the lovely charcuterie before her.

"Pft. It is nothing. This is what I do." She sat opposite Pippin and raised her glass. *À ta santé,"* she said. "To your health, *ma petit."*

Pippin knew enough French to recognize that Collette had called her *little one*. Because Pippin was younger by at least two decades? Or maybe it was because Collette stood close to a head taller than Pippin. Maybe both. The reason why didn't matter. Pippin felt the warmth from the woman, and her sincere desire to sit with her and just be. "Well. It's beautiful and I appreciate it. I've had...a lot on my mind."

"In France, *un fromager*—a cheesemonger, you say here —is like a bartender. I am a good listener. *Très bon."*

Pippin hesitated, but the idea of laying everything out on the table like scrambled pieces of a puzzle was too tempting. Maybe Colette de Maurin could help her put it all back together. She sipped from her glass of rosé—dry and refreshing—and picked from the charcuterie, organizing her thoughts. The first question she asked would direct the rest of the conversation. "Have you ever heard of bibliomancy?"

"*Mais bien sûr*. Of course. *Bibliomancie*."

At this, Pippin's brows shot up. "Really?"

"*Ma petit*, I am from Provence, the same as Nostradamus. You know of him?"

"I've heard of him," she said. She had a vague recollection of seeing a book with his name on it in the Burrow, in fact.

"He was also born in Provence, many centuries earlier than me, of course. People thought he was magical. An astronomer. Physician. And a...mmm...*voyant*."

Pippin shook her head slightly. "*Voyant*?"

"Mmm...*prophète*?"

"Oh! Yes. A prophet? Or a fortune-teller?"

Colette snapped her fingers. "Correct. Nostradamus, he predicted the future. He wrote a book *telling* the future. *Les Prophèties*." Pippin popped another bit of cheese into her mouth, followed by an olive, nodding so Colette would continue. "Another man, Peter Lemesurier, studied Nostradamus. My family in Provence, they read this book and shared much of it. Monsieur Lemesurier believes Nostradamus used the ancient divination of *bibliomancie* in his...mmm...*prophètisation*."

Pippin repeated the French word in her head a few times, coming up with the translation. "In his prophesizing? Fortune-telling?"

She broke into a wide smile. "*Exactement*," she said. "So yes, I know the *bibliomancie*."

The word was the same in English and French but sounded so much more mysterious on Colette's tongue with her French accent. "Do you believe it's true?" Pippin asked.

Colette tilted her head to one side, considering Pippin. "That Nostradamus used this divination? *Mais bien sûr.* It was practiced among the Romans. *Sortes virgilianae.* They used the poems of Virgil. Many did. Emperors. Claudius II. Even St. Augustine is said to have used *bibliomancie* with the letters of St. Paul. This is how he chose his future path as a theologian."

Pippin stared in awe. "How do you know all of this?"

Colette laughed. "I have a very deep desire to read and learn. And I also have something of a...mmm, how do you say? A...*mémoire photographique.*"

"A photographic memory?" Pippin translated.

"Yes. Correct." She laughed again. "Of course, you see that at photographic memory does not apply to translating words from French to English. Now. Why the question about the *bibliomancie*?"

Pippin released the breath she hadn't known she'd been holding. She placed her palm to her chest. "Because *I* am a bibliomancer."

If Colette was surprised to hear the confession, she didn't show it. She wore a perpetual closed lip smile, which didn't waver, and she gave a single nod as if to say she understood. She took a sip of her wine and leaned back against the wooden slats of the chair. "Tell me more," she said.

Over the charcuterie and wine, Pippin did just that. She told Colette de Maurin about her mother, Cassie, who'd left Laurel Point, Oregon, and their family's used bookstore at Cape Misery for the unknown Outer Banks island of Devil's Cove; of Leo, who'd fallen in love with Cassie from the first moment he'd laid eyes on her; of Morgan Dubhshláine and her lover, the Roman soldier Titus; of the deal Morgan had made with the sea god, Lir; and of the curse the Lane family had endured ever since.

Colette seemed to process it all instantaneously. "And you need to stop the curse before it takes you." She'd breezed past the murder at the inn, the treasure hunters, and every other detail, zeroing in on what Leo had tried to do, and what Pippin wanted to finish.

"Yes," Pippin said. She sat up straighter. "Yes. My father's research has led me this far, but I don't know what else to do—"

Colette waited patiently, her brown eyes calm and watchful.

Pippin came close to telling her about the idea that something was still around today, that people were after it— whatever *it* was—, and about the sword hilt and the letter. But she kept these bits to herself. She didn't know Colette de Maurin, and though her instinct was to trust her, Pippin's years of only trusting only herself and Grey were as ingrained in her as the rings inside a tree's trunk. She'd let a few people in. Ruby and Daisy. Cyrus McAdams. And Jamie.

For the moment, that was enough. She'd told Colette de Maurin as much as she felt she could.

"Part of the curse on your family is the *bibliomancie*, then," Colette said.

"Yes. Maybe that's a gift. But the rest—"

"The curse of dying in childbirth for the women, and at sea for the men." Colette spoke softly, almost to herself.

"If I could keep the bibliomancy, I would," she said.

Colette raised her eyes to Pippin, sipping on her rosé. "You like it, then, doing the book magic?"

Pippin hesitated. She'd taught herself how to use books

to tell her about the past, or to predict the future. She stifled a laugh. Just like Nostradamus. "I do like it," she finally said. It was the first time she'd admitted that aloud. "And I think it can help me get to the truth."

"The truth about the curse?"

That, and all the rest of it. But all she said to Colette was, "Yes, the truth about the curse. I've used *The Odyssey*."

"Homer. *Intéressant*," Colette said softly and with a tone that made Pippin think she was trying to figure something out.

"And more contemporary. *Gulliver's Travels*."

At this Colette arched one brow. "And why is that? Did your mother or father have that book?"

"My mother stayed away from books. She didn't practice bibliomancy," Pippin said. "And no, I don't think my father had *Gulliver's Travels*. Not that I've seen, anyway."

"How did you choose it?"

"I came across it in the book shop," Pippin said. "It's more like it chose me."

"*Très intéressant*." Only the remains of the cheese and a few crumbs remained on the charcuterie board and Pippin had finished her glass of wine. She thanked Colette and as she stood in the threshold of the cheese shop loaded down with her earlier purchases, Colette stopped her. "I suggest you consider Nostradamus and Virgil, *ma petit*. And as for Lir..." She dipped her chin and looked at Pippin through her lashes. "Consider making your own offering. The gods, you know, they are a fickle bunch. He may be willing to negotiate. *Après tout*, it has been more than two thousand years."

Chapter 30

*"Water reveals the sounds of the Otherworlds, to those who
know how to listen."*

~Author Jennifer McKeithen

By the time she got back to the inn, she found Zoe
waiting for her. "I thought I should stick around
till you to get back," she said.

Pippin thanked her, but her conversation with Colette
de Maurin had expanded to fill every recess of her mind.
Ron Baxter, Dr. Baxter's box, and her murder had been
shoved to the back. She managed to ask Zoe if the drop-in
had booked a stay at the inn. "No luck. Just a lookie-loo," she
said with a French accent. Because of the cheese, no doubt.
Zoe helped her deposit the cheese and meats from Charcuterie in the refrigerator before she left for the night. Pippin
put the other purchases in an empty cupboard then took
Sailor for a walk. She went up one side of Rum Runner's
Lane, crossed the street after three blocks, then came back

on the other side. All the while, she pondered what Colette de Maurin had said to her as she left the shop. *"Consider making your own offering. The gods, you know, they are a fickle bunch. He may be willing to negotiate. After all, it has been more than two thousand years."*

Pippin didn't know the first thing about making a deal with an ancient Celtic god, let alone what to offer and what words to say. She thought she knew where to look for guidance, though. Nostradamus. She picked up her pace, turning so Sailor could see her and gave the sign for *come on*.

"Ahoy there!"

Pippin practically jumped out of her skin. Her hand flew to her chest, pressing into her flesh to calm her nerves.

"Whoo-hoo! Over here, Pippin."

This time, she could pinpoint the location. She looked over and saw Hattie waving to her from her lavender and teal house. Pippin's heart slid from her throat back to her chest cavity. Good Lord. All the talk of curses and gods and offerings had her jumpy.

She detoured into Hattie's yard and went up the walkway. Hattie's house was the most colorful one on the street, and certainly fit its owner. She sat on one of the rocking chairs, another woman in the one beside her. They were complete opposites. Hattie's clothes, as usual, were inspired by the color of the rainbow. Tie-dyed Crocs, bright blue ankle socks, either a skirt or culottes—Pippin couldn't be sure which—with vertical stripes in bright orange, yellow, blue, and green, and a solid lime green shirt. Once the sun set, she just might glow in the dark. Despite the warm evening, the other woman wore black clothing with a high neckline, and folds down to her toes. Her shoulders hunched slightly, and as Pippin looked at her, she was reminded of the old crone from Sleeping Beauty. Pippin couldn't even begin to place the woman's age. Seventy? Eighty? Ninety? A hundred? Hattie's face was a map of wrinkles, but this woman's skin was shriveled like a shrunken apple.

They rocked in unison.

Hattie eyed her, as if she could see right into Pippin's mind. Her eyes burned with curiosity, but her face split into a smile, her bright pink lipstick—the color a perfect match to the hot pink in her outfit—revealing teeth yellowed by age and cigarettes. Pippin spied Hattie's ever-present unlit smoke dangling from between her fingers. "Pippin, my darlin' girl, meet Wenna."

Pippin held Sailor on a short lead. She was still thinking about the curse. The name went in one ear, and right back out the other. She lifted her free hand in a quick wave, trying to recall it. It started with a W. Wi...Win...Oh! It was Winnie, or something like that. "I'm sorry, I'm a little distracted. Your name is...?"

Hattie waggled her head. She had her hair pulled back. Streaks of blue and pink sliced across her head, ending in a ponytail. "Wenna. Like Gwen, but without the G."

She'd been close. "Got it. It's nice to meet you."

Hattie flung her hand out toward her friend, then moved it toward herself, her unlit cigarette like a laser pointer stuck to her fingers. "We go way back." Hattie turned to Wenna. "What would you say, twenty-five, thirty years?"

"About that, I'd say," Wenna agreed. She had an indefinable accent, her voice both lilting and warm. Her voice was strong and youthful, not wavering with age like Pippin half expected. She wore black flats to match her black dress, pushing her feet against the floor, keeping her chair in constant movement. Pippin watched the chair rock forward and backward, forward and backward, forward and backward, mesmerized.

"That's right. About the time Cassandra first came to Devil's Cove."

Pippin blinked, snapping back to the moment, at Hattie's mention of her mother. "Did you know her?" she asked Wenna.

"I believe I did meet her once or twice. She lived just there, didn't she?" Wenna lifted a hand to point a curved finger with enlarged knuckles at the inn.

"That's right. Good memory. Pippin owns it now," Hattie said. "Turned it into an inn, as I'm sure you can see from the sign there."

"My brother and I own it together. We inherited it," Pippin said.

Hattie waved her hand around. "He's more of a silent partner now. Has a woodworkin' business on the east side of the island. Now it's just Pippin runnin' the place."

Pippin just smiled and nodded.

"Where are you off to in such a hurry?" Hattie asked, that naked curiosity vivid in her eyes again.

Anyone else would have thought Pippin was just out for a leisurely stroll with Sailor, but Hattie Juniper Pickle knew her pace had been faster than normal, and her gaze had been down and distracted, rather than taking in the fun colors of the beach houses or breathing in the salty air.

"Just back home. Thinking about my father," she said, which was partially true. She was going to look for her father's book by Nostradamus. And then there was Colette's suggestion that she make an offering to the sea god Lir.

A loud snap brought Pippin out of her thoughts. She looked at the two women. Wenna still rocked, but Hattie had both her Croc'd feet flat on the ground. She backed her unlit cigarette between her pink lips and stared at Pippin. "Girl, what in tarnation is wrong with you? You're a million and one miles away!"

It was true. A million and two, she'd venture. "I'm sorry. Just a lot on my mind. I'll see you tomorrow, okay?" She smiled at Wenna. "Nice to meet you."

"The pleasure was mine," the elderly woman said.

Pippin moved in front of Sailor, tapping under her snout to get her attention. She made the beckoning sign, then gave a small tug on the lead. Sailor stood, turned, and walked by Pippin's side back across the street and into the old inn.

There was no sign of the Lees. She presumed they were out for dinner. They had the code to get in, so she locked up, immediately went to her room, then to the secret door in the wall which led up to the Burrow. Sailor circled then settled in the dog bed Pippin had gotten for the corner of the small study. Seconds later, the Vizsla was asleep, and Pippin got to work. She searched her father's bookshelves and ten minutes later, had a translated version of Nostradamus's book, *Les Prophèties*, in hand.

She flipped through it, stopping on a random page, and saw the list of prophecies. Page after page after page. She riffled the pages, looking for any scribblings or dog-eared corners, but other than the broken spine, there was nothing to indicate this book had been any more meaningful to her father than the other books on the shelves. Still, she went through her developing ritual of sitting cross-legged on the floor, placing the spine of the book on the ground in front of her, took a bolstering breath before asking the question: What can you tell me? And then she let go.

The front and back covers fell to either side and the pages fluttered for a split second before the book opened to a page about three-quarters of the way through. She scanned the pages, her gaze floating across the words. After what felt like a few hundred beats of her heart, she saw it start. The words in one passage darkened. They undulated. Began to peel off the page until they hovered just above where they'd been. They were now separate from the book in which they belonged.

Tomorrow at sunrise I shall no longer be here.

PIPPIN STARED at the nine words, reading them slowly, then repeating them. "Tomorrow at sunrise," she murmured. "Tomorrow at sunrise, what? What happens? Who won't be here any longer?"

Her brain jolted and Grey flashed in her mind. Surely this wasn't about him. Oh God, no.

She drew in a sharp breath. She grabbed the book up, shaking it. Talking to it as if it were alive and could answer her. "It's not Grey, is it?"

Of course, it said nothing. Remained an inanimate object, light in her hands. She exhaled. Set the book down. Went through her ritual again. Deep breath. Closed eyes. Question. "What can you tell me?" Letting go.

The book fell open and once again Pippin scanned the pages. A longer passage—three sentences—lifted off the page. But this was different. She stared. Only *some* of the words had darkened into boldface. Others remained unchanged. They dropped beneath the others, as if they were less important.

She read the entire passage first, all three sentences.

The army of the sea shall stand before the city, then shall go away for a passage that shall not be very long, as a great prey of citizens shall be holding the ground. The fleet returns. The great emblem recovered.

SHE CONCENTRATED, focusing only on the bolded text. "The...sea shall stand..., then shall go away...a citizen...shall be holding the ground...The great emblem recovered."

She shook her head, trying to make sense of the words and what they might mean. Something tapped on the wavy glass of the old window, interrupting her thoughts. "Shoo!" Pippin looked around for something to throw. That bird was going to break the glass one of these days. She jumped up, grabbed a pillow from one of the chairs, and hurled it at the window. It made contact without even a thud, landing on the floor and looking as if it had been ruefully discarded. Pippin snatched it up and cocked her arm back, ready to heave it again, but stopped. The bird was gone.

"And stay away," she said, as if her voice could travel through the window and be carried by the wind, right to the annoying bird. She tossed the pillow back onto the chair and sank down to the floor. She looked at the page, settled her frustration at the bird, and tried again. "The...sea shall stand..., then shall go away...a citizen...shall be holding the ground...The great emblem recovered."

Grey had driven home the point that she was the one to assign meaning to whatever passages struck her. She may or may not be right, but she had to start somewhere. "The sea." The sea shall stand because it's going to fight against some-one? The same answer came to her. Grey. He no longer cared about the curse. He was going to end up facing the sea, and he'd lose. Unless...

She read the words again, trying to put a more positive spin on it. If she looked at her book magic as a gift, wouldn't it be trying to help her? What if "the...sea shall stand..., then shall go away..." referred to the curse? To her *stopping* the curse? Her pulse quickened. What if *she* was the citizen standing strong against the sea?

All her fear about losing Grey dissipated. She was right. She *knew* she was right. The lines hovered just above the page. Her eyes zeroed in on the last four words. "The great emblem recovered," she said aloud. What great emblem?

She took out her phone, opened the internet browser, and typed in *emblem definition*, then read it slowly into the room, working through the twisted and reversed letters of the unfamiliar words. "A heraldic device or symbolic object as a distinctive badge of a nation, organization, or family."

Oh God. This was going to be like going on a rabbit trail. She looked up heraldic, then heraldry. Coats of arms and symbols. That didn't help her much. She decided to ignore that part of the definition, instead only focusing on the second half. "A distinctive badge of a nation, organization, or family."

An emblem. A distinctive badge of a...of a...

She mentally crossed out the words *nation* and *organization*, focusing only on the remaining word: *family*. "A distinctive badge of a family," she said. Her pulse ratcheted up again. That had to be it. An emblem was something relating to her family, and that could only mean one thing. The hilt of the sword.

Chapter 31

"What would an ocean be without a monster lurking in the dark? It would be like sleep without dreams."

~Werner Herzog

*N*ow, thirty minutes later, Pippin had a plan. She could see the very beginnings of orange and pink streaks stretching across the western horizon. There wasn't much time before the sun disappeared and darkness would fall.

The Atlantic.

She had to get off the island and get to the Atlantic side of the barrier islands. That meant driving across the old swing bridge to Sand Point, heading east, driving across Roanoke Island, and straight into Nags Head. It would take an hour. Maybe more.

She threw her blue canvas bag into the passenger seat and took off. Somehow, she managed to keep it under the speed limit driving to Grey's new place. Barely. She found him in his workshop. She saw the boat he was restoring, and dread filled her, like burning rays from the fiery sun exploding from the center of her body. She swallowed. Pushed them away. Flung herself out of the car. "Grey!"

He heard her. Removed one of his white earbuds. She could see worry instantly cloud his face. No wonder. She must look like a mad woman, her hair still wild from her bike ride earlier, her eyes wide with urgency.

Grey started toward her. "Peevie? Are you okay?"

She grabbed his hand. Dragged him toward her Jeep. "Get in. We have to go."

He pulled back, forcing her to stop. "What the hell's going on? Go where?"

She turned to face him. Her heart had climbed to her throat. Every second, darkness grew that much closer. The beaches would be pitch black before long. She yanked him forward again. "Please. I'll explain on the way."

He reluctantly agreed. He moved her bag to the back as he slid into the passenger seat. As soon as she started driving, the words tumbled from Pippin like a waterfall. She told him everything, from her discovery of the stolen artifact in Lambay to Jamie's discovery that Dr. Baxter had been in Ireland at the same time, from her conversation with Colette to the idea of trying to stop the curse, from Leo's book by Nostradamus to the passages she'd found. She'd written them down and now thrust the sheet of notepaper at Grey. "The sea shall stand, then shall go away. A citizen shall be holding the ground. The great emblem recovered. Tomorrow at sunrise I shall no longer be here."

He stared at the paper. Turned to stare at her. She didn't trust herself to let either of her shaking hands off the steering wheel, or to look at him. She was too excited. Too nervous. This could be it. What they were about to do could stop the curse that had plagued their family for millennia.

Grey held up the paper, crumpled in his hand. "I don't know what the hell this means."

"It means we can stop the curse. We're going to face the sea god Lir. We're going to hold strong against him. And we're going to make an offering."

He turned in his seat to face her. She briefly glanced at him before giving him her profile again. "What are you talking about? Like a sacrificial lamb?" He twisted in his seat, looking in the back as if she might have an animal back there.

"No, not like a sacrificial lamb," she said with a sigh. "But an emblem from our family."

Vertical lines carved into the space between his pinched brows. "What emble—?" he asked, but the last letter of the word fell away, and he frowned with realization. "Oh no, Pippin. We can't."

"Oh, but we can."

He spun around and peered into the backseat. "It's not there," Pippin said.

Pippin watched Grey as he turned around. As his gaze landed on her purse sitting between them. As his eyes met hers in the rearview mirror.

They were twins. She knew exactly what he was thinking. They reacted at the same time. The car jerked as she let go of the wheel and grabbed for the purse at the same time he did. He tugged. She pulled back and clenched her teeth. "Let go, Grey."

A horn blared. The car swerved. Another horn blasted. "Watch the road, Pippin," Grey barked.

Pippin released her hold on her bag and grabbed hold of

steering wheel with both hands. She wrenched it, bringing the car back into the right lane.

She watched Grey out of the corner of her eye as he dug one hand into the bag. A second later, the ancient sword hilt lay in its wrapping on his lap. "This is valuable," he said. "And it's stolen. It has to be returned."

"More valuable than your life?" she shot back.

He ran his hand over his face, looking more tired than she'd could ever remember seeing him. He closed his eyes and leaned his head back against the headrest. "I love that you want to try to stop it, but it's not going to work."

Her knuckles turned white as her grip tightened on the steering wheel. "How do you know that?"

"Making some sort of pact with an ancient sea god?" His fingers clawed through his dark hair. "First of all, we're in North Carolina. Even if he does exist, wouldn't we have to do it in Ireland where Morgan and Titus were?"

That hadn't occurred to her, but the sea was the sea, wasn't it? She ignored his logic. "It'll work."

"Pippin. Get serious."

She took her eyes off the road long enough to stare at him. "I. Am. A. Bibliomancer. It's real."

His eyes clouded. He turned his head and looked out the window as they drove. She could see the conflict bubbling up inside him like a pot of water going from a low boil to a raging torrent. He believed in the curse...and yet at the same time, he didn't. That's why he was taking his chances in the sound and in the ocean. He was battling it and trying to believe that none of what had happened to the Lane family was actually real. She stared straight ahead, tamping down her frustration. "You've seen me do it, Grey. You know it's true."

He rewrapped the artifact and thrust it back into her purse. "I've seen you let books fall open, but—"

He broke off, his words failing him. She finished for him. "But you don't believe what I see is real."

"I don't know." He sighed. "I really don't know."

"It's real, Grey. Every last bit of it is real. You *know* that. Every woman in our family dying as they give birth. Every man swallowed up by the sea. That isn't coincidence."

He'd turned pallid. "It might be. A self-fulfilling prophecy."

She gripped the steering wheel even harder, barreling over the Nags Head/Manteo Causeway, which connected Roanoke Island to Nags Head on the Outer Banks. "It is self-fulfilling if you ignore it. Our mother *never* should have gotten pregnant. *I* can never get pregnant! Our great-grandfather and our grandfather should have stayed away from the ocean, just like you should. Because if you don't, it's going to take you." She turned to look at him. "Unless we stop it."

He let out a frustrated groan. "Okay, say we do this. Throw that thing into the water and say some made up incantation or something. How will we know it worked? If you don't die giving birth, I guess I'll know. You're willing to risk it? To take the chance? Because what if the curse *is* real and this *doesn't* work?"

"*You're* acting like it's not real. You're taking your life in your hands every time you go in the water, so don't tell me I'm the one taking chances! I'm trying to do something. To stop this thing once and for all." And then she swallowed hard. Softened her voice. Laid her hand on her purse. "We'll know."

Chapter 32

"The breaking of a wave cannot explain the whole sea."
  ~Vladimir Nabokov

*P*ippin and Grey stood side by side in the surf. The tide rose, the Atlantic's warm summer water swirling around their calves. Their heels sank deep into the swirling sand. And then the tide receded with a force so powerful that Pippin wondered if Lir was right here, churning around their ankles, trying to haul them into the depths. They wobbled as the water pulled them toward the vast expanse of the ocean. They intertwined arms. Braced their cores. Held each other upright against the growing force of the wind.

"What now?" Grey asked over the roar of the crashing waves.

Pippin had gone over this a multitude of times since leaving the cheese shop. Pippin didn't answer Grey's question with words. Instead, she unfurled her arm from his.

Reached into her canvas purse. Took out the wrapped hilt. Removed it from the cloth.

She threw her purse onto the dry sand behind them, safe from the tide.

Overhead, gulls squawked in the darkening sky. A murder of crows flew above them. A shiver wound through Pippin. Whatever poet had named a flock of the black birds a murder was dark indeed. Was it a bad omen coming to life in the night sky? She ignored them and outstretched her arms, the hilt cradled in her two hands.

And then she spoke a passage from *A Tale of Two Cities*. "*Nothing that we do, is done in vain. I believe, with all my soul, that we shall see triumph.*"

The tide rose in a sudden swell. She dug her heels in and spoke the prophecy from Nostradamus. "*The army of the sea shall stand before the city, then shall go away for a passage that shall not be very long, as a great prey of citizens shall be holding the ground—*"

The raucous cawing of the crows, the mewing of the gulls, and the deafening fierceness of the Atlantic's waves buried her voice. The waves pummeled the shoreline with increasing power, each receding tide pulling them deeper into the water. She wove her arm through Grey's, tethering herself to him. She started again, speaking Nostradamus's words. "*The army of the sea shall stand before the city—*"

In a split second, everything changed. Grey's body jerked forward, pulled by the force of the water. Pippin's arm slid away from his. She clutched at his forearm with one hand, her nails digging into his skin. "Grey!" She yelled at the top of her lungs, but the words were ripped from her lips and hurled into the howling wind, vanishing.

Oh God, oh God, oh God. The water rose. Crashed over her head. She watched in horror as Grey was swept away from her, carried by an unseen wave. He flung his arms toward the darkening sky, fighting against the unseeable power, and then he suddenly stopped fighting. His head disappeared under water. Pippin screamed, plunging herself deeper into the water, reaching for him, but he was gone.

She screamed at the top of her lungs. "Grey!"

Her breath turned ragged. Tears streamed down her fact. "Grey," she sobbed. "Where are you?"

As if he heard her, his body resurfaced a yard away. Two yards away.

He managed to regain some footing and yelled something to her, but the words were gone, stolen by the wind, before they reached her ears. His head bobbed again, and he was pulled further out. He yelled again, and this time she thought she read on his lips the word *riptide*.

Panic rose up in her like a fire's backdraft, ready to explode. He wouldn't be able to fight against the riptide. It would exhaust him in minutes, and he'd be pulled under.

Swallowed by the sea.

Pippin reacted without thinking. Held up the hilt with one hand, her eyes glued to Grey. "Release us from the curse, Lir!" she screamed, and she hurled what was left of the ancient sword into the water.

Saltwater careened upward in a column as the hilt met the water, as if from a whale's blowhole. Pippin searched for Grey. She spotted a dark form moving farther away from shore, and she dove. Swam with all her might. She dove under the waves. Kicked her feet. Her shoes were long gone, ripped away by the vicious water.

By Lir.

She had no idea if she was caught in the riptide. She came up for air, reorienting herself with her back to the shoreline. There. She spotted Grey. He'd flipped onto his back. He wasn't fighting. Wasn't swimming.

If Pippin didn't get to him soon, they'd both lose their fight, against both the curse and the water.

She kept eyes on him as she made slow progress swimming toward him. The thunderous crashing of the water seemed to lesson. The caws and mews of the crows and gulls reached her ears. She saw them swoop down, first one, then another, and another. Then they arced back into the sky, each with their prey held tightly in their beaks.

She forced her arms to pull her through the water until, at long last, her fingertips brushed something hard. Grey. She propelled herself forward one last time. First her fingertips, then her hands grabbed hold of his shirt, his arm. "Grey!"

He didn't move. Didn't respond. "Greevie, come on!"

No response. Her head pounded. She panted with exhaustion. She couldn't be too late.

It took her a moment before she realized she no longer felt the pull of the riptide. The howling wind had calmed, and the waves deflated.

She could do this.

She summoned up every bit of strength she had, first wrapping her arm around her brother's torso, then flipping herself onto her back to tow him to shore. The fatigued muscles of her arm strained but she kept her arm wrapped around him, holding onto him for dear life.

They'd be okay. She lay back, still for a moment in the water, her heart beating against her brother's slack body on top of hers. And then she continued toward shore.

Chapter 33

"We don't even know how strong we are until we are forced to bring that hidden strength forward. In times of tragedy, of war, of necessity, people do amazing things. The human capacity for survival and renewal is awesome."

~Isabel Allende

*P*ippin held out hope that Grey would be okay. That the curse had finally been broken.

With every strained breath she took as she slowly pulled her brother and herself toward shore, she asked Lir for her family's freedom.

For their safety.

For Grey.

Finally, her feet found purchase on the moving sand under the water and then, as if in answer to a prayer, Grey sputtered. Water dribbled from his mouth. He coughed and she released her hold on him. As he flipped himself over, falling onto all fours in the now shallow surf, all the fear that had coursed through Pippin evaporated. She reached for him again, draping her arm over him, helping him to stand and stagger out of the water and onto the sand.

He'd survived a battle with the ocean. That had to mean it worked. Pippin smiled. Almost jumped for joy, but as quickly as elation had flowed through her, it dried up, because there, on the sand not three yards from where she'd tossed her bag, lay the ancient relic she'd hurled into the Atlantic as an offering to Lir.

Her heart instantly seized, a low moan sliding up her throat. "Noooo."

Grey lifted his head, following her gaze just as his legs gave out. He collapsed onto the sand. "It didn't work," he murmured.

"But you survived!" she cried. How could she have failed when Grey was still very much alive right next to her? The next second she realized what he'd said. She slumped down next to him. "You believe it's real?"

He pointed to the hilt. "You threw it into the water, didn't you?"

Slowly, she nodded. She'd hurled it with all her might before plunging herself into the riptide to get to Grey. So how was the hilt now on the dry sand?

The mew of the gulls grew loud in the darkening sky above. The crows were long gone. Pippin had a sudden recollection of the birds diving into the water, emerging with their prey. One of them may have thought they'd snatched a fish when, in fact, it had been the hilt. The idea gave Pippin a burst of hope. If the hilt was here now because of a crow or a gull, and *not* because Lir had rejected the offering, then maybe they *had* broken the curse. She just had to throw it into the water again, this time hoping the tide would eventually take it out to the deep.

She scrabbled up and ran to the object, scooping it into one hand. Without breaking stride, she ran into the surf until the water circled her knees. Grey hollered at her above the crashing waves. "What the hell are you doing? Pippin, get out of there!"

She turned to yell over her shoulder. "I have to give it back!" She closed her eyes for a moment to summon up the passage her bibliomancy had shown her. She cocked her arm back, but just as she started to hurl the hilt as far into the Atlantic as her waning strength would allow, a hand grabbed her arm, holding it firm and blocking her momentum. Grey grabbed the hilt from her hand as he pulled her back out of the water.

"Stop!" Pippin cried, trying to pull her arm free of his grip.

He only tightened it. "It's not going to work, Peevie."

"We have to—" she started, but the growing strength of the water trying to pull them in again stopped the words on her lips. A wave came out of nowhere, crashing down on them both. They lost their footing, falling to their knees.

Another pounded down on them. Pippin's head plunged into the water. She choked on a mouthful of saltwater. Sputtered. Tried to pull herself up against the force of another wave battering her. Panic flared. If they didn't get out, the sea would take them both this time. And then, once again, she felt a hand grip her arm. She felt herself being lifted out of the water.

She and Grey pushed through the water, their knees lifting high, their feet dragging. Grey held tight to her arm, but his breath was ragged, and he started to trail behind her. He'd nearly drowned, yet here he was fighting for her, just as she'd fought for him. For the first time in a long time, Pippin felt connected to her twin brother. She twined her arm around his. He gripped her forearm just as she gripped his.

Together they slogged toward the shore.

GREY SLEPT SOUNDLY on Pippin's bed, his breathing deep and heavy. She sat on the chair, her head reclined, and her eyes closed, but for her, sleep wouldn't come. She'd failed. At least she thought she had. He'd been right, of course. She couldn't risk testing the theory by thrusting her brother into another body of water, threatening his life again. She thought she might feel different, as if a weight had been lifted from her shoulders. But she didn't. It hadn't. She felt the same.

Her biggest hope was that the experience they'd gone through that night had shaken him enough that he'd stop putting himself at risk. Maybe he'd even get rid of that boat.

He shifted in his sleep and seemed to murmur, "Mmm mmm," as if he'd heard and taken exception to her silent wish.

Her mind replayed every element of the trip to the beach from picking up Grey to collapsing onto the sand and staring up at a spattering of stars twinkling in the dark sky. At long last, she drifted to sleep, awakening to sunlight creeping in through the French doors, filtered by the covered porch. She peered at the bed—at the spot where Grey had slept. Vacant. He always had been an early riser. She resisted the urge to call him. To check in. She knew he needed space and time to process what had happened the night before.

She'd call him later. She cupped her hand over her fore-head, pressing her temples to chase away the headache forming there. Only then did she peer at the clock. She bolted upright. Eight-fifteen! She swung her legs out of bed. She had to hurry and get breakfast ready for the Lees.

Fifteen minutes later, she was showered, dressed in a light sundress, had her hair pulled into a messy topknot, and had unlocked the front door. Open for business.

From what she could tell, the Lees hadn't made it downstairs yet. Relief flooded her. It was bad enough that there had been a death on the premises. She didn't want to add dissatisfaction in the inn's overall services, including breakfast, to that. She sliced strawberries, mixed them together with fresh blueberries, set out a tray of muffins Zoe had baked the day before, and placed cups, plates, and cutlery on the counter.

As she waited for the coffee to finish percolating so she could pour herself a bolstering cup, she heard the squeak of the screen door followed by a woman saying, "Hello?"

Pippin recognized Ruby's voice. She headed toward the entryway as Ruby crossed toward the kitchen. They met in the middle of the great room. From the forlorn expression Ruby wore, Pippin instantly knew something was wrong. She put her hands on Ruby's arms. "What is it? Are you okay?"

Ruby's face crumpled, tears pooling in her eyes. "I have to leave for a few days," she said, her voice cracking with the emotion she held in.

Pippin led Ruby into her little office, directing her to the chair facing her desk. She crouched in front of her. "What happened?"

"My cousin was in a car accident."

Pippin dropped to the floor, leaning her back against the hard back of her desk. She held Ruby's hand. "Oh no, I'm so sorry."

"Yeah," Ruby croaked.

"Is she okay?"

Ruby shook her head. "It was touch and go. She died yesterday."

Pippin remembered seeing Ruby on the phone, closing Devil's Brew early. She was up in an instant and enveloped Ruby in a hug. "I'm so sorry. Can I do anything to help?"

Ruby buried her face into Pippin's bare shoulder. Her body shook with her sobs. "She has a...*had* a daugh—"

"Pippin?" The front door to the inn slammed closed and Zoe's voice reached her.

Pippin couldn't answer. She just held Ruby.

A second later, Zoe poked her head through the door saying, "Gin White left a message yesterday. She said she'll be here with the beer delivery from The Brewery at nine..."

Her voice faded to nothing when she saw Pippin holding Ruby's trembling figure.

Pippin mouthed, "Okay," and waved Zoe away.

The interruption had been enough to snap Ruby out of her despair. She pulled herself from Pippin's arms and stood abruptly. "I'm sorry. I didn't mean to break down."

Pippin jumped up. "Don't go yet."

But Ruby was already halfway to the front door. "I have to."

Pippin scurried after her. Her big toe, exposed by her sandals, caught the corner of Dr. Baxter's banker box. She skirted around it. "What about Devil's Brew? Can I help there?"

Ruby stopped at the door. "I put up a sign. Closed due to an emergency. I'll be back Sunday."

In the time Pippin had known Ruby, Devil's Brew had never been closed during business hours. "Are you okay to drive?" she asked, because Ruby's hands visibly trembled and a layer of her ebony skin seemed to have paled.

Her nostrils flared as she drew in a deep breath. She let out an audible exhalation. "I will be. I just...I can't deliver your bakery order tomorrow."

"Oh God, don't worry about that." The last thing she wanted was for Ruby to be concerned about a few scones and sweet breads when she was grieving for her cousin.

Another sob escaped Ruby's pale lips. "Thanks, Pip."

Pippin squeezed her friend's hand. Zoe came to stand beside her on the porch. Together, they watched until Ruby was in her car and driving away.

"Is she okay?" Zoe asked.

"I don't know," Pippin said. She hoped so. She gave instructions to Zoe to make room in the refrigerator for the beer. She retreated to her office feeling helpless. She knew firsthand there was no way to help a person deal with grief. She'd lost her mother. Her father. Her grandparents. She'd had to process through it in her own way, in her own time.

Ruby would have to do the same.

She picked up Dr. Baxter's box and put it on her desk. Searching for clues about the archaeologist's death would be a good distraction.

Chapter 34

"Acting is magical. Change your look and your attitude, and you can be anyone."

~Alicia Witt

The phone call to Lieutenant Jacobs was short and sweet. Pippin told him about Mrs. Lee finding Dr. Baxter's jacket and the return of the box. "I found a stub of an airline ticket from Ireland to Raleigh-Durham Airport," she said, and then she told him about the theft in Lambay and the hilt she'd found in the guest safe.

Thirty minutes later, the door opened and in walked the lawman. Pippin handed the Dickens book to Zoe to re-shelve. She disappeared into the kitchen as Pippin met the portly man in the entryway to turn over the items. He looked the same as he always did, dressed in his navy uniform, his gray hair shorn close to the scalp. He rocked back on his heels, arms folded across his chest, the hilt tucked safely into a plastic evidence bag. "This will have to be returned."

She nodded. Hugh had said it belonged to Pippin and Grey, and that he relinquished any claim to it as a descendent of the Roman soldier Titus. Pippin had offered it to Lir, but it had come back to her. In her gut, she knew Jamie and Grey were both right. It had to go back to Ireland as a piece of the country's history.

She was about to get Dr. Baxter's box from her office but stopped when the lieutenant spoke. "There's a problem with the timeline."

Pippin stared at him blankly. "What timeline?"

"You saw Dr. Baxter leave the house Sunday morning at approximately seven forty-five a.m., correct?"

"Yes."

"Her body was discovered approximately fourteen hours later, at nine-thirty p.m. But based on lividity and rigor mortis, the ME believes the time of death was at least fifteen to eighteen hours *prior* to the discovery of the body."

Pippin stared. "What does that mean?"

"It means that either moments after Dr. Baxter left the inn Sunday morning, she turned around and came back, went upstairs without your knowledge, went to the widow's walk, with her killer, mind you, and was killed, all within minutes of you seeing her leave, or..."

"Or?" Pippin prompted.

"Or you have the time wrong, and she left earlier than you thought."

Pippin scraped her fingernails over her scalp. She racked her brain, thinking back to Sunday morning. Dr. Baxter had been explicit on the online registration form. She wanted breakfast at seven-fifteen. By the time the Lees were finished eating, Dr. Baxter still hadn't shown up. Zoe went off to start the morning chores, Pippin started another pot of coffee, and that's when she saw Dr. Baxter leave. "But that doesn't make sense," she finally said, "I *did* see her leave."

Lieutenant Jacobs shook his head, looking as baffled as Pippin felt. "Something's not right," he said.

"I definitely saw her leave between seven forty-five and eight o'clock." She was absolutely sure because Zoe had mentioned the time when they'd been on the back deck with the Lees. "I'm not mistaken."

"I don't know then. I'm sure the ME isn't wrong about the time of death." Jacobs cleared his throat. "Where's this airline stub and the box of Dr. Baxter's things?"

She went to her office to retrieve the box, setting it on the registration desk and laying the red jacket on top of it. "I thought now that you know Dr. Baxter was probably the one to steal that in the first place—" she nodded at the evidence bag in his hand, "—you'd want to take another look at all of this. In case there's something else that can help prove it. Not that it matters since she's dead."

Lieutenant Jacobs's brow furrowed as he looked at the box and jacket. "Ms. Hawthorne, I've never seen that box. We didn't find it with the doctor's effects," he said.

Her lungs felt as if they'd popped like balloons. If Jacobs and his people hadn't taken it, then how had Ron Baxter gotten a hold of it, and why had he brought it back?

A KNOCK JOLTED Pippin from her thoughts. She was glad for the interruption, though, since her thoughts were getting her nowhere fast. She opened the door to Gin White, her usual crossbody bag slung around her body, two cases of beer from The Brewery stacked next to her. Pippin stepped back. Gin swung her bag to her back, crouched down, and picked up one of the boxes. "Take it to the kitchen?" she asked.

"Yes." Pippin knelt to pick up the second box, heaving it up with effort. Gin had made it look easy, lifting it like it was filled with feathers instead of heavy bottles. She was stronger than she looked. In the kitchen, they placed the cases next to the refrigerator.

"If you want to empty them, I'll take the boxes back," she said.

Zoe had her back to them. She was bent over the dishwasher. Like so many other women, the sliver of skin showing from between her jeans and tee shirt revealed a sliver of a tattoo on her lower back. Zoe heard Gin's voice and stood, tugging her shirt back into place. She removed her earbuds, saw the beer, and helped Pippin loading the bottles into the refrigerator. "The rest will have to go in the mud room," Pippin said, once the bottom shelf was filled.

"Zoe, we need to make scones," Pippin said as Gin easily picked up the full box and headed for the mudroom on the opposite side of the kitchen. "Ruby can't do them tomorrow."

"Got it," Zoe said, back to being a brit. She replaced her earbuds and went back to the dishwasher.

"I talked to that Dr. Bligh guy," Gin said when she came back to the kitchen. She swung her bag around to her front again and patted it. "He said he'll take a look at my Dare Stone."

Pippin smiled. "That's great news! I hope you get the answer you want."

"I'll let you know." She glanced around. "Now, where is that sweet pup?"

"Right over there," Pippin said, pointing to the deck where Sailor lay in a sliver of sunlight.

Gin scurried over and bent to run her fingers through Sailor's hair. Sailor's tail started wagging. She opened one sleepy eye and looked up at Gin, then plopped it down again. When Gin came back, Pippin handed her the empty case. "Thanks," she called as Gin sauntered through the great room.

At the front door, Gin raised her hand in a quick wave. "Call over to The Brewery if you need anything else," she said, barely turning her head.

A sudden feeling of déjà vu washed over Pippin. The way Gin stopped and waved—it was just like Dr. Baxter had Sunday. "I will," she said to Gin.

She shook the feeling away, left Zoe to the scones, and started for her office. A book lying on the coffee table caught her eye. It was her copy of *A Tale of Two Cities*, which she'd set down when Lieutenant Jacobs had shown up. She scooped it up to return it to one of the bookshelves, but it slipped from her fingers and fell upside down, open, the pages folded and wrinkled against the table.

"Damn." She wasn't an avid reader by any stretch of the imagination, but she didn't like to see the pages of books dogeared, let alone mangled. She picked it up and started to close it but stopped when a few lines darkened and seemed to shudder on the paper.

"Judged!"... swinging his hammer. "Ay! and condemned as a traitor."

PIPPIN NEARLY DROPPED THE BOOK. It felt like a hot potato in her hands. She hadn't done her ritual—hadn't even asked a question, but the book had conveyed a message to her. It was obviously important. She perched on the edge of the couch, staring at the words for a long time as she tried to work out what they meant. *Who* had been judged? *Who* was a traitor?

Ron Baxter? To her mind, he was the leading suspect in both the murder of Dr. Baxter and as the treasure hunter invading the Lane family. He was lying about his identity, for starters, he was avoiding her, and he was clearly looking for something that had been in Monique Baxter's possession —either the hilt or something else connected to Titus and Morgan—because he'd come looking for it twice. He'd also somehow gotten his hands on Dr. Baxter's box of papers, then brought it back.

Her mind shifted to Hugh. She was still very uncertain about him. She didn't trust him, but she also didn't *not* trust him. He'd had the hilt in his possession and hadn't kept it for himself. In fact, he'd made sure that Pippin got it. She hadn't seen or heard from him since the summoning to the library. If he'd killed Monique, she had no idea why.

A smattering of other possible suspects came to mind:

Dr. Bligh, because Dr. Baxter had interrupted his dig. But, on the other hand, it seemed clear Dr. Baxter hadn't come to Devil's Cove because of the Lost Colony, and Dr. Bligh had given no indication that he cared one iota about Pippin, the Lanes, or Irish artifacts.

The Lees and Paul Marshall had been present at the inn when the murder had taken place, but there was no evidence of any connection to Dr. Baxter. The Lees were on island for their vacation, and Mr. Marshall had been elusive, but nothing seemed out of the ordinary.

Instead of standing, Pippin sat back on the couch and let her brain rearrange everything she knew. While Ron Baxter and Hugh were mysterious and both had spent time sneaking around the inn, could either of them be defined as a traitor? Well, yes, she supposed they could, actually. Ron was lying and presumably trying to steal something that didn't belong to him. And Hugh...well, Hugh she just didn't know enough about. It seemed to her, though, that he had his own agenda that didn't necessarily have much to do with Dr. Baxter.

And then there was Gin White. She *could* be the traitor. She was a local. A friend, of sorts. An island institution, for sure. She'd been touting her claim to be a descendant of John White, the grandfather of Eleanor Dare, for as long as anyone could remember, and she claimed the Dare Stone she carted around was authentic.

If she murdered an innocent woman, that might not make her a traitor like, say, Edward Snowden or Benedict Arnold, but it was still bad.

And, Pippin thought, Gin White had a potential motive. Dr. Baxter hadn't had any real interest in the Dare Stone. She was also lacking in friendly bedside manner. She could have rebuffed Gin White so harshly that it sent the latter woman into a rage.

But there were so many problems with that scenario. Number one, if what Lieutenant Jacobs said about the timeline was true, then Dr. Baxter had been killed just after Pippin had seen her leave. She must have turned right around and come back in with her killer by her side. Or...what if her killer had been waiting for her already? But, no, that scenario didn't work. How would Gin—or any of the others, for that matter—have gotten into the house to lie in wait?

Pippin didn't unlock the door until she came down for breakfast.

Something about Dr. Baxter's red jacket niggled at her brain. She'd been wearing her hood, but it hadn't been raining, or even misty. And then there was the déjà vu moment with Gin. Whatever it all meant, it was just out of reach.

A low, gravelly voice came from the kitchen, quickly followed by a cockney Eliza Doolittle. Zoe acting out the parts of a movie interrupted Pippin's thoughts for a moment, but she came back to the all the same questions. She hadn't gotten any closer to answering them.

She stood, trying to smile at Zoe's animated voice playing two different characters, but her brain skittered from thought to thought, each like a separate pinball in a supercharged machine. A door upstairs closed and a second later, the Lees ambled down the stairs, suitcases in hand. She turned to her departing guests, forcing her faltering smile wider. "I hope you'll come back."

"If I have any say in the matter, we definitely will." Mrs. Lee patted her husband's shoulder. "Now if only that company you work for will honor your vacation days. I don't want to wait another ten years."

A lot could happen in ten years, Pippin thought. "Zoe, could you print out a receipt for the Lees?"

Zoe scooted out from the kitchen, heading straight to the registration desk. A small printer was housed on one of the shelves underneath. She opened the laptop, logged in, and tapped away. A minute later, the receipt printed, and the Lees were on their way to the front door. Zoe followed them. As she stood at the door and waved, Pippin slipped back into her thoughts about Dr. Baxter, the curse, and everything else. Salty's words pushed into her mind. *People show you what they want you to see.* Hugh had shown her just enough to make him believable. She suddenly doubted that he was actually a descendant of Titus. It must have been a story he'd spun so she'd trust him.

The Dickens passage she'd just seen resurfaced. *"Judged!"... swinging his hammer. "Ay! and condemned as a traitor."*

"Oh! I forgot to tell you. We got a reservation for Halloween," Zoe said as she turned away from the door.

Pippin's mind felt a million miles away, but something suddenly triggered that déjà vu feeling again, followed by a rogue thought. It had to do with playing two parts. Pretending to be one thing when you were something else entirely. Lieutenant Jacobs had given her two scenarios about the timeline of Dr. Baxter's death. Either Pippin had gotten the time she'd seen her leave Sunday morning wrong, or Dr. Baxter had come right back without Pippin seeing.

But what if there was a third scenario? What if it wasn't Dr. Baxter at all that she'd seen leave that morning? What if she'd been killed much earlier and someone else had *pretended* to be her to confuse the time of death?

A detail slammed into her mind. The Lees had mentioned the thin walls. Mr. Lee had had heard Dr. Baxter talking with someone late Saturday night. Pippin gasped. What if she had seen the killer walk right out of the house?

Her lungs felt empty of breath, as if she was pressed down by the waves that had crashed down on her and Grey. She buckled over, hands on her knees. In a flash, Zoe was at her side. "Pippin, are you okay?"

"Yeah, yeah. I'm fine." She pushed herself upright and waved her away, but her brain stuttered. "I have...I have to go...I'll be back..."

And then she was out the door.

Chapter 35

"By doubting we are led to question, by questioning we arrive at the truth."

~Peter Abelard

*T*raitor. *Traitor. Traitor.* The word ricocheted in Pippin's head as she pedaled down Rum Runner's Lane toward The Open Door. Her thoughts crashed against each other like bumper cars on a collision course. She tried to hold on to each one long enough to process through it. Hugh said he knew Dr. Baxter had the hilt. He'd gone to her room to look for it. She thought back to her conversation with him in the library. She'd never actually asked him, point blank, why he'd given Titus's hilt to Zoe to put in the safe. What if he never found the hilt because it was already missing?

Hugh had warned her that there were others. That Dr. Baxter wasn't the only one who knew about the legend of Titus giving something to his beloved Morgan.

Like a computer presentation progressing to the next slide, Salty's words played in her head. *"If ya think Jimmy'n me are the only ones prowlin' 'round your family tree, you'd be mistaken. That woman who was killed—she ain't the only one, you know. There are other people who know, you're right about that, and you best watch your back, 'cause people show ya what they want ya to see. No more, no less. And on of 'em'll find what they're after."*

People show you what they want you to see.

Her breath lodged in her throat. It was as if all roads suddenly pointed to a single person, someone she hadn't even considered. Someone she'd trusted.

She lifted up on the handlebars, bouncing her bike onto the sidewalk on Main Street. Past The Taco Shop. Past Sprinkles, the ice cream parlor. Past a kitschy tourist shop with Devil's Cove baubles. She skidded as she braked hard, nearly crashing into one of the flowerpots in front of the bookshop. She jumped off her bike before she'd come to a complete stop. She stumbled but caught herself before toppling to the ground. She dropped her bike on its side. A second later, she stood in the doorway, panting. "Oh, thank God you're here!"

Jamie stood behind the counter ringing up a customer. He turned to look at her, giving his wire-rimmed glasses a little push up his nose. "Pip! Are you okay?"

"I need to talk to you—!" she blurted.

The customer, a young man, took his book from Jamie, dipped his chin, and started for the door. Pippin stared at him, familiarity tickling the edges of her brain.

"Hey, Bryan, your change!" Jamie called.

He looked up for a split second and it came to her. "You stopped by the inn yesterday."

The man, Bryan, gave a tentative smile. "Uh, yeah." He

backtracked for his change, but didn't meet Pippin's eyes again, and then he was gone.

The moment the door closed behind him, he vanished from Pippin's mind. "Jamie," she said, the urgency back in her voice.

"Hang on," he said, then he signaled to Noah. "I'll be outside for a few minutes."

As usual, Noah had his earbuds in, but he heard Jamie and nodded at him with a chill, "Got it."

Cars rolled down Main Street in a steady stream. Next door to The Open Door, the inside of the coffee shop was dark. Ruby had taped a sign on the door. *Due to a family emergency, Devil's Brew is closed until Monday.* She and Jamie both silently acknowledged the sign for a moment before sitting at one of the bistro tables Ruby kept on the sidewalk.

"My book magic...it showed me a new quote. 'Ay! and condemned as a traitor.'"

Jamie sat back, listening as she took him through her thoughts about Hugh and Ron Baxter. She was about to tell him her theory, but stopped herself. It was ridiculous. It didn't make sense. "I don't know, maybe I'm wrong—"

She broke off when she saw a dark sedan coming down Main Street. A navy four door car just like the one she'd almost rammed her bike into. The cars in front of it forced it to slow. It rolled past. As if in slow motion, the man in the passenger seat turned his head and looked right at her.

It was Bryan, the man she'd just seen in the bookshop. The same man who'd come to the inn the day before.

And in the driver's seat was the man calling himself Ron Baxter.

Pippin froze, her brain rearranging information as if it was computer calculating a complex math problem.

'...*There are people who have traced the ancestry of this...
treasure...to you,*' Hugh had said.

'...*There are other people who know...And one of 'em'll find
what they're after...*' Salty had told her.

Blood pulsed in her temples. Like Tetris blocks dropping
from the top of the game, the pieces of came together. Not so
ridiculous after all.

She pointed to the car, now driving past the bookshop
and turning left just past the library. "It's all of them.
Together. And Zoe," she said almost under her breath, then
louder, "And Zoe."

Chapter 36

"The dead cannot cry out for justice. It is a duty of the living to do so for them."

~Lois McMaster Bujold

Within minutes, Pippin had Lieutenant Jacobs on the phone again. She put him on speaker, gave him a description of the car, then launched into her theory. "I know it sounds crazy, but it's all true."

"Treasure," Jacobs mulled, as if he were tossing the word out to see how it sounded.

"Yes. But listen," she said, telling him her idea that Zoe had impersonated Dr. Baxter Sunday morning. "But..." She gave a dramatic pause... "Dr. Baxter was already dead."

"Let's go through this again," Jacobs said after a solid twenty seconds of silence over the line.

Pippin took a deep inhalation before rewinding to the beginning. "Zoe and the other two—Ron and Bryan—must be part of that group Hugh—"

Jacobs interrupted. "The man with the clear eyes."

"Right. They have to be part of that group Hugh and Dr. Baxter were in." Now, looking back, it seemed too perfect. She'd come at the just the right time. Pippin hadn't advertised a position. She didn't even know what to call it. Jill-of-all-trades fit the bill. Zoe filled the position perfectly, ever accommodating, always coming in early, staying late, never complaining about Pippin running out. She came up with new ideas about cleaning and organizing, searching through this cupboard, or that nook.

"Maybe Dr. Baxter recognized her," Jamie suggested.

The thought had crossed her mind. "Or knew *of* her."

"So, *Zoe* stole the hilt from Dr. Baxter's room," Jamie said. "She's the one who stashed it in the guest safe, but not for Hugh?"

Pippin pointed into the air. "Hugh never actually said he took the hilt," she said. "I just assumed. But it had to be Zoe. She banked on the fact that Dr. Baxter wouldn't notice and that I'd have no reason to look in the safe." Pippin had provided Zoe with an opportunity by getting her to make sure Hugh left during the party. She was a clever thing, coming up with the story that he'd given it to her for safekeeping. "If Dr. Baxter *did* recognize her *and* noticed the hilt was gone, that could have led to a confrontation. Oh!"

Jamie watched her as if he could see the wheels turning inside her head.

"Oh, what?" Jacobs asked through the speaker.

"*That* could be the conversation Mr. Lee heard late Saturday night. Zoe knows the walls are thin. She could have taken Dr. Baxter up to the widow's walk for privacy."

"She had to have something with her to smash her head in when it all went south," Jacobs said.

Pippin thought for a moment. The answer came to her in a rush. "The cement frogs!"

The skepticism was back in Jacobs's voice. "What's that? A frog?"

Zoe had left the damaged frog she'd repaired to cure under the bathroom sink upstairs. She could have grabbed it before she followed Dr. Baxter up the ladder to the widow's walk. "Check the cement frogs on the back deck of the inn." If she was right, there had to be traces of blood invisible to the naked eye on one of them.

Pippin felt Jacobs frown skeptically at the suggestion, but the more she thought about it, the more sure she was. It would have made the perfect murder weapon.

"Is there more?" Jacobs asked.

Pippin yanked apart the Tetris blocks. "*She* probably took Dr. Baxter's box. She said she hadn't seen Ron Baxter the day I'd almost crashed my bike into that car, but my bet is that she had the box stashed somewhere at the inn so they could go through it together. If they all think there's some treasure, they would have wanted to know if Dr. Baxter had found anything besides the hilt. She lied. Ron *had* been at the inn before he'd raced back to the car I'd almost hit, leaving the box for Zoe to dispose of." She pulled apart another block, remembering something. It all played in her head like a scene from a movie. Zoe had gone upstairs. Turned on the vacuum. She raced downstairs in the red jacket, sure the noise from the vacuum would catch Pippin's attention. It had been risky, but it had worked. Zoe employed her voice skills, uttering two words in the gruff tone that mimicked Dr. Baxter. Once outside, she had flown into super-speed, stashing the jacket under the porch stairs, circling the house, and coming back in through the mudroom. "The sand," she muttered. Sailor had gone into the mudroom. Something had caught her attention. Not a sound, but Zoe's shadow as she came into the mudroom, trailing sand. She'd flown up the back stairs, turning off the vacuum before Pippin went up to investigate. Just in time, in fact. It had been risky, and the timing had been crucial. "The Sea Captain and the Hidden Treasure," she said to herself. Jamie raised a brow at her in question. "Zoe said I should make up some new stories about the inn. She suggested, The Sea Captain and the Hidden Treasure."

"Because that's what she was looking for," he said.

Another block tumbled away, revealing another clue. Zoe had been conducting a methodical cleaning of the house. Pippin thought she was conscientious, but Zoe's motive was more nefarious than simply cleaning. Room by room, she was searching for a hidden treasure.

"I concede, it's worth having a talk with her. I'm on my way." Lieutenant Jacobs grunted, adding, "Stay away from the inn," but Pippin had already hung up the phone. She was on her bike and pedaling before Jamie registered what was happening.

"You can't go back!" Jamie shouted after her.

Like hell she couldn't. She pedaled harder. Faster. Seconds and minutes zipped by. She approached the inn in record time. A car roared up behind her. Passed her up. Jamie in his sporty silver Audi. He threw his car into park just as Pippin jumped off her bike and raced up the walkway. He was just yards behind her as she flew up the porch steps. She yanked open the screen door, nearly pulling it off its hinges, and she barreled through the front door.

"Zoe—!"

Jamie's hand clamped around her arm. He yanked her back. "Wait for Jacobs," he hissed.

Pippin's jaw tightened. She spoke from between her clamped teeth. "No. Way. *She's* the traitor."

From the corner of her eye, she caught a flash of movement upstairs. Zoe. She appeared at the top of the stairs. Her entire persona changed before their eyes. She must have suspected that Pippin was putting the pieces together when she'd raced out. Now, she seemed to know the jig was up. Gone was the sweet, brown-eyed twenty-something. In her place was a manipulative woman who'd ingratiated herself into Pippin's life and business for her own gain. "You won't be able to hide it forever, you know," she snarled.

Pippin met her, tone for tone. "I'll damn well try."

Zoe's eyes went wide for second. Her expression changed from angry to stunned. "So, you know. You know what it is?"

Pippin knew about the hilt and nothing more, but that was information Zoe didn't need to know. "Of course. And no one will ever find it."

Zoe narrowed her gaze as she edged down the stairs. "Oh, we'll find it."

"Not likely," Jamie muttered.

"Right. More like you're going to prison for murdering Dr. Baxter," Pippin said. "You *and* your friends—"

Zoe caught her breath.

"That's right, we know about Bryan and Ron Baxter, or whatever his name is. Accessories after the fact, or coconspirators? Either works for me."

She made it to the bottom step. Moved in front of the fireplace. "You can't prove anything," she snapped.

"You think?" Pippin looked past her toward the deck. "Did you get all the microscopic blood off the frog? That's what you used, isn't it?"

Zoe's skin turned ashen. She started to look over her

shoulder, as if she could make the cement weapon go away.

Jamie smirked. "Not as smart as you think you are, eh?"

Zoe had her legs spread, bent at the knees. She was ready to bolt the second she thought she could get away from them. The French doors to the deck were her only option.

"The sheriff's on his way," Pippin said just as Sailor appeared in the kitchen behind Zoe. Pippin saw Sailor's eyes register recognition as she looked at Zoe's back. Pippin reacted, lifting one arm to catch the dog's attention. Sailor stopped and looked at her. Pippin held her hand out to communicate *Stay!* Just as quickly, she bent her arm at the elbow and awkwardly rubbed the back of her head. It was a blundering effort to conceal the command, but it worked. Zoe hadn't noticed.

Sailor had. She froze. Read the room. Her tail stiffened and her stance widened. Her ears perked up straight as if she could hear.

Zoe shifted her gaze from Pippin to Jamie. "I'm going to walk right out of here," she said, edging another step backwards toward the kitchen.

The high-pitched sound of a siren wailed in the distance. Jacobs. Finally. Pippin advanced toward Zoe. "You're not leaving."

Jamie edged forward, moving cautiously.

The siren grew louder.

Jamie moved past the couch.

Louder.

Past the bar.

Louder.

Zoe's eyes darted to the front door. For the first time, they clouded with fear.

The siren blared outside. A door slammed.

In a sudden move, Zoe spun around. She stopped short when she saw Sailor. "Stupid dog," she ground out. "Move."

If there was a sign for *attack!,* Pippin didn't know it. She released Sailor from the *stay* command and held two fingers parallel to the floor—their hand signal for *stand up*—and yelled, "Don't let her go, Sailor!"

Sailor registered the urgency in Pippin's body language. She threw her head back and barked. Only a low guttural sound emanated from deep in her throat, but it was enough to startle Zoe and break her focus. Sailor gave a deaf dog's growl. Zoe tried to dodge, but Pippin lunged and caught her arm with one hand, jerking her back.

The front door flung open and Jacobs burst in. He took in the scene and in a split second, his gun was drawn and aimed at Zoe. "You got nowhere to go," he said, his voice measured and calm.

Zoe tried to shake off Pippin's grip, but Pippin held tight. Behind them, Sailor guarded the French door with silent growls. Zoe rooted her feet against the floor and tried to pull free. A deputy appeared on the back deck. Pippin let go, and Zoe careened back, slamming against the kitchen island then falling to the floor in a heap, the air knocked out of her.

Pippin released the breath she'd been holding, a flood of anxiety flowing away at the same time. She waved her arms to get Sailor's attention. The second the dog's eyes landed on her, she beckoned for her to come with both hands. In an instant, the silent growls stopped, and Sailor trotted past Zoe and into Pippin's open arms. "Good girl," Pippin said, raking her fingers through the honey-colored hair then burying her face against Sailor's side. "Such a good girl."

Zoe got onto all fours. She tried to stand but the deputy, a short, trim woman in her mid-thirties, had her gun drawn. Zoe collapsed. She had nowhere to go.

Chapter 37

"If you live to be a hundred, I want to live to be a hundred minus one day so I never have to live without you."

~A.A. Milne, from Winnie the Pooh

*R*umors in the small town of Devil's Cove fly faster than a group of sailfish torpedoing after schools of sardines and anchovies. Case in point, less than an hour after Lieutenant Jacobs hauled Zoe Ibis off in his SUV, Quincy Ratherford from the Gazette burst through the door of the inn, notebook and pen in hand. His face was more flushed than usual, and he'd rushed from the office without his beret. Despite that, he was still the most fashionable man on the island with his pink peg-legged pants and multicolored checkered shirt. His penchant for color rivaled only Hattie's. Pippin would lay money down that there was not a scrap of black or gray in either of their closets.

He spotted Pippin on the floor leaning against the fireplace. Sailor sprawled out in front of her. He'd clearly heard about the arrest, but Pippin had no idea how. She asked him with a silent arch of her brow.

"I have a police scanner," he said with a shrug. "I high-tailed it over here just as fast as I could. How are you holding up, sweetheart?"

There wasn't an easy answer to that question. For starters, Ron Baxter and Bryan whatever-his-last-name-was had been stopped and brought to the sheriff's station for questioning, along with Zoe. But their pending arrests didn't resolve the bigger problems. Were Zoe and her accomplices the only people after whatever mythical treasure Titus supposedly gave to Morgan, a treasure that had survived two thousand years and had purportedly traveled from Ireland to America in the process? Not according to both Hugh and Salty.

Zoe had been willing to kill over it. Pippin had no way of knowing just how much danger she and Grey were in.

And where *was* Hugh?

Then there was the curse. Had she and Grey broken it with their attempted offering to Lir? If she had to give an answer, she'd say no. They'd failed—and they'd barely escaped with their lives.

So how *was* she holding up? The truth was, she was exhausted and wanted nothing more than to collapse onto her bed and sleep for twenty-four hours straight. The reality was, she had charcuterie to set up for the women's group meeting tonight, sweet and savory treats to make for the upcoming men's discussion group, and new guests were scheduled to arrive within the next two hours. "Ask me tomorrow. I might be able to answer by then."

She stood up, noticing the notepad and pen clutched in his hands. "You want the story?"

"Of course. On the record, hopefully, but I'll settle for off if you prefer."

She gave him the story on the record, omitting Hugh and the curse. "So, they were after the hilt that Dr. Baxter had with her?" Quincy asked.

"Apparently so. Lieutenant Jacobs has it now. It'll be returned to Lambay."

"No photograph of this hilt, I suppose?"

"I do have a few on my phone. I'll email them to you."

Quincy beamed his thanks. He asked a few follow up questions, scribbled down a few more notes, and within fifteen minutes, he was back at the door. "Look for it in tomorrow's paper," he said about the article. "And you take care, Pippin. Remember, the good guys won."

Pippin thought about that after he left. The good guys may have won this battle, but they were still fighting the war, and the enemies were invisible.

Daisy burst through the front door a few minutes later. "I took the rest of the day off. I'm here to help!" she announced as soon as she laid eyes on Pippin. "What can I do?"

Pippin's heart ballooned. She surged forward and fell into a hug, letting Daisy wrap her arms around her. "Hey, I gotcha," Daisy said.

Daisy released her with a final squeeze when the front door opened again. "We're back, Miss Pippin. We're back!"

Pippin wiped away the tears that had pooled in her eyes. She spun around at the sound of Mathilda's excited voice. The little girl jumped up and down on her tiptoes, her amber eyes glowing. She ran back onto the porch and yelled, "Hurry up, y'all. You're slowpokes!"

A few seconds later Jamie and Heidi appeared next to Mathilda. Pippin broke into a smile. She'd grown so used to seeing the girls at the bookshop that she'd missed them. "You're back!" She rushed to the entryway. Mathilda launched herself into Pippin's arms. "The beach was fun, fun, fun, but there's no place like home." She grinned. "That's what Dorothy says."

"You should have read it in the book instead of just seeing it on TV," Heidi commented, but there was no bite in her tone. Pippin opened her arm. Heidi gave her a crooked closed-lip smile and slid in to join the hug.

Jamie stood back, one arm crossed over his chest and propping up the opposite elbow, his fingertips resting against his smiling lips. He caught Pippin's eye and mouthed to her, "Are you okay?"

So, he'd heard. "Yes," she replied silently. Hugs from these girls, and Jamie and Daisy both being here were more than enough to bring her out of her dark mood.

Jamie chuckled. "What a reunion. I think you missed Pippin more than you missed me," he quipped.

"Oh Daddy." Mathilda pulled free and ran to Jamie, wrapping her arms around him. "We love you the most. You know that."

Jamie ruffled her hair. "I do know that, squirt. I love you both the most, too."

Heidi pulled back from Pippin and put her hands on her hips. "I have a new book for us."

Pippin met her gaze with equal seriousness. "I'm ready. Lay it on me."

"*The Secret Garden*. It's a classic English book—English as in *from England*, not English as in the *language*—and it's a children's book, but don't worry about *that* because it's very grown up."

A sliver of elation carved through the brick of anxiety in Pippin's gut. In the letter Aunt Rose had sent, she'd said *The*

Secret Garden was Cassie's favorite book when she was a girl. How serendipitous that it was Heidi's choice for their next shared read.

"We have a copy at the library," Daisy said. "I can hold it for you if you want—"

Heidi stopped her with an emphatic shake of her head. "No, no, Pippin should have her own copy of it." She looked up at Jamie. "Don't you think so, Dad?"

A sudden ache, deep and mournful, filled Pippin. She wanted her mother's old copy, the one with name on the flyleaf with the curlicue C. "Actually," she said with a sad smile, "that was my mother's favorite book. My aunt still has her copy. I think I'll ask her to send it to me."

She caught Jamie's gaze. He nodded at her with a smile, then clapped his hands. "Okay, girls, let's help Pippin."

HAVING a network of friends was like being wrapped up in a cashmere blanket under a velvety night sky. Each glistening star was a supportive influx of warmth. The chores were done, the new guests were checked in and off exploring the island, Jamie and his girls went home to settle back into their everyday life, Kyron picked up Daisy for date night, and the women's club would start in an hour.

Pippin slid her copy of *Gulliver's Travels* next to *The Tale of Two Cities* on the bookshelf in the great room. She'd put Nostradamus's book of prophesies back in the Burrow with all the other books her father kept safe there. With Sailor as her shadow, she went out to the front porch to call Grey. They hadn't talked since the near-death calamity at Nag's Head.

He answered the phone in the middle of the first ring.

"Peevie! I've been in the shop all day. I just heard. Are you okay?"

"Working on the boat?" she asked, as if that was more important than everything else that had happened. To her mind, it was. She didn't know if he fully believed in the curse again, or if he'd stop taking risks.

"I'm not getting rid of it—"

She breathed out a tired sigh. "Grey—"

"—but I'm not taking it out anytime soon, so don't worry."

It was better than nothing. "If anything happens to you..."

"Nothing's going to happen to either of us, Peevie. I'm going to help you. We'll figure out how to break the curse. Together."

The very thought bolstered her. In the distance, a crow cawed. It glided closer. Not just any crow. *Her* crow. She'd taken Hattie's words to heart. Cassie had gleaned comfort from the crow hanging around when she'd been in this house. Pippin was beginning to feel the same way. "Morgan," she murmured.

"What?" She'd loosened her grip on the phone, so Grey's voice sounded distant. "What about Morgan?"

"I'm going to call you Morgan, after Morgan Dubhshláine," she said, as if the crow could hear her. It cawed as it vanished over the house. Grey's voice brought her back. "Pippin, what are you talking about?"

"Nothing," she said quickly, holding the phone to her ear again. "It's just that crow hanging around."

A car drove up and parked in front of the house. Ruby! Pippin jumped up. The movement startled Sailor, but she settled back to her sleeping position when Pippin bent to quickly scratch her head. "Grey, I gotta go." she said. "Talk tomorrow?"

"Are you sure you're okay?" he asked. "You didn't tell me what happened."

"I'm fine. Ruby just pulled up, so I'll tell you tomorrow," she said.

By the time Pippin hung up the phone, Ruby was out of the car and holding open the back driver's side door. Pippin was halfway down the porch steps when a little girl appeared from the backseat. Her skin was a few shades lighter than Ruby's mahogany skin. She wore a somber expression and clutched a stuffed penguin to her chest. Pippin jogged down the rest of the steps while Ruby ushered the girl up the walkway. She gave a wan smile. It didn't quite reach her red-rimmed eyes, but Pippin got the feeling she was trying extra hard. "Pippin, this is Sasha."

A charge of electricity shot through Pippin. She remembered what Ruby had said through her tears when she told her about her cousin's accident. Now Pippin crouched down so she was eye-to-eye with the quiet girl. "Well, hello there, Sasha. It's very nice to meet you."

She looked over the girl's head at Ruby. Her sad nod confirmed it. This was her cousin's daughter. "She wants to meet Sailor," Ruby said.

Pippin jumped up with exaggerated excitement. Anything to lift this girl's spirits. "She's right on the porch. Come with me." Sasha took Pippin's proffered hand and they walked side-by-side up the stairs. After a moment, Ruby followed. "How old are you?" Pippin asked.

Sasha squeezed her penguin tight and for a second Pippin didn't think she was going to answer. Then her small voice said, "I'm six."

"Well," Pippin said, "maybe tomorrow you can meet Mathilda. She's six, too, and I bet you'll get along great."

Sailor raised her head as Sasha fell to her knees in front of her. "Hi Sailor," she said softly, and she buried her fingers in the dog's hair.

THE END

DEAR READER,

I know you have many book choices when it comes to books. I'm thrilled you selected Murder at Sea Captain's Inn, the second installment in the Book Magic Mystery series. Readers often decide what to read based on reviews. If you would, please take a moment to share your thoughts about this book. Thank you, and happy reading!

LEAVE A REVIEW HERE.

PRE-ORDER MURDER THROUGH AN OPEN DOOR, book 3 in the Boom Magic series.

JUMP BACK to a Book Magic Prequel! Read Cassie's story in The Secret on Rum Runner's Lane, a Book Magic Mini Mystery

Turn the page to learn how to create a charcuterie board.

And keep turning to read and excerpt from Death at Cape Misery, the third Book Magic Mystery coming in September 2021.

HOW TO CREATE A
CHARCUTERIE BOARD

Dear Reader,

I'm in love with charcuterie boards. Charcuterie is traditionally preparing and assembling cured meats, but it's now evolved to include meats, cheeses, breads, olives, nuts, and fruit. It's all artfully arranged on a board. The artfully part takes practice, I've discovered!

Below are tips on how to put together a charcuterie board.

Charcuterie

The goal is to balance flavors and textures that compliment each other, and also contrast each other.

You want to include a variety of textures, as well as sweet and salty elements.

A spattering of dried fruits, such as cranberries, gives the board a pretty finishing touch.

One or two smoked meat options is plenty.

Adding crackers or sliced baguette on the board or on the side is important.

Fruit preserves are a fantastic compliment to soft bloomy cheeses like brie or camembert.

Add little dishes of mustard or olive oil for added flavors.

Ingredients to consider:

- 2 or 3 meats like prosciutto, dry salami, pepperoni, ham
- 3-4 cheese—consider those from the following list:
- A bloomy cheese like brie or camembert (or Mt. Tam, one of my favorites)
- Parmesan, gouda, or asiago
- Gruyere, cheddar, or manchego
- Softer cheeses like havarti
- Blue like gorgonzola
- Crumbly cheese like feta. I don't love goat cheese, but if you do, include it!
- 2-3 dips, spreads, or other condiments (Whole Foods has a delicious cherry jam that goes beautifully with bloomy cheese), mustard, flavored olive oil, hummus, or baba ganoush (another of my faves!)
- Something briny like capers, pickles, or olives (I like a variety of olives!)
- Other accents like nuts, dried fruit, fresh fruit

(grapes, thin slices of apples or pears,
strawberries, blueberries), and chocolate

Fold the pieces of meat by folding in half, then in half again, the pinch together to make them like little fans.
Put the bloomy cheese out whole.
Put chunks of the other cheeses.
Enjoy!!

READ AN EXCERPT FROM THE SECRET ON RUM RUNNER'S LANE

A Book Magic Mini Mystery

~

The Secret on Rum Runner's Lane, by Melissa Bourbon
  A Book Magic Mini Mystery

Laurel Point. It was a spit of a town nestled between a forest of evergreens and the vast Pacific Ocean, a place stuck in time. Quaint, most people said, but to Cassandra Lane in had become stifling.

Laurel Point wasn't precisely home for Cassie. She'd grown up in Cape Misery.

Being stuck on the cape was isolating. On top of that, she was burdened with a fate from which she wanted—no, needed—to escape.

She couldn't wait to get away from the everything Cape Misery represented.

She couldn't wait to get away from the *magic*.

From the moment they could verbalize, and possibly

even before, Cassandra and Lacy Lane had known they were different from other people. For starters, they had no mother and no father. Oh, of course, they'd *come* from a union between two people, but Edgar had died in a tragic fishing accident in 1969. Later that same year, when Cassie was just three years old, Annabel died giving birth to Lacy.

The weight of responsibility for their mother's death lay heavy with Lacy, though Cassie never blamed her. The fact was, Annabel and Edgar had fallen victim to the Lane Family curse: the men were taken by the sea and the women lost their lives during childbirth.

It simply was the way things were. The girls' fate was written. The sisters had vowed from the beginning never fall in love and to never, ever—under any circumstance, get pregnant.

The Lane sisters didn't live in an ordinary house in an ordinary town. Instead, they lived in the lighthouse on Cape Misery.

Edgar and Annabel, in the decade before they'd died, had taken over the family's lighthouse, turning it into the bookstore it now was.

"How many kids can say they live in a lighthouse," Cassie asked her sister at least once a year, trying to make it sound more exciting than it was. "Not many," Lacy always answered with a smile. She didn't seem to mind the isolation. She immersed herself in the volumes shelved in Books by Bequest, happy as a pirate with a jug of Jamaican rum.

Cassie didn't want her classmates to whisper about her behind her back, but they did it anyway. The girls came from a family of bibliomancers, and while the townspeople visited Aunt Rose for guidance in the way one might see a therapist, the town's kids made fun of what they didn't understand.

"Witch!" some hollered.

"Unnatural!" others said, mimicking what their parents said in the privacy of their own homes.

Cassie and Lacy had each other. That had to be enough.

When Edgar and Annabel both died, the girls' eccentric Aunt Rose had taken over their upbringing. Rose was the only mother the girls had ever known. She was their rock, even if her presence in their lives was more an ever-shifting tidal pool than a sturdy, unyielding lighthouse.

Growing up, Cassie's favorite spot in the world had become the bench at the top of the hill near her parents' graves. Sitting on the bench, the Lane family graveyard was to her left. To her right and down the hill was the white stone tower that was the lighthouse, with its arched wooden door, red reflectors and black iron accents at the windows. The blue expanse of the Pacific Ocean lay beyond, its white-caps churning wildly, its secrets buried, never to be revealed.

The small cemetery was dotted with gravestones made from slate or sandstone. Each of the tablet stones was placed vertically at the head of its particular plot, a few tilted one way or the other, but most upright, standing sentry to the souls of the people buried beneath. Cassie supposed it was because of this little graveyard that she'd come to love the earth so much. The flowers that bordered the picket fence around the space. The flowers she and Aunt Rose planted alongside each headstone every spring while Lacy holed up inside Books by Bequest, reading every ancient tome she could get her hands on.

That was the core difference between the sisters. Lacy loved the family's gift of bibliomancy. She loved books, the stories they told, the secrets they held, and the future they predicted, while Cassie preferred life outside and the way flowers in the spring gave the promise of a new tomorrow and how the falling leaves in autumn meant a cleansing of the soul and a time to reflect and rebuild. She *wished* she could read the books in the store, but the truth was, she didn't trust the messages the books gave, and lately she'd begun to wonder if Lacy trusted them, either. So many times, Cassie had seen Lacy absorbed in her divination, gleaning messages about the past, or predictions about the future, only to see frustration take hold as Lacy slammed closed the book that had been open in her lap, or on the table before her, or on the pillow of her bed.

Cassie had eventually become convinced that the Lane women's divination was actually another part of the curse that plagued her family. Learning how to use their gift of bibliomancy had been Aunt Rose's greatest joy when the sisters were younger, but now she furrowed her brows at Lacy when the books didn't tell her what she wanted to hear, and at Cassie when she refused to even pick up a book. "I don't want to know," Cassie would say, and Aunt Rose would nod as if she understood, but deep down, Cassie knew she didn't. Aunt Rose wondered how a person could deny such a big part of herself, and though she worried about Lacy getting lost in it, she also worried that Cassie having nothing to do with it would end badly.

Because, Aunt Rose always told the girls, you can't run from who and what you are.

But that was exactly what Cassie was going to do. The first opportunity she had, she was getting away Laurel Point. Away from Oregon. Putting her past behind her.

Leaving Lacy, Aunt Rose, Annabel and Edgar, and the lighthouse wouldn't be easy, but it was essential, because no book was going to tell Cassie what her future held. This place that tried to hem her in with its coastal fog, its isolating cape, it's stone-walled lighthouse—this place would not contain her.

She was going to make her own destiny.

Growing up, Cassie's natural propensity was to act as the protector of her little sister, who never, ever wanted protecting.

When Cassie tried to brush Lacy's hair, Lacy snatched the brush and ran across the room. "I can take care of myself, thank you very much."

When Cassie wanted to hold Lacy's hand as they found their footing on the jagged rocks along the shore, Lacy pulled free, scurrying at a dizzying pace, with reckless abandon that made Cassie hold her breath and pray.

When Cassie tried to get Lacy to come up to the grave-yard with her to talk to their parents, Lacy eschewed the very idea. "I talk to them in the books."

Despite their differences, they were thick as thieves, as Aunt Rose always said. Even though she wouldn't let Cassie touch her locks, Lacy always wanted to brush Cassie's hair, and she dragged Cassie with her to the beach to see a blinking light far out at the horizon, sure it was a morse code message from one of the Lane ancestors.

The sisters even looked alike—both petite and with eyes that were as blue as the cerulean skies above. Cassie's hair was more blonde, with a touch of strawberry like their mother's, or so they were told, while Lacy's had the brown tint of their father's. They both had curls that bounced and framed their faces like wispy halos that became instant bird's nests of leaves and twigs when the wind came, which was often living on the Oregon coast. Their curls had still been the envy of every school girl they'd ever encountered. The jealousy of school girls was not to be taken lightly and had stuck with them through their adolescence. Another line on Cassie's list of reasons to leave.

They both steered clear of eating any living thing that came from the sea, fearful that their ancestors' blood coursed through the bottom-feeding shrimp or the white-fleshed halibut. They cooked the meals for their little family because Aunt Rose lost track of time, and if Cassie and Lacy left it to her, they'd eat a breakfast of leathering steak at midnight and a dinner of runny scrambled eggs at four in the afternoon.

Cassie found the recipes, wrote them out by hand so as not to depend on an open book, and added the ingredients to Aunt Rose's market list, then she and Lacy would prepare the meals together, each working through the steps, moving around each other wordlessly, as if they'd done it a thousand times. Which by the time they were in their teens, it felt as if they had.

Where Cassie cooked by using precise measurements, Lacy, let loose in the kitchen. She was like a chemist—or, Cassie thought wryly, like a witch. Lacy tossed handfuls of herbs or flours or whatever she was drawn to into a boiling pot of soup as if it was a caldron and she was crafting a potion to end all potions.

They were opposites, but they complemented one another like dark chocolate and red wine, or salt and caramel.

They'd been parentless, but Aunt Rose had done her very best. She'd never had children of her own, and inheriting Cassie and Lacy had been an unexpected. Truth be told, Aunt Rose had been ill-equipped to raise the sisters. She practiced her bibliomancy for the same people in the town whose children steered clear of the sisters, and for the people who came to Books by Bequest explicitly to get a 'reading'. She lived in her books more than she lived in the real world.

Cassie became the keeper of the schedule and her organization was the thing that kept her and Lacy on track, despite Lacy's wild tendencies. But now, with Lacy and Cassie sixteen, nearly seventeen, and nineteen, nearly twenty, respectively, their paths were clear. Lacy could have her books. Cassie would take flowers and fresh air any day of the week.

Cassie stood, brushing dirt from her knees and peeling off her garden gloves. She left the flat of impatiens, only half planted, and walked into the fenced area and right up to Annabel's and Edgar's graves. She spoke to her parents whenever she needed an ear, which lately was nearly every day.

If only Annabel and Edgar could answer.

"I want to go," Cassie usually said, always followed by a hasty, "but I can't leave you...or Lacy...or Aunt Rose."

Sometimes the leaves on the trees would rustle and Cassie would imagine that the breeze was Annabel trying to hug her.

Most often, there was just silence.

This time though, Cassie was actually saying goodbye. More than anything, Lacy didn't want Cassie's mothering anymore. Something had caused her sister to shut her out, and Aunt Rose had her books and her divination.

It was time.

Cassie had just opened her mouth to speak—to tell her parents that this time she was really going—when a scream came from somewhere below. Her heart shot to her throat. Was it from the lighthouse, or had it carried up from the beach? Was it Aunt Rose or...oh no, was it—?

"Lacy!" she yelled. She started to run, but her legs felt like they were moving in slow motion.

The scream came again, this time followed by a string of cursing. Cassie stopped in her tracks. Closed her eyes. "Oh, thank God," she whispered. It *was* Lacy, but she wasn't in trouble. Probably some book had given her a glimpse into a past or a future she didn't want to see. That was par for the course. Lately Lacy's abilities seemed to fail her more and more.

Now Cassie went back to her parents. "It's just Lacy," she said with a sigh. It felt like a refrain she kept repeating lately. "It's just Lacy."

Keep Reading

ACKNOWLEDGMENTS

The Lost Colony of Roanoke is a fascinating piece of American folklore and a truly unsolvable mystery. I am fascinated with the history of John White, his granddaughter, Eleanor Dare, who was the first English child to be born in the Americas, and the Dare Stone hoax.

Connections between people can be beautifully serendipitous. A friend in my town happens to have a sister who is an archeologist and scholar. Melissa Darby has drawn connections between the hoax of Sir Francis Drake's Brass Plate on the West Coast, and the Dare Stone hoax clear across the country. Melissa's book, Thunder Go North: The Hunt for Sir Francis Drake's Fair and Good Bay, is thought-provoking and helped me add depth and layers to the history of the fictional island of Devil's Cove. So, thank you to Nancy Baker for connecting me with her sister, Melissa Darby. I appreciate you both!

Finding great people to be part of my publishing team is always thrill. I'm so glad I found you, Sarah Simonic! You helped make this book stronger.

Finnegan Count Smooshie Tushie is the sweet rescue Vizsla who was the inspiration behind Sailor. He's featured on the cover of the first two Book Magic books—with more modeling to come. A heartfelt thanks to Gwen Romack and Finn for sharing his likeness and his antics with me.

Finally, a huge thank you to my mom and dad for always being my fiercest allies, to my husband, Carlos, for supporting my writing career, and to Wendy Lyn Watson, for being my Book Magic partner. XO

ABOUT MELISSA

Melissa Bourbon is the national bestselling author of more than 20 mystery books, including the Lola Cruz Mysteries, A Magical Dressmaking Mystery series, the Bread Shop Mysteries, written as Winnie Archer, and the brand new Book Magic Mysteries.

She is a former middle school English teacher who gave up the classroom in order to live in her imagination full time. Melissa, a California native who has lived in Texas and Colorado, now calls the southeast home. She hikes, practices yoga, cooks, and is slowly but surely discovering all the great restaurants in the Carolinas. Since four of her five amazing kids are living their lives, scattered throughout the country, her dogs, Bean, the pug, and Dobby, the chug, keep her company while she writes.

Melissa lives in North Carolina with her educator husband, Carlos, and their youngest son. She is beyond fortunate to be living the life of her dreams.

VISIT Melissa's website at http://www.melissabourbon.com

JOIN her online book club at https://www.facebook.com/groups/BookWarriors/

JOIN her book review club at https://facebook.com/melissaanddianesreviewclub

ALSO BY MELISSA BOURBON

Book Magic Mysteries

The Secret on Rum Runner's Lane, a Book Magic Mini Mystery (prequel)

Murder in Devil's Cove

Murder at Sea Captain's Inn

Bread Shop Mysteries, *written as Winnie Archer*

Kneaded to Death

Crust No One

The Walking Bread

Flour in the Attic

Dough or Die

A Murder Yule Regret

Magical Dressmaking Mysteries

Pleating for Mercy

A Fitting End

Deadly Patterns

A Custom-Fit Crime

A Killing Notion

A Seamless Murder

Mystery/Suspense

Silent Obsession

Silent Echoes

Deadly Legends Boxed Set

Paranormal Romance

<u>Storiebook Charm</u>

CPSIA information can be obtained
at www.ICGtesting.com
Printed in the USA
LVHW020436310822
727204LV00002B/186

9 780997 866162